Paolo Giordano was born in Turin in 1982. He is working on a doctorate in particle physics. *The Solitude of Prime Numbers*, his first novel, has sold over a million copies and has been translated into more than thirty languages. It won Italy's premier book prize, the Premio Strega award.

THE SOLITUDE OF PRIME NUMBERS

A prime number is a lonely thing: it can be divided only by itself, or by one; it never truly fits with another . . . Alice and Mattia are alone. Alice bears the scars of a skiing accident that nearly killed her, and Mattia lives with a guilty secret that lies at the heart of his disabled twin sister's disappearance. They each recognize in the other a kindred, damaged spirit — their destinies seem irrevocably intertwined. But when Mattia accepts a mathematics posting that takes him thousands of miles away, it seems that love might just be a game of numbers after all; until a chance sighting by Alice of a woman who could be Mattia's sister forces a lifetime of hidden emotion to the surface.

PAOLO GIORDANO
Translated by Shaun Whiteside

◆

THE SOLITUDE
OF PRIME
NUMBERS

Complete and Unabridged

CHARNWOOD
Leicester

First published in Great Britain in 2009 by
Doubleday
an imprint of Transworld Publishers, London

First Charnwood Edition
published 2010
by arrangement with Transworld Publishers
A Random House Group Company, London

British Library CIP Data

Giordano, Paolo, *1982* –
    The solitude of prime numbers.
    1. Solitude- -Fiction. 2. Friendship- -Fiction.
    3. Life change events- -Fiction. 4. Large type books.
    I. Title
    853.9′2–dc22

    ISBN 978–1–44480–080–7

Published by
F. A. Thorpe (Publishing)
Anstey, Leicestershire

Set by Words & Graphics Ltd.
Anstey, Leicestershire
Printed and bound in Great Britain by
T. J. International Ltd., Padstow, Cornwall

This book is printed on acid-free paper

To Eleonora,
because in silence
I promised it to you

Her old aunt's richly ornamented dress was a perfect fit for Sylvie's slender figure, and she asked me to lace it up for her. 'It has tight sleeves; how ridiculous!' she said.

Gérard de Nerval, *Sylvie*, 1853

Contents

The Snow Angel (1983) 1

The Archimedes Principle (1984)..............15

On the Skin and Just Behind It (1991) 31

The Other Room (1995) 115

In and Out of the Water (1998) 129

Getting Things in Focus (2003) 199

What Remains (2007)........................215

Acknowledgements 329

The Snow Angel
(1983)

1

Alice Della Rocca hated ski school. She hated getting up at half past seven in the morning during the Christmas holidays. She hated her father staring at her over breakfast, his leg dancing nervously under the table as if to say hurry up, get a move on. She hated the woollen tights that made her thighs itch, the mittens that kept her from moving her fingers, the helmet that squashed her cheeks and the boots that were always too tight and made her walk like a gorilla.

'Are you going to drink that milk or not?' her father said.

Alice gulped down three inches of boiling milk that burned all the way down to her stomach.

'OK, today you can show us what you're really made of.'

He shoved her outside, mummified in a green ski suit dotted with badges and the fluorescent logos of the sponsors. It was minus ten degrees and a grey fog enveloped everything. Alice felt the milk swirling around in her stomach as she sank into the snow. Her skis were over her shoulder, because you had to carry your skis yourself until you got good enough for someone to carry them for you.

'Keep the ends facing forwards or you'll kill someone,' her father said.

At the end of the season the Ski Club gave you a pin with little stars on it. One star every year,

3

from when you were four years old and just tall enough to slip the little disc of the ski-lift between your legs, until you were nine and you managed to grab the disc all by yourself. Three silver stars and then another three in gold: a pin every year to tell you you'd got a bit better, a bit closer to the skiing competitions that terrified Alice. She'd already started thinking about it when she only had three stars.

The rendezvous at the ski-lift had been arranged for exactly half past eight, when it opened. The other kids were already there, standing in a loose circle like little military recruits, wrapped up in their uniforms and numb with sleep and cold. They stuck their ski-poles into the snow and leaned on them, wedging them in their armpits. No one felt like talking, least of all Alice. Her father tapped her twice on the helmet, too hard, as if trying to plant her in the snow.

'Pull out all the stops,' he said. 'And remember: keep your bodyweight forward, OK? Bo-dy-weight for-ward.'

'Bodyweight forward,' Alice echoed.

Then he walked away, blowing into his cupped hands. Two steps and the fog swallowed him up.

Alice clumsily dropped the skis on the ground and slapped the bottom of her boots with the ski-pole to knock off the clumps of snow. If her father had seen her he would have slapped her right there, in front of everyone.

She was already desperate for a pee; it was pushing against her bladder like a pin stuck in her belly. Yet again, she wasn't going to make it.

It was the same every morning. After breakfast she would lock herself in the bathroom and push and push to get rid of every last drop, contracting her abdominal muscles until the effort gave her a headache and she felt as if her eyes were going to pop out of their sockets. She would turn the tap on as far as it would go so that her father couldn't hear the noises, pushing and pushing, clenching her fists, to squeeze out the very last drop. She would sit there until her father knocked hard on the bathroom door and called all right, Miss, have we finished? We're late again.

Reaching the bottom of the first ski-lift she would be so desperate that she would have to crouch down in the fresh snow and pretend to tighten her boots in order to have a pee inside the ski suit while all her classmates looked on. It's such a relief, she thought each time, as the lovely warmth trickled between her shivering legs. Or it would be, if only they weren't all there watching me.

Sooner or later they're going to notice.

Sooner or later I'm going to leave a stain in the snow and they'll all make fun of me.

One of the parents walked over to Eric and asked him if it wasn't too foggy to go to a high altitude. Alice pricked up her ears hopefully, but Eric just smiled broadly.

'It's only foggy down here,' he said. 'At the top the sun is warm enough to split stones. Come on, let's go.'

On the chair-lift Alice was paired with Giuliana, the daughter of one of her father's colleagues. They didn't talk to each other on the way up; neither had anything against the other, it was just that, at that moment, neither of them wanted to be there.

They could hear the wind brushing the summit of the mountain, punctuated by the metallic rush of the steel cable from which Alice and Giuliana were suspended, their chins tucked into the collars of their jackets so that they could warm themselves with their breath.

It's only the cold, you don't really need to go, Alice said to herself.

But the closer she got to the top, the more the pin in her belly pierced her flesh. Perhaps this time she was seriously close to wetting herself. Then again, it might even be something bigger. No, it's just the cold, I can't need to go again.

Regurgitated rancid milk suddenly surged into her mouth and Alice swallowed it back down with disgust.

She needed to go; she was desperate to go.

There were two more stations before the shelter; she couldn't hold it in for that long.

Giuliana lifted the safety bar and they both shifted their bottoms forward to get off. When her skis touched the ground Alice shoved herself away from her seat. You couldn't see more than two metres ahead of you, let alone the sun splitting the stones. It was like being wrapped in a sheet, all white, nothing but white, above, below, to right and left. It was the exact opposite of darkness, but it frightened Alice in exactly the same way.

She slipped off to the side of the piste to look

for a little pile of fresh snow to relieve herself in. Her stomach made a noise like a dishwasher. Turning around, she couldn't see Giuliana any more, which meant that Giuliana couldn't see her either. She climbed a few metres up the hill with her skis in a fishbone shape, as her father had forced her to do when he had taken it into his head to teach her to ski. Up and down the nursery slope, thirty to forty times a day, sidestepping up and snow-ploughing down. It trained your legs and, anyway, buying a ski-pass for just one piste was a waste of money.

Alice unfastened her skis and took another few steps. Her boots sank into the snow halfway up her calves. At last she could sit. She stopped holding her breath and relaxed her muscles. A pleasant electric shock spread throughout her body, finally settling in the tips of her toes.

It was the milk, of course it was. And the fact that her bum was freezing from sitting in the snow at two thousand metres. It had never happened before, at least not as far as she could remember. Never, not even once.

But this time it wasn't pee. Or, not only. As she leaped to her feet she felt something heavy in the seat of her pants and instinctively touched her bottom. She couldn't feel a thing through her gloves, but it didn't matter — she had already worked out what had happened.

Eric called her but Alice didn't reply. As long as she stayed up there she would be hidden by the fog. She could pull down the trousers of her ski suit and clean herself up as best she could or go down to Eric and whisper in his ear and tell him what had happened. She could tell him she had to get back to the village, that her knees hurt. Or she could just ignore it and carry on skiing, making sure she was always at the back of the queue.

Instead she simply stayed where she was, careful not to move a muscle, shielded by the fog.

Eric called her again. Louder now.

'She must have gone to the ski-lift already,' a little boy said.

Alice heard murmuring. Someone said let's go and someone else said I'm cold from standing here. They could have been down below, a few metres away or even at the top of the ski-lift. Sounds are deceptive: they rebound off the mountains; they're absorbed by the snow. 'Damn . . . let's go and see,' Eric said. Alice slowly counted to ten, suppressing her urge to vomit as she felt something sliding down her thighs. Having got to ten, she started over again, and this time she counted to twenty. Now there wasn't so much as a sound.

She picked up her skis and carried them under her arm to the piste. It took her a little while to work out how to get the skis at right angles to the steepest bit of slope. With fog like that you couldn't even tell which way you were facing.

She put on her boots and tightened the buckles. She slipped off her goggles and spat inside them because they had misted up. She could go down to the village all on her own. She didn't care that Eric was looking for her at the top of the mountain. With her tights caked in shit, she didn't want to stay up there a second longer than she absolutely had to. She thought of the journey. She had never gone down on her own, but after all she had taken the ski-lift by herself and she'd been down that slope dozens of times.

She began to snowplough. Just the day before, Eric had said if I see you doing one more snowplough turn, I swear I'm going to tie your ankles together.

Eric didn't like her, she was sure of it. He thought she was a coward and events had proved him right. Eric didn't like her father either, because every day, at the end of the lesson, he pestered him with endless questions. So how is our Alice coming along, are we getting better, do we have a little champion on our hands, when are we going to start these competitions, on and on. Eric always stared at a spot somewhere behind her father and answered yes, no or maybe when she's gone up a size, etc.

Alice saw the whole scene superimposed through her foggy goggles as she gently edged down, unable to make out anything beyond the tips of her skis. Only when she ended up in the fresh snow did she understand that it was time to turn.

She started singing a song to herself to feel less alone. From time to time she ran a hand under her nose to wipe away the snot.

Weight upwards, pole in, wheel. Rest on your boots. Now with your bodyweight forward, OK? Bo-dy-weight for-ward. The voice was partly Eric's and partly her father's.

Her father would probably fly into a complete fury. She had to prepare a lie, a story that would stand up without gaps or contradictions. She wouldn't dream of telling him what had really happened. The fog, that was it, it was the fog's fault. She was following the others on to the big slope when her ski-pass had come off her jacket. Or no, not that, no one's ski-pass ever blew away. You'd have to be really stupid to lose it. Let's say her scarf. Her scarf had blown away and she had gone back a bit to find it and the others hadn't waited for her. She had called them a hundred times but there was no sign of them, they had disappeared into the fog and then she had gone down to look for them.

So why hadn't she gone back up? her father would ask.

Quite right, why hadn't she? When you thought about it, it was better if she lost her ski-pass. She hadn't gone back up because she'd lost her ski-pass and the man at the ski-lift wouldn't let her back up again.

Alice smiled, content with her story. It was flawless. She didn't even feel all that dirty any more. She would spend the rest of the day in front of the TV. She would have a shower and put on clean clothes and slip her feet into her furry slippers. She would stay in the warm all day. Or she would have, if only she'd looked up from her skis long enough to see the orange tape with the words *Piste Closed*. Her father was always telling her look where you're going. If only she'd remembered that in fresh snow your bodyweight shouldn't go forwards and if only

Eric, a few days before, had adjusted the fastenings better and her father had been more insistent in saying but Alice weighs 28 kilos, won't they be too tight like that?

The drop wasn't very high. A few metres, just long enough to feel a bit of a void in your stomach and nothing beneath your feet. After which Alice was already face down on the ground, skis bolt upright in the air, leaving her fibula broken.

She didn't really feel that bad. She barely felt a thing, to tell the truth. Only the snow that had slipped under her scarf and into her helmet and burned where it touched her skin.

First of all she moved her arms. When she was little and had woken up to find it had snowed, her father had wrapped her up tight and carried her downstairs. They walked to the middle of the courtyard and then, holding one another by the hand, counted to three and let themselves fall backwards like a dead weight. Then her father told her to do an angel and Alice moved her arms up and down and, when she got up and looked at her outline carved in the white cloak, it really did look like the shadow of an angel with its outspread wings.

Alice made the snow angel like that, for no reason, just to prove to herself that she was still alive. She managed to turn her head to one side and start breathing again, even though it felt as if the air that she breathed wasn't going to wherever it was supposed to go. She had the strange sensation of not knowing which way round her legs were. The very strange sensation

11

of no longer having legs at all.

She tried to get up, but she couldn't.

Without that fog someone might have seen her from above, a green stain squashed at the bottom of a gully, a few steps from the spot where a little waterfall would start flowing again in the spring. When it turned warm the wild strawberries would come out, and if you waited long enough they'd become as sweet as candy and you could fill a whole basket with them in a day. Alice cried for help, but her thin voice was engulfed by the fog. She tried to get up again, or at least to turn over, but it was no use.

Her father had told her that almost everyone who died of cold was found in their underwear. People who froze to death felt very hot and, just before they expired, felt an urge to get undressed. To make matters worse, her knickers were dirty.

She was starting to lose the feeling in her fingers. She took off one glove, blew into it and then put her clenched fist back in to warm it up. She did the same with her other hand. She repeated this ludicrous gesture two or three times.

It's your extremities that get you, her father always told her. Your toes and fingers, your nose and ears. Your heart does everything in its power to keep the blood to itself and leaves the rest to freeze.

Alice imagined her fingers turning blue and then, slowly, her arms and her legs. She thought of her heart pumping harder and harder, trying to keep in all the remaining warmth. She would go so stiff that if a wolf passed by it would snap one of her arms off just by stepping on it.

They're looking for me.

I wonder if there really are any wolves.

I can't feel my fingers any more.

If only I hadn't drunk that milk.

Bo-dy-weight for-ward, she thought.

But no, wolves would be hibernating.

Eric will be furious.

I don't want to do those competitions.

Don't talk rubbish, you know very well that wolves don't hibernate.

Her thoughts were growing more and more circular and illogical.

The sun sank slowly behind Mount Chaberton as if nothing was the matter. The shadow of the mountains spread over Alice and the fog went completely black.

The Archimedes Principle
(1984)

2

When the twins were still small and Michela was up to one of her tricks, like throwing herself downstairs in her baby-walker or getting a pea stuck up one of her nostrils, so that she had to be taken to Emergency to have it taken out with special tweezers, their father always turned to Mattia, the firstborn, and told him that his mother's womb was too small for both of them.

'God knows what the two of you got up to in there,' he said. 'I reckon you kicked your sister and did her serious damage.'

Then he laughed, even though there was nothing to laugh about. He lifted Michela in the air and plunged his beard into her soft cheeks.

Mattia watched from below. He laughed as well and let his father's words filter through him by osmosis, without really understanding them. He let them settle at the bottom of his stomach, forming a thick and sticky layer like the sediment of wine that has aged for a long time.

His father's laughter turned into a drawn smile when, at twenty-seven months, Michela couldn't utter a word that really was one. Not even mammy or poo-poo or sleepy or woof. Her inarticulate little cries came from such a solitary and deserted place that they always made their father shiver.

When she was five and a half a speech therapist with thick glasses sat Michela down in front of a piece of plywood with four different shapes cut out of it — a star, a circle, a square and a triangle — and the corresponding coloured pieces to place into the holes.

Michela looked at it with wonder.

'Where does the star go, Michela?' asked the speech therapist. Michela looked down at the toy and didn't touch anything. The doctor put the star in her hand.

'Where does this go, Michela?' she asked.

Michela looked everywhere and nowhere. She put one of the five yellow points in her mouth and began to chew it. The speech therapist took her hand out of her mouth and repeated the question for the third time.

'Michela, do as the doctor says, for goodness' sake,' snarled her father, who couldn't quite manage to stay seated where they had told him to.

'Signore Balossino, please,' the doctor said in a conciliatory voice. 'You have to let children take their time.'

Michela took her time. A whole minute. Then she emitted a heart-rending groan, that could equally well have been one of joy or of despair, and resolutely placed the star in the square hole.

★ ★ ★

In case Mattia had not already worked out for himself that there was something wrong with his sister, his classmates had no hesitation in pointing it out to him. For example, when they were in the first year and the teacher said to

18

Simona Volterra, this month you are going to sit next to Michela, she refused, crossing her arms, and saying, I don't want to sit next to *her*.

Mattia had allowed Simona and the teacher to argue for a while, and had then said Miss, I can sit next to Michela. Everyone had looked relieved: *her*, Simona, the teacher. Everyone apart from Mattia.

The twins sat at the front of the class. Michela spent the whole day colouring in, meticulously going outside the lines and picking colours at random. The skin of the children blue, the sky red, all the trees yellow. She gripped the pencil like a knife and pressed down so hard on the page that one time in three she tore it.

Sitting next to her Mattia learned to read and write. He learned his arithmetic and was the first in the class to learn how to do long division.

His brain seemed to be a perfect machine, in the same mysterious way that his sister's was so defective.

Sometimes Michela started getting agitated on her chair, crazily waving her arms around like a trapped moth. Her eyes darkened and the teacher looked at her, more frightened than she was, vaguely hoping that the poor girl really might one day take flight. Someone in the back row giggled and someone else said shhh. Then Mattia got to his feet, picking up his chair so that it wouldn't squeak on the floor, and went to Michela, who was now rolling her head from side to side and waving her arms about so fast that he was afraid they would come off.

Mattia took her hands and delicately wrapped

her arms around her chest.

'There, you haven't got any wings any more,' he whispered in her ear. It took Michela a few seconds before she stopped trembling. She stared into the distance for a few seconds, and then went back to tormenting her drawings as if nothing had happened. Mattia returned to his seat, head lowered and ears red with embarrassment, and the teacher went on with the lesson.

In the third year of primary school the twins still hadn't been invited to any of their classmates' birthday parties. Their mother had noticed and had thought she could resolve the situation by organizing a party for the twins' own birthday. At dinner, Mr Balossino had rejected the suggestion out of hand, saying for heaven's sake, Adele, it's embarrassing enough as it is. Mattia had sighed with relief and Michela had dropped her fork for the tenth time. It was never mentioned again. Then, one morning in January, Riccardo Pelotti, who had red hair and the lips of a baboon, came over to Mattia's desk.

'Hey, my mum says you can come to my birthday party as well,' he said in one breath, looking at the blackboard.

'So can she,' he added, pointing to Michela, who was carefully smoothing the surface of the desk as if it were a bed-sheet.

Mattia's face went red with excitement. He said thank you, but Riccardo, having got the weight off his chest, had already left.

The twins' mother immediately became quite anxious and took them both to Benetton to buy them new clothes. They went to three toy shops, but each time Adele couldn't make up her mind.

'What sort of things is Riccardo interested in? Would he like this?' she asked Mattia, holding up a jigsaw puzzle.

'How would I know?' replied her son.

'He's a friend of yours. You must know what games he likes.'

Mattia didn't think that Riccardo was a friend of his, but he couldn't explain that to his mother. He shrugged.

In the end Adele opted for the Lego space-ship, the biggest and most expensive toy in the department.

'Mummy, it's too much,' her son protested.

'Nonsense. And besides, there are two of you. You don't want to make a bad impression.'

Mattia knew very well that, Lego or no Lego, they would make a bad impression. With Michela, anything else was impossible. He knew that Riccardo had only invited them because he'd been told to. Michela would cling to him all the time, she'd spill orange juice over herself and then she'd start whining the way she always did when she was tired.

For the first time Mattia thought it might be better to stay at home.

Or rather, he thought it might be better if Michela stayed at home.

'Mummy,' he began uncertainly.

Adele was looking in her bag for her wallet.

'Yes?'

Mattia took a breath.

'Does Michela really have to come to the party?'

21

Adele suddenly froze and stared into her son's eyes. The cashier observed the scene indifferently, her hand open on the conveyor belt, waiting for money. Michela was mixing up the packets of sweets on the display.

Mattia's cheeks burned, ready to receive a slap that never came.

'Of course she's coming,' his mother said, and that was that.

★ ★ ★

Riccardo's house was less than ten minutes' walk away, and they were allowed to go on their own. At three o'clock on the dot Adele pushed the twins out the door.

'Go on, or you'll be late. Remember to thank his parents,' she said.

Then she turned to Mattia.

'Look after your sister. You know she mustn't eat junk.'

Mattia nodded. Adele kissed them both on the cheek, Michela for longer. She tidied Michela's hair under her hairband and said enjoy yourself.

All the way to Riccardo's house, Mattia's thoughts matched the rhythm of the pieces of Lego, which moved around inside the box making a sound like a little tide. A few metres behind him, Michela stumbled as she tried to keep up, dragging her feet along the mush of dead leaves stuck to the tarmac. The air was still and cold.

She's going to drop her crisps on the carpet, thought Mattia.

She'll take the ball and she won't want to give it back to anyone.

'Will you hurry up?' he said, turning round to his twin, who had suddenly crouched down in the middle of the pavement and was torturing a ten-centimetre worm with her finger. Michela looked at her brother as if seeing him for the first time in ages. She smiled and ran to him, holding the worm between her thumb and forefinger. 'That's disgusting. Throw it away,' Mattia ordered, recoiling.

Michela looked at the worm again for a moment and seemed to be wondering how it had ended up in her hand. Then she dropped it and started a lopsided run to join her brother who had already walked on ahead.

He looked at his twin, who had the same eyes as him, the same nose, the same colour hair and a brain that belonged in the bin, and for the first time he felt genuine hatred. He took her hand to cross the road, because the cars were going fast, and it was as they were crossing that an idea came to him.

He let go of Michela's hand in its woollen glove, instantly thinking that it wasn't right.

Then, as they were walking by the park, he changed his mind again and convinced himself that no one would ever find out.

Just for a few hours, he thought. Just this once. He abruptly changed direction, dragging Michela behind him by an arm, and went into the park. The grass was still damp from the night's frost. Michela trotted behind him, muddying her brand-new white suede boots. There was no one in the park; it was so cold that no one would have felt like going for a walk. The twins reached an area full of trees, with three wooden tables and a barbecue. They had had their lunch there once, in year one, when the teachers had taken them out collecting dry leaves to make ugly table decorations to give to their grandparents for Christmas.

'Michela, listen to me,' said Mattia. 'Are you listening?'

With Michela you always had to check that her narrow channel of communication was open. Mattia waited for a nod from his sister.

'Good. So, I'm going away for a little while, OK? But I won't be away for long, just half an hour,' he explained.

There was no reason to tell the truth, since half an hour or a whole day made little difference to Michela. The doctor had said that the development of her spatio-temporal perception had been arrested at a pre-conscious stage and Mattia had understood perfectly well what that meant.

'You sit here and wait for me,' he said to his twin. Michela stared seriously at her brother and didn't reply, because she didn't know how to reply. She gave no sign of having really understood, but for a moment her eyes lit up and for the rest of his life when Mattia thought of those eyes he thought of fear.

He moved a little way from his sister, walking backwards to make sure she didn't follow him. Only prawns walk like that, his mother had once yelled at him, and they always end up crashing into something.

He was about fifteen metres away and Michela

24

had already stopped looking at him, engrossed in the attempt to detach a button from her woollen coat.

Mattia turned round and started running, tightly clutching the bag with the present. In the box more than two hundred little plastic blocks crashed into each other and it was as if they were trying to tell him something.

★ ★ ★

'Hi, Mattia,' Riccardo Pelotti's mother said as she opened the door. 'Where's your little sister?'

'She had a temperature,' Mattia lied. 'A bit of one.'

'Oh, what a shame,' the lady said, not seeming to be displeased in the slightest. She stepped aside to let him in.

'Ricky, your friend Mattia is here. Come and say hello,' she called, turning towards the corridor.

Riccardo appeared, sliding along the floor with an unpleasant expression on his face. He stopped for a second to glance at Mattia and look for traces of the retard. Relieved, he said hi.

Mattia lifted the bag with the present under the lady's nose.

'Where shall I put this?' he asked.

'What is it?' Riccardo asked suspiciously.

'Lego.'

Riccardo grabbed the bag and disappeared along the corridor.

'Go with him,' the lady said, pushing Mattia. 'The party's down there.'

The Pelottis' sitting room was decorated with bunches of balloons. On a table covered by a red paper cloth there were bowls of popcorn and crisps, a baking tray of dry pizza sliced in squares and a row of still unopened bottles of fizzy drinks of various colours. Some of Mattia's classmates had already arrived and were standing in the middle of the room guarding the table.

Mattia took a few steps towards the others and then stopped some metres away, like a satellite that doesn't want to take up too much room in the sky. No one paid him any attention.

When the room was full of children, an entertainer with a red plastic nose and a clown's bowler hat made them play blind man's buff and pin the tail on the donkey. Mattia won first prize, which consisted of an extra handful of sweets, but only because he could see out from under the blindfold. Everyone shouted boo and you cheated as he shamefacedly slipped the sweets into his pocket.

Then, when it was already dark outside, the clown turned out the lights, made them sit in a circle and started to tell them a horror story. He held a lit torch under his chin.

Mattia thought that the story wasn't really frightening, but the face was when it was lit up like that. The light shining from below turned it all red and revealed its terrifying shadows. Mattia looked out of the window to keep from looking at the clown and remembered Michela. He hadn't really forgotten her for a minute, but for the first time he imagined her all alone among the trees, waiting for him, and rubbing her face with her white gloves to warm up a bit.

He got to his feet, just as Riccardo's mother came into the dark room with a cake covered with lit candles and everyone started clapping, partly for the story and partly for the cake.

'I've got to go,' he said to her, without even giving her time to set the cake down on the table.

'Right now? But the cake's here.'

'Yes, now. I've got to go.'

Riccardo's mother looked at him from over the candles. Lit up like that, her face was full of threatening shadows, just like the clown's. The other guests fell silent.

'It's OK,' the woman said uncertainly. 'Ricky, take your friend to the door.'

'But I've got to blow out the candles.'

'Do as I say,' his mother ordered, still staring at Mattia.

'You're such a drag, Mattia.'

Some of the children started laughing. Mattia followed Riccardo to the front door, took his jacket from the pile and said thanks and bye. Riccardo didn't reply, quickly shutting the door behind him to run back to his cake.

From the courtyard of Riccardo's block, Mattia turned towards the lit window one last time. His classmates' muffled cries filtered out like the reassuring hum of the television in the living room when his mother sent him and Michela to bed in the evening. The gate closed behind him with a metallic click and he began to run.

He entered the park, but after he had walked

for ten metres or so the light from the street lamps was no longer enough for him to make out the gravel path. The bare branches of the trees where he had left Michela were just slightly darker scratches against the black sky. Seeing them from far away, Mattia was filled with the clear and inexplicable certainty that his sister was no longer there.

He stopped a few yards away from the bench where Michela had been sitting until a few hours before, busy fiddling with her coat. He stopped and listened until he got his breath back, thinking that at any moment his sister was bound to emerge from behind a tree saying peep-bo and then run towards him, fluttering along with her crooked gait.

Mattia called Michela and was startled by his own voice. He repeated it more quietly. He walked over to the wooden tables and laid a hand on the spot where Michela had been sitting. It was as cold as everything else.

She must have got bored and gone home, he thought.

But what if she doesn't know the way? And she doesn't know how to cross the road on her own either.

Mattia looked at the park, which was disappearing into the darkness in front of him. He didn't even know where it stopped. He thought that he didn't want to go on and that he had no choice.

He walked on tiptoes to keep the leaves from crunching under his feet, turning his head from side to side in the hope of spotting Michela crouching behind a tree to ambush a beetle or who knows what.

He walked into the playground. He tried to remember the colours of the slide in the Sunday afternoon light, when his mother gave in to Michela's cries and let her have a few goes, even though she was too old for it.

He walked along the hedge as far as the public toilets, but wasn't brave enough to go inside. He found his way back to the path, which was now just a thin strip of soil marked by the footsteps of passing families. He followed it for a good ten minutes until he no longer knew where he was. Then he started crying and coughing at the same time.

'You're so stupid, Michela,' he said under his breath. 'A stupid retard. I've told you a thousand times to stay where you are if you get lost . . . But you never understand anything . . . Nothing at all.'

He went up a slight slope and found himself looking at the river that cut through the park. His father had told him its name loads of times, but Mattia couldn't remember it. The water reflected a bit of light coming from somewhere unknown and it seemed to quiver in his tear-filled gaze.

He went over to the river-bank and had a sense that Michela must be somewhere close by. She liked the water. His mother always told him that when they were little and she bathed them both together, Michela shrieked like a mad thing because she didn't want to get out, even after the water was cold. One Sunday his father had taken them to the river-bank, perhaps even to this very spot, and taught him to throw flat stones so that they bounced on the surface. As he was showing him the best way to exploit his wrist muscles to make the stone spin, Michela had leaned forward and slipped into the water up to her waist before their father caught her by the arm. He had given her a smack and she had started whining and then all three of them had gone home in silence, with long faces.

The image of Michela playing with a twig and breaking up her own reflection in the water before sliding into it like a sack of potatoes ran through his head with the force of an electric shock.

Exhausted, he sat down a couple of feet from the river's edge. He turned round to look behind him and saw the darkness that would last for many hours to come.

He started staring at the gleaming black surface of the river. Again he tried to remember its name, but it wouldn't come. He plunged his hands into the cold earth. On the bank the dampness made it softer. He found a piece of a bottle, a sharp reminder of some night-time festivity. The first time he stuck it into his hand it didn't hurt, perhaps he didn't even notice. Then he started twisting it round in his flesh to get it deeper in, without taking his eyes off the water. He waited for Michela to rise to the surface, and in the meantime he wondered why some things float while some others don't.

On the Skin and Just Behind It
(1991)

3

The horrible white ceramic vase, decorated with a complicated gold floral motif, which had always occupied a corner of the bathroom, had been in the Della Rocca family for five generations. But no one really liked it. On several occasions Alice had felt an urge to hurl it to the floor and throw the tiny, inestimable fragments into the rubbish bin at the front of the house, along with the Tetra Pak mashed-potato containers, used sanitary towels — although certainly not used by her — and the empty blister-packs of her father's anti-depressants.

Alice ran a finger along the rim and thought how cold, smooth and clean it was. Soledad, the Ecuadorian housekeeper, had become more meticulous with the passing of the years; in the Della Rocca household attention was paid to detail. When Sol had first arrived, Alice was only six and studied her suspiciously from behind her mother's skirt. Soledad had crouched down and looked at her with wonder. What lovely hair you have, she had said, can I touch it? Alice had bitten her tongue to keep from saying no and Soledad had lifted one of her chestnut curls as if it was a swatch of silk and then let it fall back. She couldn't believe that hair could be so soft.

Alice held her breath as she slipped off her vest and automatically shut her eyes tight for a moment.

When she opened them again she saw herself reflected in the big mirror above the washbasin and felt a pleasurable sense of disappointment. She rolled down the elastic of her knickers a few times so that they just revealed the scar and were stretched tightly enough to leave a little gap between the edge and her belly, forming a bridge between the bones of her pelvis. There wasn't quite room for her index finger; but being able to slip her little finger in drove her mad.

There, it should blossom right there, she thought.

A little blue rose like Viola's.

Alice turned to stand in profile, her right side, the good one, as she was used to telling herself. She brushed all her hair forward and thought it made her look like a child possessed by demons. She tried to gather it up in a ponytail and then scooped it higher up on her head, the way Viola wore hers, which everyone always liked.

It didn't work like that either.

She let her hair fall on her shoulders and with her usual gesture pinned it back behind her ears. She rested her hands on the basin and pushed her face towards the mirror so quickly that her eyes seemed to superimpose themselves into one single, terrifying Cyclops eye. Her hot breath formed a halo on the glass, covering part of her face.

She couldn't really work out where Viola and her friends got the looks with which they went around breaking boys' hearts. Those merciless, captivating looks that could make or break you with a single, imperceptible flicker of the eyebrow.

Alice tried to be provocative with the mirror,

but saw only a gracelessly embarrassed girl shaking her shoulders and moving as if she were anaesthetized. The real problem was her cheeks: too puffy and blotchy. They suffocated her eyes, when all the while she wanted her gaze to land like a dagger in the stomach of the boys whose eyes she met. She wanted that gaze to spare no one, to leave an indelible mark.

Instead only her belly, bum and tits got slimmer, while her cheeks stayed as they were, two round baby's pads.

Someone knocked at the bathroom door.

'Alice, it's ready,' her father's hateful voice rang out through the frosted glass.

Alice didn't reply and sucked her cheeks into her mouth to see how much better they would be like that.

'Alice, are you in there?' her father called.

With her mouth puckered, Alice kissed her reflection. She brushed her own tongue against the cold of the glass. She closed her eyes and, as if it was a real kiss, made her head sway back and forth, too regularly to be believable. She hadn't yet found the kiss she really yearned for on anyone's mouth.

Davide Poirino had been the first to use his tongue, in the third year of secondary school, after losing a bet. He had rolled it mechanically around Alice's tongue three times, clockwise, and then turned to his friends and said OK? They had burst out laughing and someone had said you've kissed the cripple, but Alice was pleased anyway, she had been given her first kiss and Davide wasn't bad at all.

35

Then there had been others. Her cousin Walter at their grandmother's party, and a friend of Davide's whose name she didn't even know, and who had asked her in secret if he could have a go too. In a hidden corner of the school playground they had pressed their lips together for a few minutes, neither of them daring to move a muscle. When they had parted, he had said thank you and walked off with his head held high and the springy step of a grown-up man.

Now she was lagging behind. Her classmates talked about positions, love-bites and how to use your fingers, and discussed whether it was better with or without a condom, while Alice's lips still bore the insipid memory of a mechanical kiss in third grade.

'Alice? Can you hear me?' her father called again, louder this time.

'Shush. Yes, I hear you,' Alice replied irritably, in a tone of voice that could barely be heard from outside.

'Dinner's ready,' her father repeated.

'I heard you, damn it,' Alice said. Then, under her breath, she added, 'Pain in the arse.'

★   ★   ★

Soledad knew that Alice threw her food away. At first, when Alice started leaving her dinner on her plate, she said *mi amorcito*, eat it all up, in my country children are dying of hunger.

One evening Alice, furious, looked her straight in the eyes.

'Even if I stuff myself till I burst, the children

36

in your country won't stop dying of hunger,' she said.

So Soledad said nothing now, but put less food on her plate. It made no difference anyway. Alice was quite capable of weighing up her food with her eyes and choosing her 300 calories for dinner. The rest she got rid of, somehow or other.

She ate with her right hand resting on her napkin. In front of the plate she put her wine glass, which she asked to be filled but never drank, and her water glass, in such a way as to form a glass barricade. Then, during dinner, she strategically positioned the salt-cellar and the oil cruet too. She waited for her family to be distracted, each absorbed in the difficult process of mastication. At that point she very carefully pushed her food, cut into small pieces, off the plate and into her napkin.

Over the course of a dinner she made at least three full napkins disappear into the pockets of her sweatpants. Before brushing her teeth she emptied them into the toilet and watched the little pieces of food disappearing down the drain. With satisfaction she ran a hand over her stomach and imagined it as empty and clean as a crystal vase.

'Sol, damn it, you put cream in the sauce again,' her mother complained. 'How many times do I have to tell you that I can't digest it?'

Alice's mother pushed her plate away in disgust.

Alice had come to the table with a towel wrapped around her head like a turban in order

37

to justify all the time she had spent locked up in the bathroom.

She had thought about whether or not to ask for it. But she would do it anyway. She wanted it too much.

'I'd like to get a tattoo on my belly,' she began.

Her father pulled his glass away from his mouth.

'Excuse me?'

'You heard,' said Alice, defying him with her eyes. 'I want to get a tattoo done.'

Alice's father ran his napkin over his mouth and eyes, as if to erase an ugly image that had run through his mind. Then he carefully refolded it and put it back on his knees. He picked up his fork again, trying to display all his irritating self-control.

'I don't even know how you get some of these things into your head,' he said.

'And what would you like to have tattooed? Let's hear,' her mother broke in, the irritable expression on her face probably due more to the cream in the sauce than her daughter's request.

'A rose. Tiny. Viola's got one.'

'And forgive me, who might Viola be?' her father asked with an ironic inflection that was a little too marked.

Alice shook her head, looked at the middle of the table and felt insignificant.

'Viola's a classmate of hers,' Fernanda replied. 'She must have mentioned her a million times. You're not really with it, are you?'

Mr Della Rocca looked disdainfully at his wife, as if to say no one asked you.

'Well I'm sorry, but I don't think I'm very interested in what Alice's classmates get drawn on them,' he pronounced at last. 'At any rate she's not getting a tattoo.'

Alice pushed another forkful of spaghetti into her napkin.

'You can't stop me,' she ventured, still staring at the vacant centre of the table. Her voice cracked with a hint of insecurity.

'Could you repeat that?' her father asked, without altering the volume and calm of his own voice.

'Could you repeat that?' he asked more slowly.

'I said you can't stop me,' replied Alice, looking up, but without being able to endure her father's deep, chilly eyes for more than half a second.

'You think not? As far as I'm concerned you're fifteen years old and this binds you to the decisions of your parents for — the calculation is a very simple one — another three years,' the lawyer intoned. 'Once that period has concluded you will be free to adorn your skin with flowers, skulls or whatever takes your fancy.'

The lawyer smiled in the direction of the plate and slipped into his mouth a well-rolled forkful of spaghetti.

There was a long silence. Alice ran her thumb and forefinger along the edge of the tablecloth. Her mother nibbled on a bread stick and allowed her eyes to wander around the dining room. Her father pretended to eat heartily. He chewed with rolling motions of his jaw and at the first two seconds of each mouthful he kept his eyes closed, in ecstasy.

Alice chose to deliver the blow because she really detested him, and seeing him eat like that made even her good leg go stiff.

'You don't give a damn if no one likes me,' she said. 'If no one ever will ever like me.'

Her father looked at her quizzically, then returned to his dinner, as if no one had spoken.

'You don't care if you've ruined me for ever.'

Mr Della Rocca sat with his fork in mid-air. He looked at his daughter for a few seconds.

'I don't know what you're talking about,' he said, a slight quaver to his voice.

'You know perfectly well,' Alice said. 'You know that it'll be your fault alone if I'm like this for ever.'

Alice's father rested his fork on the edge of the plate. With one hand he covered his eyes as if he was thinking deeply about something. Then he got up and left the room, his heavy footsteps ringing out from the gleaming marble of the corridor.

Fernanda said, oh Alice, without compassion or reproach, just a resigned shake of the head. Then she followed her husband into the next room.

Alice went on staring at her full plate for about two minutes, while Soledad cleared the table, silent as a shadow. Then she stuffed the full napkin into her pocket and locked herself in the bathroom.

4

It had been some time since Pietro Balossino had tried to penetrate his son's obscure universe. When, by accident, he glimpsed Mattia's arms, devastated by scars, he thought back to the sleepless nights spent scanning the house for sharp objects left lying around, the nights when Adele, full of sedatives, slept on the sofa with her mouth open because she no longer wanted to share the bed with him. The nights when the future seemed to come only in the morning and he counted the hours, all of them, by the chimes of distant church bells.

The conviction that one morning he would find his son face down on a blood-soaked pillow had taken root so firmly in his head that he was now used to thinking as if Mattia had already ceased to exist, even at times like this, when he was sitting next to him in the car.

He was driving him to his new school. Outside it was raining, but the rain was so fine that it didn't make a sound.

A few weeks before, the head of the E. M. scientific high school had called him and Adele to his office to *inform them of a situation.* When the time came for the meeting, he had skirted the issue, dwelling on the boy's sensitive temperament, his extraordinary intelligence, his solid 90 per cent average in all subjects.

Mr Balossino had insisted on his son being

41

present for the discussion, for reasons of correctness which doubtless interested him alone. Mattia had sat down next to his parents and throughout the whole session he had not raised his eyes from his knees. By clenching his fists tightly he had managed to make his left hand bleed very superficially. Two days before, in a moment of distraction, Adele had only checked the nails on his other hand.

Mattia listened to the headmaster's words as if he wasn't really talking about him and he remembered that time in the fifth year of primary school when his teacher Rita, after he hadn't uttered a word for five days in a row, had made him sit in the middle of the room, with all the others arranged around him in a horseshoe. The teacher had begun by saying that Mattia plainly had a problem that he didn't want to talk to anyone about. That Mattia was a very intelligent child, perhaps too intelligent for his age. Then she had invited his classmates to sit close to him, so that they could make him understand that they were his friends. Mattia had looked at his feet and, when the teacher had asked him if he wanted to say something, he had finally spoken and asked if he could go back to his chair.

Once the plaudits were finished, the head got to the *situation*. Mr Balossino finally understood, although only a few hours later, that Mattia's teachers had expressed a peculiar unease, an almost impalpable feeling of inadequacy, with regard to this extraordinarily gifted boy, who seemed not to want to form bonds with any of his contemporaries.

The headmaster paused. He leaned back into his comfortable armchair and opened a folder, although he didn't seem to be reading anything. Then he closed it again, as if remembering all of a sudden that there were other people in his office. With carefully chosen words he suggested to the Balossinos that perhaps the E. M. high school was not capable of responding fully to their son's needs.

When, at dinner, Mattia's father had asked him if he really wanted to change schools, Mattia had replied with a shrug and studied the dazzling reflection of fluorescent light on the knife with which he was supposed to be cutting his meat.

★ ★ ★

'It isn't really raining crooked,' said Mattia, looking out of the car window and jerking his father out of his thoughts.

'What?' said Pietro, instinctively shaking his head.

'There's no wind outside. Otherwise the leaves would be moving on the trees as well,' Mattia went on.

His father tried to follow his reasoning. In fact none of it meant anything to him and he suspected that it was merely another of his son's eccentricities.

'So?' he asked.

'The raindrops are running down the window at an angle, but that's just an effect of our motion. By measuring the angle with the vertical, you could also calculate the fall velocity.'

Mattia ran his finger along the trajectory of a drop. He brought his face close to the windscreen and breathed on it. Then, with his index finger, he drew a line in the condensation.

'Don't breathe on the windows, you'll leave marks.'

Mattia didn't seem to have heard him.

'If we couldn't see anything out of the car, if we didn't know we were moving, there would be no way of telling whether the raindrops were to blame or we were,' said Mattia.

'To blame for what?' his father asked, bewildered and slightly annoyed.

'To blame for them coming down so crooked.'

Pietro Balossino nodded seriously, without understanding. They had arrived. He put the car in neutral and pulled on the handbrake. Mattia opened the door and a gust of fresh air blew inside.

'I'll come and get you at one,' said Pietro.

Mattia nodded. Mr Balossino leaned slightly forward to kiss him, but the belt restrained him. He leaned back into the seat and watched his son get out and close the door behind him.

⋆ ⋆ ⋆

The new school was in a lovely residential area. It had been built in the twenties, and in spite of its recent refurbishment it remained a blot on the landscape amid a row of sumptuous villas; a parallelepiped of white concrete, with four horizontal rows of equidistant windows and two

44

green iron fire escapes.

Mattia climbed the two flights of steps leading to the main door and remained apart from all the little groups of kids who were waiting for the first bell, getting wet from the rain.

Once he was inside, he looked for the map with the layout of the classrooms, so that he wouldn't have to ask the janitors for help.

F2 was at the end of the corridor on the first floor. Mattia took a deep breath and walked in. He waited, leaning against the wall at the back of the classroom, with his thumbs pressed to the straps of his backpack and the look of someone who wanted to disappear into the wall.

As they were taking their seats, the new faces glanced at him apprehensively. No one smiled at him. Some of them whispered in each other's ears and Mattia was sure that it was about him.

He kept an eye on the desks that were left free and, when one next to a girl with red nail varnish was occupied, he felt relieved. The teacher came into the classroom and Mattia slipped on to the last empty chair, next to the window.

'Are you the new boy?' asked his neighbour, who looked just as alone as he did.

Mattia nodded without looking at him.

'I'm Denis,' he said, extending his hand.

Mattia shook it weakly and said nice to meet you.

'Welcome,' said Denis.

5

Viola Bai was admired and feared with equal passion by her classmates, because she was so beautiful she made people uneasy, and because at the age of fifteen she knew more about life than any of her contemporaries; or at least that was the impression she gave. On Monday mornings, during break, the girls congregated around her desk and listened greedily to the account of her weekend. Most times this was a skilful reimagining of what Serena, Viola's older sister, had told her the day before. Viola switched everything to herself, but enriched the stories with sordid details, often completely invented, which to the ears of her friends sounded mysterious and disturbing. She talked about various bars, without ever having set foot in them, and she was capable of giving minute descriptions of the psychedelic lighting, or of the malicious smile that the barman had flashed at her as he served her a Cuba libre.

In most cases she ended up either in bed with the barman or out behind the bar, among the beer-kegs and the cases of vodka, where he took her from behind, covering her mouth with a hand to keep her from screaming.

Viola Bai knew how to tell a story. She knew that all the violence is contained in the precision of a detail. She was good at calculating pace so that the bell rang just as the barman was about

46

to open the zip of his name-brand jeans. At that moment her devoted audience slowly dispersed, their cheeks red with envy and indignation. Promises were extracted from Viola that she would go on with her story at the next bell, but she was too intelligent actually to do it. She always ended up dismissing the event with a pout of her perfect mouth, as if what had happened to her was of no importance. It was just one more detail in her extraordinary life and she was already light years ahead of everyone else.

She had actually tried sex, and also some of the drugs whose names she liked to list, but she had only been with one boy, and only once. It had happened at the seaside. He'd been a friend of her sister's who had smoked and drunk too much that evening to realize that a little thirteen-year-old girl was too young for certain things. He had fucked her hastily, in the street, behind a rubbish bin. As they came back, heads lowered, to rejoin the others, Viola had taken his hand but he had snatched it away and asked what are you doing? Her cheeks burned and the heat still trapped between her legs had made her feel alone. Over the days that followed the boy didn't say a word to her and Viola had confided in her sister, who had laughed at her naivety and said wise up, what did you expect?

Viola's devoted audience was made up of Giada Savarino, Federica Mazzoldi and Giulia Mirandi. Together they formed a compact and ruthless phalanx: the four bitches, as some of the boys at the school called them. Viola had chosen them one by one and from each of them she had demanded a little sacrifice, because her friendship was something you had to earn. She alone decided if you were in or out and her decisions were obscure and unmistakably her own.

Alice observed Viola on the sly. From her desk, two rows back, she fed off the broken sentences and fragments of torrid tales; then in the evening, alone in her room, she savoured every one.

Before that Wednesday morning Viola had never addressed a word to her. The event was to be a kind of initiation and had to be done properly. None of the girls ever knew for sure whether Viola was improvising or whether she planned the torture beforehand — but they all agreed that she was a complete genius.

Alice hated the changing-room. Her oh-so-perfect classmates stood around in their bras and knickers for as long as possible to be properly envied by the others. They assumed stiff and unnatural poses, pulling in their bellies and thrusting out their tits. They pouted away at the half-broken mirror that occupied one of the walls. They said look here, measuring with their hands the width of their pelvises, which could not have been more well proportioned and seductive.

On Wednesday Alice left home with her shorts under her jeans so that she wouldn't have to undress fully. The others looked at her suspiciously, imagining the horrors that were surely hidden under those clothes. She took off her sweater with her back turned to them so that they wouldn't see her belly.

She put on her trainers and pushed her shoes against the wall, arranging them parallel to one another. Her jeans were carefully folded, whereas her classmates' clothes dangled chaotically from the wooden benches, their shoes scattered over the floor and turned the wrong way round because they had taken them off using only their feet.

'Alice, have you got a sweet tooth?' Viola said to her.

Alice took a few seconds to convince herself that Viola Bai was actually talking to her. She was sure that she was invisible. She pulled the two ends of her shoelaces, but the knot came apart between her fingers.

'Me?' she asked, looking uneasily around.

'I don't see any other Alices.'

The others exploded with laughter.

'No. Not particularly.'

Viola rose from the bench and came closer to her. Alice felt those marvellous eyes on her, bisected by the shadow that her fringe cast over her face.

'But you like sweets, don't you?' Viola continued in her honeyed voice.

'Yes. I suppose. Pretty much.'

Alice bit her lip and rebuked herself for her idiotic insecurity. She pressed her bony back against the wall. A tremor ran down her good leg. The other remained inert, as ever.

'What do you mean pretty much? Everyone likes sweets. Isn't that right, girls?' Viola addressed the three friends without turning round.

'Mhmmm. Everyone,' they echoed. Alice noticed a strange trepidation in the eyes of Federica Mazzoldi, who was staring at her from the far end of the changing room.

'Yes, actually, I do like them,' she corrected herself. She was starting to get frightened, although she didn't yet know of what.

In the first year, the four bitches had grabbed Alessandra Mirano, the one who ended up being thrown out and training as a beautician, and dragged her into the boys' changing room. They had shut her inside and two boys had got their cocks out in front of her. From the corridor Alice had heard their shouts of encouragement, mixed with the wild laughter of the four torturers.

'I thought so. Now would you like a sweet?' Viola asked.

If I say yes, what are they going to make me eat?

If I say no, Viola might get angry and then they'll put me in the boys' changing room as well.

She sat in silence like a moron.

'Come on. It isn't that hard a question,' Viola said mockingly. She took a handful of fruit gums from her pocket.

'You girls behind me, which ones do you want?' she asked.

Giulia Mirandi came over to Viola and looked into her hand. Viola didn't take her eyes off Alice, who felt her body crumpling under the gaze like a sheet of newspaper burning in the fireplace.

'There's orange, raspberry, blackberry, strawberry and peach,' Giulia said. She darted a fleeting and apprehensive glance at Alice, unseen by Viola.

50

'I'll have raspberry,' said Federica.

'I'll have peach,' said Giada.

Giulia threw them the sweets and unwrapped her own orange one. She slipped it into her mouth and then took a step back to return the stage to Viola.

'Blackberry and strawberry are left. So do you want them or not?'

Maybe she just wants to give me a sweet, Alice thought.

Maybe they just want to see whether I eat or not.

It's just a sweet.

'I prefer strawberry,' she said quietly.

'Damn it, that's my favourite too,' Viola said, giving a terrible performance of disappointment. 'But I'll happily give it to you.'

She unwrapped the strawberry fruit gum and let the paper fall to the ground. Alice held out her hand to take the sweet.

'Wait a moment,' Viola said. 'Don't be so greedy.'

She bent to the ground, holding the sweet between thumb and index finger. She rubbed it along the sweaty floor of the changing room. Walking with her knees bent, she dragged it slowly along the whole of the wall to Alice's left and round the corner, where the dirt had coagulated in balls of dust and tangles of hair.

Giada and Federica laughed fit to burst. Giulia nervously chewed on a lip. The other girls had figured out where things were going and left, closing the door behind them.

Reaching the end of the wall, Viola moved towards the washbasin, where the girls splashed their armpits and faces after gym. She used the sweet to collect the whitish slime that covered the inner wall of the outflow.

She turned back towards Alice and held the revolting object under her nose.

'There,' she said. 'Strawberry, the one you wanted.'

She wasn't laughing. She had the serious and determined look of someone doing something painful but necessary.

Alice shook her head to say no. She pressed herself even closer against the wall.

'What is it? Don't you want it any more?' Viola asked her.

'Go on,' Federica cut in. 'You asked for it and now you can eat it.'

Alice gulped.

'What if I don't?' she summoned the courage to say.

'If you don't eat it, you'll take the consequences,' Viola replied enigmatically.

'What consequences?'

'You can't know the consequences. You can't ever know them.'

They want to take me to the boys, Alice thought. Or else they'll strip me and not give me back my clothes.

Trembling, but almost imperceptibly, she held her hand out towards Viola, who dropped the filthy sweet into her palm. She slowly brought it to her mouth.

The others had fallen silent, and seemed to be thinking she isn't really going to do it. Viola was impassive.

Alice put the sweet on her tongue and felt the hairs that were stuck to it drying up her saliva. She chewed only twice and something squeaked between her teeth.

Don't throw up, she thought. You mustn't throw up.

She choked back an acidic spurt of gastric juices and swallowed the sweet. She felt it struggling its way down, like a stone, along her oesophagus.

The fluorescent light on the ceiling gave off an electrical hum and the voices of the boys in the gym were a formless mixture of shouts and laughter. In the basement rooms the air was heavy and the windows were too small to allow it to circulate.

Viola stared seriously at Alice. Without smiling she gave a nod of the head that meant now we can go. Then she turned round and left the changing room, passing the other three without so much as a glance.

6

There was something important that you had to know about Denis. To tell the truth, Denis thought it was the only thing about him worth knowing, so he had never said it to anyone.

His secret had a terrible name, which settled like a nylon cloth over his thoughts and wouldn't let them breathe. There it was, weighing heavily inside his head like an inevitable punishment with which he would sooner or later have to come to terms.

When, at the age of ten, his male piano teacher had accompanied his fingers all the way along the D major scale, pressing his hot palm down on the back of his hand, Denis had been unable to breathe. He had bent his torso slightly forward to cover the outline of the erection that had exploded in the trousers of his tracksuit. All his life he would think of that moment as being true love, and would fumble around every corner of his existence in search of the adhesive warmth of that contact.

Each time memories like this came back to his mind, making his neck and hands sweat, Denis locked himself in the bathroom and masturbated fiercely, sitting back to front on the toilet. The pleasure only lasted a moment and spread just a few inches around his penis. The sense of guilt, on the other hand, plunged down on him from above like a shower of dirty water. It ran down his skin and nestled in his guts, making everything slowly rot, the way that damp eats away at the walls of old houses.

During biology class, in the basement laboratory, Denis watched Mattia dissecting a piece of steak, separating the white fibres from the red. He wanted to stroke his hands. He wanted to discover whether that cumbersome lump of desire that had taken root in his head would really melt like butter simply through contact with the classmate he was in love with.

They were sitting close to one another. Both rested their forearms on the lab bench. A row of transparent flasks, beakers and test tubes separated them from the rest of the class and deflected the rays of light, distorting everything beyond that line.

Mattia was concentrating on his work and hadn't looked up for at least a quarter of an hour. He didn't like biology, but he pursued the task with the rigour he applied to all subjects. Organic matter, so violable and full of imperfections, was incomprehensible to him. The vital odour which the soft piece of meat gave off aroused nothing in him but a faint disgust.

With a pair of tweezers he extracted a thin white filament and deposited it on the glass slide. He brought his eyes to the microscope and adjusted the focus. On the squared notebook he wrote down every detail and made a sketch of the enlarged image.

Denis gave a deep sigh. Then, as if taking a backward dive, he found the courage to speak.

'Mattia, have you got a secret?' he asked his friend.

Mattia seemed not to have heard, but the scalpel with which he was cutting another section of muscle slipped from his hand and rang out on the metal surface. Slowly he picked it up again.

Denis waited for a few seconds. Mattia was motionless, and held the knife a few inches above the piece of meat.

'You can tell it to me; you can tell me your secret,' Denis went on. His veins pulsed with trepidation. Now that he had pushed himself over the edge and into his classmate's fascinating intimacy, he had no intention of letting go.

'I've got one too, you know,' he said.

Mattia cleanly sliced the muscle in half, as if he wanted to kill something that was already dead.

'I haven't got a secret,' he said under his breath.

'If you tell me yours, I'll tell you mine,' Denis pressed. He moved his stool closer and Mattia visibly stiffened. He stared without expression at the scrap of meat.

'We've got to finish the experiment,' he said in a monotonous voice. 'Otherwise we won't be able to complete the module.'

'I don't give a damn about the module,' said Denis. 'Tell me what you've done to your hands.'

Mattia counted three breaths. Light molecules of ethanol stirred in the air, and some of them penetrated his nostrils. He felt them rising like a pleasant burning sensation along his septum, up to a point between his eyes.

'You really want to know what I've done to my

56

hands?' he asked, turning towards Denis but looking at the jars of formalin lined up behind him: dozens of jars containing foetuses and limbs amputated from various animals.

Quivering, Denis nodded.

'Then look at this,' said Mattia.

He gripped the knife with all five fingers. Then he plunged into the hollow between his index and middle fingers and dragged it down to his wrist.

7

On Thursday Viola was waiting for her outside the gate. Alice was already passing, head lowered, when Viola called her name and grabbed her sleeve. Alice immediately thought about the sweet again and gave a start, the nausea making her head spin. Once the four bitches had you in their sights, they didn't let you go.

'I've got a maths test,' Viola said. 'I don't know anything and I don't want to go.'

Alice looked at her uncomprehendingly. She didn't seem hostile, but Alice didn't trust her. She tried to pull away. Let's go for a walk, Viola continued. Me and you? Yes, me and you. Alice looked around in terror. Come on, get a move on, Viola urged, they mustn't see us out here. But . . . Alice tried to object. Viola didn't allow her to continue; she pulled her harder by the sleeve and Alice had no choice but to follow, hobbling as they ran to the bus stop.

They sat down side by side, Alice resting her back against the window so as not to steal Viola's space. From one moment to the next she expected something to happen, something terrible, but Viola was radiant. She took a lipstick from her bag and ran it over her lips. Want some? she asked. Alice shook her head. The school shrank in the distance behind them. My father will kill me, Alice whispered. Her legs were shaking. Viola sighed. Come on, show me the absence card. Studying the signature of Alice's father, she said it's easy . . . I'll do it. She showed Alice her own card, the signatures that she faked every time she didn't feel like going to a lesson. Anyway first class tomorrow is old Follini, she said, and she can't see a thing.

Viola started talking about school, about how she didn't give a stuff about maths because she was going to do law anyway. Alice struggled to hear her. She thought about the day before, about the changing room, and she couldn't give a name to this sudden confidence.

They got off in the square and started walking under the arcades. Viola slipped into a clothes shop with fluorescent windows in which Alice had never set foot. She was acting as if they were lifelong friends. She asked Alice her size and she was ashamed to say thirty-eight. The shop assistants watched them suspiciously, but Viola paid no attention. They shared a changing room and, surreptitiously, Alice compared her own body with her friend's. In the end they didn't buy anything.

They went into a bar and Viola ordered two coffees, without asking Alice what she wanted. Alice hadn't a clue what was going on, but a new and unexpected happiness was spilling into her head. Slowly she forgot all about her father and about school. She was sitting in a bar with Viola Bai and time seemed to belong to them alone.

Viola smoked three cigarettes and insisted that Alice try one too. She laughed, with her perfect teeth, every time her new friend exploded in a fit of neophyte coughing. She subjected her to a little quiz, about the boys she hadn't had and the kisses she hadn't given. Alice replied with her eyes lowered. Are you trying to make me believe you've never had a boyfriend? Never ever ever? Alice shook her head. It's impossible. It's a tragedy. We've absolutely got to do something. You don't want to die a virgin!

The next day, at ten o'clock break, they had walked around the school in search of the boy for Alice. Viola dismissed Giada and the others, saying we've got things to do, and they watched her leave the classroom hand in hand with her new friend.

She had already organized everything. It would happen at her birthday party the following Saturday. They just had to find the right boy. As they walked down the corridor she pointed to this one and that one and told Alice, look at the arse on that one, not bad at all, I bet he knows what to do.

Alice smiled nervously and couldn't make her mind up. In her head she imagined with unsettling clarity the moment when a boy would slip his hands under her jumper. When a boy would discover that, beneath the clothes that covered her body so well, there was nothing but chubby flesh and flabby skin.

Now they were leaning on the rail of the fire escape, on the second floor, watching the boys play football in the playground with an under-inflated yellow ball.

'What about Trivero?' Viola asked.

'I don't know who he is.'

'What do you mean you don't know who he is? He's in the fifth year. He used to row with my sister. They say interesting things about him.'

'What sort of things?'

Viola made a gesture with her hands to indicate length and then laughed loudly, enjoying the disconcerting effect of her allusions. Alice felt a flash of shame rising to her face, along with the marvellous certainty that her loneliness was really over.

They went down to the ground floor and passed by the snack and drinks machines. The students formed a chaotic queue, chinking coins in their jeans pockets.

'OK, you've got to decide,' said Viola.

Alice spun on her heels. She looked around, disoriented.

'That one looks cute,' she said, pointing at two boys some distance away, beside the window. They were standing close together, but not talking or looking at each other.

'Who?' Viola asked. 'The one with the bandage or other one?'

'The one with the bandage.'

Viola stared at her. Her sparkling eyes were as wide as two oceans.

'You're crazy,' she said. 'You know what he did?'

Alice shook her head.

'He stuck a knife in his hand, on purpose. Here at school.'

Alice shrugged.

'He looks interesting,' she said.

'Interesting? He's a psychopath. With a guy

like that you'll end up in pieces in a freezer.'

Alice smiled, but went on looking at the boy with the bandaged hand. There was something in the way he kept his head thrust down that made her want to go over to him, lift his chin and say to him look at me, I'm here.

'Are you absolutely sure?' Viola asked her.

'Yes,' said Alice.

Viola shrugged.

'So let's go,' she said.

She took Alice by the hand and pulled her towards the two boys at the window.

8

Mattia was looking out of the opaque windows of the hall. It was a bright day, an anticipation of spring at the beginning of March. The strong wind that had cleared the air during the night seemed to sweep time away too, making it run at a faster pace. Mattia tried to estimate how far away the horizon was by counting the roofs of the houses that he could see from his vantage point.

Denis was surreptitiously staring at him, trying to guess his thoughts. They hadn't spoken of what had happened in the biology lab. In fact, they didn't speak much at all, but spent time together, each in his own abyss, held safe and tight by the other's silence.

'Hi,' Mattia heard someone say, too close to him.

Reflected in the glass he saw two girls standing behind him, holding hands. He turned round.

Denis looked at him quizzically. The girls seemed to be waiting for something.

'Hi,' Mattia said gently. He lowered his head, to protect himself from one of the girls' keen eyes.

'I'm Viola and this is Alice,' she continued. 'We're in 2B.'

Mattia nodded. Denis's mouth fell open. Neither of them said anything.

'Well?' Viola said. 'Aren't you going to

introduce yourselves?'

Mattia spoke his name in a low voice, as if he was reminding himself of it. He offered a soft hand, the one without the bandage, to Viola and she shook it powerfully. The other girl barely brushed it and smiled, looking in another direction.

Denis introduced himself next, rather clumsily.

'We wanted to invite you to my birthday party the Saturday after next,' said Viola.

Again Denis sought Mattia's eyes, but Mattia responded by staring at Alice's shy half-smile. He thought her lips were so pale and thin that her mouth seemed to have been traced by a keen-bladed scalpel.

'Why?' he asked.

Viola looked at him askance and turned towards Alice, with an expression that meant I told you he was mad.

'What do you mean why? Obviously because we feel like inviting you.'

'No, thanks,' said Mattia. 'I can't come.'

Denis, relieved, hurried to say he couldn't come either.

Viola ignored him and concentrated on the boy with the bandage.

'You can't? I wonder what could be keeping you so busy on a Saturday evening,' she said provocatively. 'Do you have to play video games with your little friend? Or were you planning on cutting your veins again?'

Viola felt a tremor of terror and excitement as she uttered those last words. Alice gripped her hand harder to make her stop.

Mattia reflected that he had forgotten the number of roofs and wouldn't have time to count them again before the bell.

'I don't like parties,' he explained.

Viola forced herself to laugh for a few seconds, with a sequence of piercing, high-pitched giggles.

'You really are strange,' she said, tapping herself twice on the right temple. 'Everyone likes parties.'

Alice had withdrawn her hand and unconsciously rested it on her belly.

'Well, I don't,' Mattia snapped back.

Viola stared defiantly at him and he blankly held her gaze. Alice had taken a step back. Viola opened her mouth to give some kind of reply, but the bell rang just in time. Mattia turned round and headed resolutely towards the stairs, as if the discussion for him was over. Denis followed, dragged along in his wake.

9

Since entering the service of the Della Rocca family, Soledad Galienas had only blundered once. It had happened four years previously, one rainy evening when the Della Roccas were out dining with friends.

Soledad's wardrobe contained only black clothes, underwear included. She had spoken so often of her husband's death in a work accident that she sometimes believed it herself. She imagined him standing on a scaffolding, 60 feet off the ground, cigarette between his teeth, as he levelled a layer of mortar before laying another row of bricks. She saw him tripping over an abandoned tool or perhaps a coil of rope, the rope with which he was supposed to make a harness and which instead he had thrown aside because the harness was for softies. She imagined him wobbling on the wooden planks before plummeting without a sound. The image panned out so that her husband became like a little black dot waving its arms against the white sky. Then her artificial memory ended with an overhead shot: her husband's body splattered on the dusty ground of the building site, lifeless and two-dimensional, with his eyes still open and a dark pool of blood oozing out from under his back.

Thinking of him like that gave her a pleasurable tremor of anguish and, if she lingered on it long enough, she managed to squeeze out a few tears, which were entirely for herself.

The truth was that her husband had walked out. He had left her one morning, probably to remake his life with a woman she didn't even know. And she had never heard anything more about him. When she arrived in Italy she had made up the story of widowhood to have a past to tell people about, because there was nothing to say about her real past. Her black clothes and the thought that the others might see the traces of a tragedy in her eyes, a pain that had never been assuaged, gave her a sense of security. She wore her mourning with dignity and until that evening she had never betrayed the memory of the deceased.

On Saturdays she went to six o'clock mass, to be back in time for dinner. Ernesto had been pursuing her for weeks. After the service he stood waiting for her in the porch and, always with the same precise degree of ceremony, offered to walk her home. Soledad shrank into her black dress, but in the end she agreed. He told her about the Post Office where he used to work, and how long the evenings were at home alone, with so many years behind him and so many ghosts to come to terms with. Ernesto was older than Soledad and his wife really had died, taken away by pancreatic cancer.

They walked arm in arm, very composed. That evening Ernesto had given her room under his umbrella, and he had allowed his head and coat to get soaked the better to shelter her. He had complimented her on her Italian, which was getting better week by week, and Soledad had laughed, pretending to be embarrassed.

It had been because of a blunder, a lack of coordination, that instead of saying goodbye to each other as friends with two chaste kisses on the cheek, their mouths had touched outside the door of the Della Rocca house. Ernesto had asked her forgiveness, but then he had bent to her lips again and Soledad had felt all the dust that had settled in her heart whirling up and ending in her eyes.

She had been the one who invited him in. Ernesto had to stay hidden in her room for a few hours, just long enough to give Alice something to eat and send her to bed. The Della Roccas would be going out soon and they would be back late.

Ernesto thanked someone up there for the fact that such things could still happen at his age. They entered the house furtively, Soledad leading her lover by the hand, like a teenager, and with her finger to her mouth she told him not to make a sound. Then she hastily made dinner for Alice, watched her eat it too slowly and said you look tired, you should go to bed. Alice protested that she wanted to watch television and Soledad gave in, just to get rid of her, as long as she watched it in the loft. Alice went upstairs, taking advantage of her father's absence to drag her feet as she walked.

Soledad returned to her lover. They kissed for a long time, sitting side by side, not knowing what to do with their own hands, clumsy and out of practice. Then Ernesto plucked up the courage to pull her to him.

As he was fiddling with the devilish thing that fastened her bra, apologizing under his breath for being so clumsy, she had felt young and beautiful and uninhibited. She closed her eyes and, when she opened them again, she saw Alice, standing in the doorway.

'*Coño*,' she exclaimed. '*¿Qué haces aquí?*'

She slipped away from Ernesto and covered her bosom with one arm. Alice tilted her head to one side and observed them without surprise, as if they were animals in an enclosure.

'I can't get to sleep,' she said.

★ ★ ★

By some mysterious coincidence Soledad was thinking back to that very moment when, turning round, she saw Alice standing in the study doorway. Soledad was dusting the library. She took out the heavy volumes of the lawyer's encyclopaedias in blocks of three, the ones with the dark green binding and the gilded spines. She held them with her left arm, which was already beginning to ache, as with her right she ran the duster over the mahogany surfaces all the way into the most hidden corners, because the lawyer had once complained that she only dusted around things.

It was years since Alice had entered her father's study. An invisible barrier of hostility kept her frozen in the doorway. She was sure that if she had put as much as a toe on to the regular, hypnotic geometry of the parquet, the wood would crack under her weight and send her plunging into a black abyss.

The whole room was saturated with her father's intense smell. It lay on the papers stacked neatly on the desk, and the thick, cream-coloured curtains were drenched with it. As a little girl Alice had come in on tiptoe to call her father for dinner. She always hesitated for a moment before speaking, absorbed by the posture with which her father loomed over his desk while he studied his complicated documents from behind silver-framed glasses. When the lawyer noticed his daughter he slowly pulled up his head and frowned, as if to ask what she was doing there. Then he nodded and gave her a hint of a smile. I'm coming, he said.

Alice was sure that she could hear those words echoing against the wallpaper in the study, trapped for ever in these four walls and inside her head.

'*Hola, mi amorcito*,' said Soledad. She still used that expression, even though the now pencil-thin girl standing in front of her was a far cry from the sleepy child that she had once dressed each morning and walked to school.

'Hi,' replied Alice.

Soledad looked at her for a few seconds, waiting for her to say something, but Alice glanced nervously away. Soledad returned to her shelves.

'Sol,' Alice said at last.

'Yes?'

'There's something I've got to ask you.'

Soledad set the books down on the desk and walked over to Alice.

'What is it, *mi amorcito?*'

'I need a favour.'

'What sort of favour? Of course, tell me.'

Alice rolled the elastic of her trousers around her index finger.

'On Saturday I have to go to a party. At my friend Viola's house.'

'Oh, how lovely,' smiled Soledad.

'I'd like to bring a pudding. I'd like to cook it myself. Would you help me?'

'Of course, darling. What sort of pudding?'

'I don't know. A cake. Or a tiramisu. Or that pudding that you make with cinnamon.'

'My mother's recipe,' said Soledad with a hint of pride. 'I'll teach you.'

Alice looked at her pleadingly.

'So we'll go shopping together on Saturday? Even though it's your day off?'

'Of course, darling,' said Soledad. For a moment she felt important, and in Alice's insecurity she recognized the little girl she had brought up.

'Could you take me to another place as well?' Alice ventured.

'What place?'

Alice hesitated for a moment.

'To get myself tattooed,' she said hastily.

'Oh, *mi amorcito,*' sighed Soledad, vaguely disappointed. 'Your father doesn't want you to, you know that.'

'We won't tell him. He'll never see it,' Alice insisted with a whine.

71

Soledad shook her head.

'Go on, Sol, please,' she begged. 'I can't get it done on my own. I need my parents' permission.'

'So what can I do?'

'You pretend to be my mother. You'll only have to sign a piece of paper, you won't have to say anything.'

'But it's impossible, my dear, it's impossible. Your father will fire me.'

Alice suddenly grew more serious. She looked Soledad straight in the eyes.

'It'll be our secret, Sol.' She paused. 'After all, the two of us already have a secret, haven't we?'

Soledad looked at her, puzzled. She didn't understand, at first.

'I know how to keep secrets,' Alice continued slowly. She felt as strong and ruthless as Viola. 'Otherwise he'd have fired you ages ago.'

Soledad was suddenly unable to breathe.

'But — ' she said.

'So you'll do it?' Alice cut in.

Soledad looked at the floor.

'OK,' she said quietly. Then she turned her back on Alice and adjusted the books on the shelf as her eyes filled with two fat tears.

10

Mattia deliberately made all his movements as silent as he could. He knew that the chaos of the world would only increase, that background noise would grow until it covered every coherent signal, but he was convinced that by carefully measuring each of his gestures he would be less guilty of that slow undoing.

He had learned to set down first his toe and then his heel, keeping his weight towards the outside of the sole to minimize the amount of surface area in contact with the ground. He had perfected this technique years before, when he got up at night and stealthily roamed the house; when the skin of his hands had become so dry that the only way of being aware that they were still his was to pass them over a blade. Over time that strange, circumspect gait had become his normal way of walking.

Often his parents would suddenly find themselves face to face with him, like a hologram projected from the floor, a frown on his face and his mouth always tight shut. Once his mother had dropped a plate with fright. Mattia had bent down to pick up the bits and had resisted the temptation of the sharp edges. Embarrassed, his mother had thanked him, and when he left she had sat down on the floor and stayed in that position for a quarter of an hour, defeated.

Mattia turned the key in the front-door lock.

He had learned that by turning the handle towards himself and pressing his palm over the keyhole, he could eliminate almost entirely the metallic click of the opening. With the bandage on it was even easier.

He slipped into the hallway, put the keys back in from the inside and repeated the operation, like a burglar in his own home.

His father was already home, earlier than usual. When he heard him raise his voice he froze, unsure whether to cross the sitting room and interrupt his parents' conversation or go out again and wait until he had seen the living-room light go out from the corridor.

' . . . I don't think it's right,' his father concluded with a note of reproach in his voice.

'Right,' Adele shot back. 'You'd rather pretend nothing was wrong, act as if there was nothing strange going on.'

'And what's so strange?'

There was a pause. Mattia could clearly imagine his mother lowering her head and pulling back one corner of her mouth as if to say there's no point with you.

'What's so strange?' she said, pointedly. 'I don't . . . '

Mattia stayed a step back from the ray of light that spilled from the sitting room into the hall. Rolling his eyes he followed the line of shadow from the floor to the walls and then to the ceiling. He convinced himself that it formed a trapezium, and that it was only one more trick of perspective.

His mother often abandoned her sentences

halfway through, as if she had forgotten what she was going to say as she was saying it. Those interruptions left bubbles of emptiness in her eyes and in the air and Mattia always imagined bursting them with a finger.

'The strange thing is that he stuck a knife in his hand in front of all his classmates. The strange thing is that we persuaded ourselves that those days were over and in fact we've been wrong all over again,' his mother went on.

Mattia had no reaction when he realized that they were talking about him, just a slight sense of guilt at overhearing a conversation he shouldn't have been listening to.

'That's not a good reason to go and talk to his teachers without him,' his father said, but in a more moderate tone. 'He's old enough to have the right to be there.'

'For God's sake, Pietro,' his mother exploded. She never called him by name. 'That's not the point, can't you see? You have to stop treating him as if he were . . . '

He froze. The silence stuck in the air in the form of an electrostatic charge. A slight shock made Mattia's back contract.

'As if he was what?'

'Normal,' his mother confessed. Her voice trembled slightly and Mattia wondered if she was crying. She had cried often since that afternoon. Most of the time she did it for no reason. Sometimes she cried because the meat she had cooked was stringy or because the plants on the balcony were full of parasites. Whatever the reason, her despair was always the same. As if, in any case, there was nothing to be done.

'The teachers say he has no friends. He only talks to the boy who sits next to him and he spends the whole day with him. And boys of his age go out in the evening, they try it on with girls — '

'You don't think he's . . . ' his father interrupted. 'Well, you know . . . '

Mattia tried to complete the sentence, but nothing came to mind.

'No, that's not what I think. Perhaps I'd rather it was just that,' said his mother. 'Sometimes I think that part of Michela passed into him.'

His father sighed, deeply and noisily.

'You promised not to talk about that any more,' he said vaguely irritated.

Mattia thought of Michela, who had disappeared into the void. He only thought of her for a fraction of a second. Then he was distracted by the faded image of his parents, which he discovered reflected in miniature on the smooth, curved surfaces of the umbrella stand. He started scratching his left elbow with the keys. He felt the joint jumping between one tooth and the next.

'Do you know what makes me shiver even more?' said Adele. 'It's all those high marks he gets. Always nine, ten, always the maximum. There's something frightening in those marks.'

Mattia heard his mother sniff, once. Then again, but now as if her nose was pressed up against something. He imagined his father taking her in his arms, in the middle of the sitting room.

'He's fifteen,' said his father. 'It's a cruel age.'

His mother didn't reply and Mattia listened to those rhythmic sobs rising to a peak of intensity and then slowly ebbing, to re-establish silence.

At that point he walked into the sitting room. His eyes closed slightly as he passed into the beam of light. He stopped two steps away from his hugging parents, who looked at him in alarm, like two kids caught in a fumble. Stamped on their expressions was the question of how long he'd been out there.

Mattia looked at a point midway between them. He said, simply, I do have friends, on Saturday I'm going to a party. Then he continued towards the hall and disappeared into his room.

11

The tattoo-artist had first looked Alice suspiciously up and down and then the woman with the unusually dark skin and the frightened expression that the girl had introduced as her mother. He hadn't believed it for a second, but it was none of his business. He was used to tricks of that kind, and he was used to capricious teenage girls. They were getting younger and younger: this one couldn't be as much as seventeen, he thought. But he certainly wasn't in a position to refuse a job for a question of principle. He'd showed the woman to a chair and she'd sat down and hadn't said another word. She held her handbag tightly in her hands, as if she wanted to leave at any moment. She looked everywhere except in the direction of the needle.

The girl hadn't flinched. He had asked does it hurt, because that's a question you ask, and she had said no through clenched teeth.

Then he had recommended that she keep the gauze on for at least three days and to clean the wound morning and evening for a week. He had given her a jar of Vaseline and put the money in his pocket.

Back home in the bathroom, Alice took off the white tape that held the bandage on. Her tattoo had been in existence for a few hours and she had already taken a peek at it ten times or so.

Each time she looked part of the excitement dispersed, like a pool of shining water evaporating beneath the August sun. This time she thought only of how the skin had turned red, all the way around the design. She wondered if her skin would ever regain its natural colour and for a moment her throat tightened with panic. Then she banished that stupid anxiety. She hated the fact that her every action always had to seem so irremediable, so definitive. In her head she called it *the weight of consequences* and she was sure that it was another awkward part of her father that had wormed its way into her brain. How she longed for the uninhibitedness of her contemporaries, their vacuous sense of immortality. She yearned for all the lightness of her fifteen years, but in trying to grasp it she became aware of the fury with which the time at her disposal was slipping away. This was how the weight of consequences was becoming increasingly unbearable and her thoughts began whirling faster and faster, in ever smaller circles.

At the last moment she had changed her mind. That was what she had said to the young man who had already turned on the whizzing machine and was bringing the needle to her belly, she had said I've changed my mind. Unsurprised, he had asked her don't you want to do it any more? Alice had said yes I want to do it. But I don't want a rose any more. I want a violet.

The tattooist had looked at her, puzzled. Then he had confessed that he didn't know how to do a violet. It's more or less like a pansy, Alice had explained, with three petals at the top and two at the bottom. And it's violet in colour. The tattooist had said OK and set to work.

Alice looked at the livid little flower that now framed her navel and wondered if Viola would understand that it was for her, for their friendship. She decided she wouldn't show it to her till Monday. She wanted to present it cleaned of its scabs, bright against her pale skin. She imagined what it would be like to show it secretly to that boy she had invited to the party. Two days before Mattia had appeared in front of her and Viola, with his sunken air. He'd said Denis and I are coming, to the party. Viola hadn't even had time to come up with an unpleasant remark before he was back at the end of the corridor, back turned to them and head lowered.

She wasn't sure she wanted to kiss him, but it was all decided now and she would look like an idiot in front of Viola if she backed down.

She measured the precise point where the top of her pants must be, to be able to see the tattoo but not the scar that appeared immediately beneath it. She slipped into a pair of jeans, a T-shirt and a sweatshirt big enough to cover the lot — the tattoo, the scar and her bulging hips, then she left the bathroom, to join Soledad in the kitchen and watch her make her special cinnamon pudding.

12

With long, deep breaths, Denis tried to fill his lungs with the smell of Pietro Balossino's car. There was a slightly harsh smell of sweat, which seemed to emanate not so much from the people as from the fireproof covers of the seats, and a whiff of something damp which had lain there for too long, perhaps hidden under the mats. Denis felt the mixture wrapping itself around his face like a hot bandage.

He would happily have spent all night in that car, driving around the half-dark streets of the hill, watching the lights of the cars on the opposite lane striking his companion's face and leaving it in the shade again, unharmed.

Mattia was sitting in the front, beside his father. To Denis, who had been secretly studying the absence of any expression on both their faces, it seemed that father and son had agreed not to utter a single word during the whole journey, and to ensure that their eyes didn't meet even by accident.

He noticed that they had the same way of gripping objects, framing them with their fingers tensed, in contact with surfaces but not really resting on them, as if they feared deforming what they held in their hands. Mr Balossino seemed barely to touch the steering wheel. Mattia's frightened hands followed the edges of the present that his mother had bought for Viola and which he was now holding on his knees.

'So you're in the same class as Mattia,' Mr Balossino forced himself to say, without a great deal of conviction.

'Yeah,' said Denis, in a shrill voice that seemed to have been trapped for too long in his throat. 'We sit next to each other.'

Mattia's father nodded seriously and then returned, conscience assuaged, to his thoughts. Mattia seemed not even to have noticed that scrap of conversation and didn't move his eyes from the windscreen, through which he tried to work out whether his perception that the interrupted white line in the middle of the road was in fact a continuous line was due only to the slow response of his eye or to some more complicated mechanism.

Pietro Balossino braked about a metre away from the big gate of the Bai family's property and pulled on the handbrake because the road was on a slight slope.

'She's pretty well off, your friend,' he observed, leaning forward to see beyond the top of the gate.

Neither Denis nor Mattia admitted that they barely knew the girl's name.

'So I'll come back for you at midnight, OK?'

'Eleven,' Mattia replied quickly. 'Let's make it eleven.'

'Eleven? But it's nine o'clock now. What are you going to do for only two hours?'

'Eleven,' insisted Mattia.

Pietro Balossino shook his head and said OK.

Mattia got out of the car and Denis did

likewise, reluctantly. He was worried that Mattia might make new friends at the party, funny, fashionable boys who, in the bat of an eye, would take him away for ever. He was worried that he would never again get into that car.

He politely said goodbye to Mattia's father and, to make himself seem like a grown-up, also held out his hand. Pietro Balossino performed a clumsy acrobatic manoeuvre to shake it without unfastening his seat-belt.

The boys stood stiffly at the gate and waited for the car to turn around before deciding to ring the bell.

★ ★ ★

Alice was crouching at one end of the white sofa. She was holding a glass of Sprite and from the corner of her eye she peeked at Sara Turletti's voluminous thighs, crammed into a pair of dark tights. Squashed on to the sofa they became even fatter, almost twice as broad. Alice thought about the space that she occupied in comparison to her classmate. The idea of being able to become so thin as to be invisible gave her a pleasant pang in the stomach.

When Mattia and Denis came into the room, she suddenly stiffened her back and looked desperately around for Viola. She noticed that Mattia wasn't wearing the bandage any more and tried to see if a scar had been left on his wrist. She instinctively ran her index finger along the trace of her own. She knew how to find it even under her clothes; it was like an earthworm lying on her skin.

The boys looked around like hunted prey, but no one among the thirty or so young people scattered around the room paid them any attention. No one apart from Alice.

Denis followed Mattia's movements, going where he went and looking where he looked. Mattia walked over to Viola, who was busy telling one of her made-up stories to a group of girls. He didn't even wonder whether he'd ever seen those girls at school. He placed himself behind the birthday girl with the present in his hands, holding it stiffly at chest height. Viola turned around when she noticed that her friends had taken their eyes off her irresistible mouth and were looking over her shoulder.

'Ah, you're here,' she said charmlessly.

'Here,' said Mattia, placing the present in her arms. Then he added a mumbled happy birthday.

He was about to go when Viola shouted in an over-excited voice, 'Alice, Alice, come quickly. Your friend's here.'

Denis gulped down the lump in his throat. One of Viola's little friends cackled into the ear of another.

Alice got up from the sofa. In the four paces that separated her from the group she tried to mask her syncopated gait, but she was sure that that was what they were all looking at.

She greeted Denis and then Mattia with a quick smile, ducking her head and saying hi in a faint voice. Mattia said hi back and his eyebrows gave a jerk that made him look even more spastic in Viola's eyes.

There was an uncomfortably long silence that only she was able to break.

'I've discovered where my sister keeps the pills,' she said, beaming. 'Do you want some?'

She turned to face Mattia, certain that he wouldn't have the slightest idea what she was talking about. She wasn't mistaken.

'Girls, come with me and get them,' she said. 'You too, Alice.'

She gripped Alice by an arm and the five girls jostled each other into the corridor.

Denis found himself alone with Mattia again and his heartbeat resumed its regular frequency. They both walked over to the drinks table.

'There's whisky,' Denis observed, slightly shocked. 'And vodka, too.'

Mattia didn't reply. He took a plastic cup from the little column in which they were stacked and filled it to the brim with Coca-Cola, trying to get as close as possible to the limit at which the surface tension of the liquid prevented it from spilling over. Then he set it down on the table. Denis poured whisky into his own, looking cautiously around and hoping secretly to impress Mattia, who didn't even notice.

Two rooms along, the girls had sat Alice down on Viola's sister's bed to instruct her about what to do.

'Don't take it in your mouth. Not even if he asks you, you understand?' advised Giada Savarino. 'The first time the most you can give him is a hand-job.'

Alice laughed nervously and couldn't work out whether Giada was being serious.

85

'Now you go back in there and start talking to him,' explained Viola, who had a plan in mind and a very clear one. 'Then you come up with an excuse to take him to my room, OK?'

'And what excuse do I come up with?'

'What do I know? Anything. Tell him you're fed up with the music and you want a bit of peace.'

'And his friend? He's always glued to him,' Alice said.

'We'll take care of him,' said Viola with her most ruthless smile.

She climbed on to her sister's bed, trampling the light green cover with her shoes. Alice thought of her father, who wouldn't even let her walk on the carpet with her shoes on. For a moment she wondered what he would have said if he had seen her there, but then she swallowed that thought back down into her stomach.

Viola opened a drawer in the cupboard above the bed. She rummaged around, unable to see inside, and took out a little box covered with red fabric, adorned with gilded Chinese characters.

'Take this,' she said. She held her hand out towards Alice. In the middle of her palm there was a bright blue pill, square and with rounded corners, in the centre of which was carved a butterfly. For a moment Alice saw the filthy fruit gum that she had accepted from the same hand and felt it trapped once more in her throat.

'What is it?' she asked.

'Take it. You'll enjoy yourself more.'

Viola winked. Alice thought for a moment. They were all looking at her. She thought it was another test. She took the pill from Viola's hand and put it on her tongue.

One by one the girls left the room, all of them looking down and with a wicked smile on their faces. Federica pleaded with Viola, please, let me have one too. And Viola brusquely told her to wait her turn.

'You're ready,' Viola said with satisfaction. 'Let's go.'

Alice was the last to leave. As all the others turned their backs on her, she brought a hand to her mouth and spat the pill into it. She put it in her pocket and turned out the light.

13

Like four beasts of prey, Viola, Giada, Federica and Giulia surrounded Denis.

'Will you come with us?' Viola asked.

'Why?'

'We'll explain why afterwards.' Viola cackled.

Denis froze. He sought Mattia's help, but Mattia was still absorbed by the rippling of the Coca-Cola on the rim of the cup. The loud music that filled the room made the surface jerk with each beat of the bass drum. Mattia waited with strange trepidation for the moment when it would spill.

'I'd rather stay here,' said Denis.

'God, how boring you are,' Viola said, losing patience. 'You're coming with us and that's that.'

She pulled him by the arm. Denis resisted feebly. Then Giada started pulling as well and he gave in. As they were pushing him into the kitchen, he looked once more at his friend, who was still motionless.

Mattia noticed Alice when she rested a hand on the table: the balance broke and a small quantity of liquid spilled out from over the top of the cup and settled around the base in a dark ring.

He instinctively looked up and met her gaze.

'How are you?' she asked.

Mattia nodded. 'Fine,' he said.

'Do you like the party?'

'Mmm.'

'Music this loud gives me a headache.'

Alice waited for Mattia to say something. She looked at him and it seemed to her that he wasn't breathing. His eyes were meek and pain-stricken. Like the first time, she suddenly wanted to draw those eyes towards her, to take Mattia's head in her hands and tell him everything was fine.

'Will you come into the other room with me?' she ventured.

Mattia looked at the floor, as if he had been waiting for those very words.

'OK,' he said.

Alice stepped out into the corridor and he followed a short distance behind. Mattia, as always, kept his head down and looked in front of him. He noticed that Alice's right leg bent gracefully, at knee-height, like all the legs in the world, and her foot brushed the floor without a sound. Her left leg, on the other hand, remained stiff. To push it forward she had to make it perform a little arc towards the outside. For a fraction of a second her pelvis was unbalanced, as if she were about to topple sideways. At last her left foot touched the ground as well, heavily, like a crutch.

Mattia concentrated on that gyroscopic rhythm and, without realizing it, synchronized his steps with hers.

When they were in Viola's room, Alice slipped up beside him and, with a daring that startled even her, closed the door. They were standing, he on the rug and she just off it.

Why doesn't he say anything? Alice wondered.

For a moment she wanted to drop the whole thing, to open the door again and leave, to breathe normally.

But what am I going to tell Viola? she thought.

'It's better in here, isn't it?' she said.

'Yeah,' nodded Mattia. He let his arms dangle at his sides like a ventriloquist's dummy. With his right index finger he was folding a short, hard bit of skin that stuck out from beside his thumbnail. It was almost like piercing himself with a needle and the sting distracted him for a moment from the charged air in the room.

Alice was sitting on Viola's bed, balancing on the edge. The mattress didn't dip beneath her weight. She looked round, searching for something.

'Why don't you sit down here?' she asked Mattia at last.

He obeyed, sitting down carefully, about a foot away from her. The music in the sitting room sounded like the heavy, panting breath of the walls. Alice noticed Mattia's hands, clenched into fists.

'Is your hand better?' she asked.

'Nearly,' he said.

'How did you do it?'

'I cut myself. In the biology lab. By accident.'

'Can I see?'

Mattia tightened his fists still further. Then he slowly opened his left hand. A furrow, light in shade and perfectly straight, cut it diagonally. Around it, Alice made out scars that were shorter and paler, almost white. They filled the

90

whole of his palm and intersected, like the branches of a leafless tree seen against the light.

'I've got one too, did you know?' she said.

Mattia clenched his fist again and trapped his hand between his legs, as if to hide it. She rose to her feet. She lifted her sweatshirt slightly and unbuttoned her jeans. He was seized by panic. He looked down as far as he could, but he still managed to see Alice's hands pulling back a corner of her trousers, revealing a piece of white gauze framed by sticky tape and, just below it, the edge of a pair of pale grey pants.

Alice pushed the elastic of her knickers aside a couple of inches and Mattia held his breath.

'Look,' she said.

A long scar ran along the protuberant bone of her pelvis. It was thick and in relief, and wider than Mattia's. The marks of the stitches, which intersected it perpendicularly and at regular intervals, made it look like the scars that children draw on their faces when they dress up as pirates for carnival.

Mattia couldn't think what to say. Alice buttoned up her jeans again and tucked her sweater inside. Then she sat down again, a little closer to him.

The silence was almost unbearable; the empty space between their faces overflowing with expectation and embarrassment.

'Do you enjoy school?' Alice asked, for the sake of saying something.

'Yes.'

'They say you're a genius.'

Mattia sucked in his cheeks and then clamped

91

them between his teeth until he felt the metallic taste of blood filling his mouth.

'Do you really like studying?'

Mattia nodded.

'Why?'

'It's the only thing I know how to do,' he said gently. He wanted to tell her that he liked studying because you can do it on your own, because all the things you study are already dead, cold and chewed-over. He wanted to tell her that the pages of the schoolbooks were all the same temperature, that they leave you time to choose, that they never hurt you and that you can't hurt them either. But he said nothing.

'And do you like me?' Alice went for it. Her voice came out rather shrilly and her face exploded with heat.

'I don't know,' Mattia answered hastily, looking at the floor.

'Why?'

'I don't know,' he insisted. 'I haven't thought about it.'

'You don't need to think about it.'

'If I don't think I can't understand anything.'

'I like you,' said Alice. 'A bit. I think.'

He nodded. He played at contracting and relaxing his retina, to make the geometric design of the carpet go in and out of focus.

'Do you want to kiss me?' Alice asked. She wasn't ashamed, but as she said it her empty stomach curled with terror that he might say no.

Mattia didn't move for a few seconds. Then he shook his head, slowly, still staring at the swirls in the carpet.

With a nervous impulse, Alice brought her hands to her hips and measured the circumference of her waist.

'It doesn't matter,' she said quickly, in a different voice. 'Please don't tell anyone,' she added.

Mattia, you're an idiot, he thought. Worse than a kid at primary school.

He got to his feet. Suddenly Viola's room seemed like a strange, hostile place. He felt himself becoming intoxicated by all the colours on the walls, the desk full of scattered make-up, the dancing shoes hanging from the wardrobe door, like a pair of severed feet, the enlargement of a photograph of Viola by the sea, stretched out on the sand looking beautiful, the cassettes stacked haphazardly beside the stereo and the clothes piled up on the armchair.

'Let's go back,' he said.

Alice got up from the bed. Mattia looked at her for a moment and Alice thought he was about to apologize. She opened the door, letting the music flood aggressively into the room. She walked a little way along the corridor on her own. Then she thought of Viola's face. She turned back, took Mattia's stiff hand without asking his permission and, joined like that, they walked into the noisy sitting room.

14

The girls had trapped Denis in the corner, beside the fridge, so as to be able to make fun of him. They had arranged themselves in front of him to form a barrier of excited eyes and flowing hair, through which Denis could no longer see Mattia in the other room.

'Truth or dare?' Viola asked him.

Denis shook his head timidly, to say that he didn't feel like playing this game. Viola looked up to the sky and then opened the fridge, forcing Denis to lean to the side to make room for the door. She pulled out a bottle of peach vodka and took a gulp, without bothering to find a glass. Then she offered him some, with a complicit smile.

He already felt dizzy and a little nauseous. The whisky had left a bitter aftertaste suspended between his nose and mouth, but there was something in Viola's behaviour that prevented him from objecting. She picked up the bottle and gulped down another mouthful. Then she passed it to Giada Savarino, who grabbed it greedily and started to pour it down her throat as if it were orangeade.

'So. Truth or dare?' repeated Viola. 'Otherwise we'll choose.'

'I don't like this game,' Denis objected unconvincingly.

'Mmm, you and your friend really are a drag,'

she said. 'Then I'll choose. Truth. Let's see.'

She brought her index finger to her chin and with her eyes traced an imaginary circle on the ceiling, pretending to be deep in thought.

'Got it!' she exclaimed. 'You have to tell us which one of us you like best.'

Denis shrugged, intimidated.

'Dunno,' he said.

'What do you mean, dunno? You must like at least one, don't you think?'

Denis thought he didn't like any of them, that he just wanted them to get out of his way and let him get back to Mattia. That he only had one more hour to be with him and watch him just existing, at a time of night when he could usually do nothing but imagine him in his bedroom, sleeping under a sheet the colour of which he didn't know.

If I choose one of them, they'll leave me alone, he thought.

'Her.' He pointed to Giulia Mirandi, because she seemed the most harmless.

Giulia brought a hand to her mouth as if she'd just been elected prom queen. Viola turned up one corner of her mouth. The other two exploded into coarse laughter.

'Great,' said Viola. 'So now the dare.'

'No, that's enough,' protested Denis.

'You really are boring. Here you are, surrounded by four girls, and you don't even want to play a bit. This can't happen to you every day.'

'But now it's someone else's turn.'

'And I say it's still your turn. You have to do

95

the dare. What do you say, girls?'

The others nodded keenly. The bottle was once more in the hands of Giada, who at regular intervals threw back her head and took a swig, as if she wanted to finish it before the others noticed.

'See?' said Viola.

Denis puffed.

'What do I have to do?' he asked with resignation.

'Well, since I'm a generous hostess, I'm going to give you a nice dare,' Viola said mysteriously. The other three hung on her words, eager to discover the new torture. 'You have to kiss Giulia.'

Giulia blushed. Denis felt a stitch in the middle of his ribs.

'Are you mad?' Giulia asked, shocked, perhaps pretending.

Viola gave a capricious shrug. Denis shook his head, two, three times in a row.

'You were the one who said you liked her,' she said.

'What if I don't do it?'

Suddenly dead serious, Viola looked him straight in the eyes.

'If you don't do it you'll have to choose truth again,' she said. 'You could tell us about your little friend, for example.'

In her keen, bright stare Denis recognized all the things he had always thought were invisible. His neck stiffened.

Holding his arms at his sides, he turned his face towards Giulia Mirandi. He narrowed his eyes and kissed her. Then he tried to draw back, but Giulia held his head in place by resting a hand on the back of his neck. She forced her tongue through his pursed lips.

In his mouth Denis tasted saliva that wasn't his and felt sick. In the middle of this, his first kiss, he opened his eyes just in time to see Mattia coming into the kitchen, hand in hand with the crippled girl.

15

The others were the first to notice what Alice and Mattia would understand only many years later. They walked into the room holding hands. They weren't smiling and they were looking in opposite directions, but it was as if their bodies flowed uninterruptedly into one another, through their arms and their touching fingers.

The marked contrast between Alice's light-coloured hair, which framed the excessively pale skin of her face, and Mattia's dark hair, tousled forwards to hide his black eyes, was erased by the slender arc that linked them. There was a shared space between their bodies, the confines of which were not well delineated, from which nothing seemed to be missing and in which the air seemed motionless, undisturbed.

Alice walked a step ahead of him and Mattia's slight drag balanced its cadence, erasing the imperfections of her faulty leg. His scars were hidden and safe in her hand.

They stopped on the threshold of the kitchen, a little way from the cluster of girls and Denis. They tried to work out what was happening. They looked dreamy, as if they had come from a distant place that they alone knew.

Denis pushed Giulia violently away and their mouths parted with a smack. He looked at Mattia and sought in his expression the traces of the thing that terrified him. He thought that he and Alice had said something to one another, something that he would never be able to know and his brain filled with blood.

He ran from the room, deliberately crashing through the couple to destroy the loathsome equilibrium. For a moment Mattia met Denis's eyes, red and upset. For some reason he remembered Michela's defenceless eyes, that afternoon in the park. Over the years those two gazes would finally merge in his memory into a single, indelible fear.

He let go of Alice's hand. It was as if his nerve-endings were all concentrated in that single point and, when he broke away, it seemed to him that his arm was giving off sparks, as if from an uncovered cable.

'Excuse me,' he whispered to her and left the kitchen to catch up with Denis.

Alice walked over to Viola, who was staring at her with eyes of stone.

'We — ' she began.

'I don't care,' Viola cut in. Looking at Alice and Mattia she had thought again of the boy by the sea, of when he had refused her hand, when she would have loved to go back to the others on the beach holding hands just like that. She was envious, with a jealousy both painful and violent, and she was furious, because the happiness she herself wanted she had just given to someone else. She felt robbed, as if Alice had taken her share too.

Alice leaned over to speak into her ear, but she turned around.

'What do you want now?' she said.

'Nothing.' Alice retreated in fear.

At that moment Giada bent forward, as if an invisible man had punched her in the stomach. With one hand she held on to the kitchen surface and with the other she gripped her belly.

'What's wrong?' Viola asked.

'I'm going to be sick,' she moaned.

'That's disgusting, go to the toilet,' Viola yelled.

But it was too late. With a jerk Giada emptied the contents of her stomach on the floor, something reddish and alcoholic, a mixture of vodka and Soledad's pudding.

The others pulled back, appalled, as Alice tried to hold her up by the hips. The air immediately turned rancid.

'Well done, you idiot,' said Viola. 'What a fucking awful party.'

She left the room, her fists furiously clenched. Alice looked at her uneasily and then went back to look after Giada, who was sobbing gently.

16

The other guests had scattered in groups around the sitting room. The boys were bobbing their heads back and forth in time, while the girls scanned the room. Some held glasses; six or seven were dancing. Mattia wondered how they could feel so at ease, moving around like that in front of everyone. Then he thought it was the most natural thing in the world, and that was precisely why he was incapable of it.

Denis had disappeared. Mattia crossed the lounge and went into Viola's room to look for him. He looked in her sister's and her parents' room. He looked in both bathrooms and in one he found a boy and girl from school. She was sitting on the toilet and he was on the floor in front of her, legs crossed. They both wore sad and questioning expressions and Mattia hastily closed the door.

He went back to the sitting room and out on to the balcony. The hill descended darkly and below them lay the whole of the city, a series of bright, white dots arranged homogeneously, as far as the eye could see. Mattia pushed himself away from the railings and looked through the trees of the grounds of Villa Bai, but he couldn't see anyone. He went back inside; anxiety began to take his breath away.

A spiral staircase led from the sitting room to a dark attic. He climbed the first steps, then stopped.

Where has he got to? he thought.

He went on, up to the top. The light that filtered from the floor below allowed him to make out the shadow of Denis, standing in the middle of the room.

He called to him. All through their friendship he had uttered his name three times at the most. He had never needed to, because Denis was always right next to him, like a natural extension of his limbs.

'Go away,' Denis replied.

Mattia looked for the switch and turned on the light. The room was enormous, surrounded by tall bookshelves. The only other furniture was a big, empty wooden desk. Mattia had the impression that no one had come up to this floor of the house for a long time.

'It's nearly eleven. We've got to go,' he said.

Denis didn't reply. He turned his back to him, standing in the middle of a big rug. Mattia walked over to his friend. He saw that Denis had been crying. He was blowing through his teeth as he breathed, his eyes fixed straight ahead and his half-open lips trembling slightly.

After a few seconds Mattia spotted a desk lamp that lay shattered at his feet.

'What have you done?' he asked.

Denis's breathing turned into a wheeze.

'Denis, what have you done?'

Mattia forced himself to touch one of his friend's shoulders, and Denis gave a violent start. Mattia yanked at him.

'What have you done?'

'I . . . ' Denis began. Then he froze.

'You what?'

Denis opened his left hand and showed Mattia a fragment of the lamp, a splinter of green glass, turned opaque by the sweat of his hand.

'I wanted to feel what you feel,' he whispered.

Mattia didn't understand. He took a step back, confused. A burning sensation exploded in his belly and filled his arms and legs.

'But then I couldn't do it,' said Denis.

He held the palms of his hands upwards, as if waiting for something.

Mattia was about to ask him why, but then said nothing. The music rose up, muffled, from below. The low frequencies passed through the floor, while the higher ones seemed trapped.

Denis sniffed. 'Let's go,' he said.

Mattia nodded, but neither of them moved from where they were. Then Denis turned around abruptly and walked towards the stairs. Mattia followed him across the sitting room and then outside, where the cool night air was waiting to give them their breath back.

17

Viola decided if you were in or out. On Sunday morning Giada Savarino's father had phoned her father, waking up everyone in the Bai household. It was a long phone call and Viola, still in pyjamas, had pressed her ear to her parents' bedroom door, but she hadn't been able to catch a single word of the conversation.

When she heard the bed creak, she ran back to her room and hid under the blankets, pretending to be asleep. Her father had woken her up saying you're going to tell me what happened, but for now you should know that there will be no more parties in this house and for a good long while, indeed you can forget parties of any kind. At lunch her mother had asked her to explain the broken lamp in the attic and her sister hadn't come to her defence, because she had noticed that Viola had laid hands on her personal stock.

She locked herself away in her room all day, disheartened and banned from using the phone. She couldn't get Alice and Mattia, and their way of holding hands, out of her head. As she scratched away the last remnants of varnish on her nails she decided: Alice was out.

On Monday morning, locked in her bathroom at home, Alice finally removed the gauze that covered her tattoo. She rolled it up and then threw it in the bin, along with the crumbled biscuits that she hadn't eaten for breakfast.

She looked at the violet reflected in the mirror and thought that, for the second time, she had changed her body for ever. She shivered with a pleasant mixture of regret and trepidation. She thought that this body was hers alone, that if she felt like it she could even destroy it, lay waste to it with indelible marks or let it dry out like a flower picked on a whim by a child and then left to die out on the ground.

That morning she would show her tattoo to Viola and the others, in the girls' toilet. She would tell them how she and Mattia had kissed for a long time. There was no need to invent anything more than that. If they asked her for details, she would merely go along with their fantasies.

In class she left her rucksack on her chair and headed for Viola's desk to join the others. As she approached, she heard Giulia Mirandi saying, here she comes. She said hi to everyone, beaming, but no one replied. She leaned over to give Viola two kisses on the cheeks, as she herself had taught her to do, but her friend didn't move a millimetre.

Alice drew herself up and found herself looking into four hostile faces.

'We were all ill yesterday,' Viola began.

'Really?' Alice asked, with genuine concern. 'What was wrong with you?'

'A terrible stomach-ache, all of us,' Giada broke in aggressively.

Alice saw her vomiting on the floor again and felt like saying I'm not surprised with the amount you drank.

'There was nothing wrong with me,' she said.

'Of course,' sneered Viola, looking at the others. 'There's no doubt about that.'

Giada and Federica laughed; Giulia lowered her eyes.

'What's that supposed to mean?' Alice asked, disoriented.

'You know very well what I mean,' Viola retorted, suddenly changing her tone and staring straight at her.

'No, I don't know,' Alice defended herself.

Giada attacked. 'You poisoned us.'

'What are you saying? What do you mean poisoned?'

Giulia butted in, timidly. 'Come on, girls, that's not true.'

'Yes it is. She poisoned us,' Giada repeated. 'Who knows what filth she put in that pudding.'

She turned back towards Alice. 'You wanted to make us all ill, didn't you? Well, well done, it worked.'

Alice listened to the sequence of words, but it took her a few seconds to reconstruct their meaning. She looked at Giulia, who, with her big blue eyes, was saying sorry, there's nothing I can do. Then she sought shelter in Viola's eyes, but Viola returned an empty gaze.

Giada held a hand over her belly, as if she was still having convulsions.

'But I made the pudding with Soledad. We bought everything at the supermarket.'

No one replied. They looked in different directions, as if waiting for the murderer to leave.

'It wasn't Sol's pudding. I ate it too, and I

wasn't ill,' Alice lied.

'You're a liar,' pounced Federica Mazzoldi, who had not said a word until that moment. 'You didn't even taste it. Everyone knows that — '

She suddenly froze.

'Please, stop,' Giulia begged. She looked as if she was about to burst into tears.

Alice brought a hand over her flat stomach. Under the skin she felt her own heart beating.

'Everyone knows what?' she asked in a calm voice.

Viola Bai slowly shook her head. Alice stared at her former friend in silence, waiting for words that didn't come but that floated in the air like tongues of transparent smoke. She didn't even move when the bell rang. Ms Tubaldo, the science teacher, had to call her twice before she finally went to sit in her place.

18

Denis hadn't come to school. On Saturday, as they were driving home, he and Mattia hadn't looked at each other once. Denis had spoken in monosyllables to Mattia's father, and when getting out of the car he hadn't said goodbye.

Mattia rested a hand on the empty chair beside him. Now and again Denis's words in that dark attic ran through his head. Then they slipped away, too quickly for him to be able to get to the bottom of their meaning.

He thought it wasn't really important to him to understand them. He only wished Denis was there, to protect him against everything beyond his desk.

The day before his parents had made him sit down on the sofa, in the sitting room. They had sat in the chairs opposite. Then his father said tell us about this party. Mattia had clenched his hands tightly, but then stretched them out on his knees so that his parents could see them. He had shrugged and replied in a quiet voice that there was nothing to tell. His mother had risen nervously to her feet and disappeared into the kitchen. His father, on the other hand, had come over to him and clapped him twice on the shoulder, as if he knew he had to console him for something. Mattia remembered that when he was a child, on the hottest days of summer, his father would blow on his and Michela's faces in turn, to cool them down. He remembered what the sweat felt like as it evaporated from his skin, very lightly, and experienced a searing nostalgia for a part of the world that had drowned in the river along with Michela.

He wondered if his classmates knew everything. Indeed if his teachers knew everything. He felt their furtive glances weaving together above his head like a fishing net.

He opened the history book at random and started learning by heart the sequence of all the dates he found printed from that page onwards. The list of numbers, lined up without any logical meaning, formed a lengthening trail in his head. As he followed it, Mattia slowly moved away from the thought of Denis standing in the shadow and forgot the void that now sat in his place.

19

During break time Alice slipped into the sick bay on the first floor, a narrow white room furnished only with a hospital bed and a mirrored cabinet containing everything needed for first aid. Once she had ended up on her own in that room when she had fainted during P.E. In the forty hours previously she had eaten only two wholemeal crackers and an energy bar. That day the gym teacher, with his green Diadora tracksuit and the whistle, which he never used, around his neck, had said to her think carefully about what you're doing, think very carefully. Then he had gone out, leaving her alone under the fluorescent light, without anything to do or look at for the whole hour that followed.

Alice found the first-aid cabinet open. She took a wad of cotton wool the size of a plum and the bottle of methylated spirits. She closed the door and looked around for a heavy object. There was only the waste-paper basket, made of hard plastic, a dull colour halfway between red and brown. She prayed that no one would hear the noise from outside and shattered the mirror of the little cupboard with the bottom of the basket.

Then, taking care not to cut herself, she pulled out a big triangular splinter of glass. She saw her own right eye crossing the reflecting side and felt proud not to have cried, not even a bit. She stuffed everything into the middle pocket of the ample sweatshirt that she was wearing and went back to class.

She spent the rest of the morning in a state of torpor. She never even glanced at Viola and the others and didn't listen to a single word of the lesson on the theatre of Aeschylus.

As she was leaving the class, bringing up the rear of her classmates, Giulia Mirandi furtively took her hand.

'I'm sorry,' she whispered into her ear. Then she kissed her on the cheek and ran after the others, who were already in the corridor.

Alice waited for Mattia in the entrance hall, at the bottom of the lino-covered staircase down which a chaotic stream of pupils were headed for the exit. She rested a hand on the banister. The cold of the metal gave her a sense of tranquillity.

Mattia came down the stairs surrounded by a foot and a half of emptiness that no one apart from Denis dared occupy. His black hair fell over his forehead in tousled curls. He watched carefully where he placed his feet and tipped slightly backwards as he came down. Alice called out to him, but he didn't turn around. She called more loudly and he looked up, said an embarrassed hi, and made as if to head towards the glass doors.

Alice pushed her way through the other students and joined him. She took him by the arm and he gave a start.

'You have to come with me,' she said.

'Where?'

'You have to help me do something.'

Mattia looked nervously around in search of

some kind of threat.

'My father's waiting for me outside,' he said.

'Your father will wait. You've got to help me. Now,' said Alice.

Mattia snorted. Then he said OK but he couldn't have said why.

'Come.'

Alice took him by the hand, as she had at Viola's party, but this time Mattia's fingers spontaneously opened around hers.

They left the crowd of students. Alice walked quickly, as if she was escaping from someone. They slipped into the deserted corridor on the first floor. The doors leading to the empty classrooms emanated a sense of abandonment.

They went into the girls' toilets. Mattia hesitated. He was about to say I'm not supposed to be here, but then he let her drag him in. When Alice took him inside a cubicle and locked the door they were so close that his legs started trembling. The space around the old-style hole-in-the-ground toilet was just a thin strip of tiles and there was barely room for their four feet. There were pieces of toilet paper scattered on the ground half-stuck to the floor.

Now she's going to kiss me, he thought. And you've got to kiss her too. It'll be easy; everyone knows how.

Alice opened the zip of her gleaming jacket and started to undress, just as she had at Viola's house. She untucked her T-shirt and lowered the same pair of jeans to halfway down over her bottom. She didn't look at Mattia; it was as if she was there on her own.

In place of Saturday evening's white gauze she had a flower tattooed on her skin. Mattia was about to say something, but then fell silent and looked away. Something stirred between his legs and he tried to distract himself. He read some of the graffiti on the wall, without grasping its meaning. He noticed how none of the writing was parallel to the line of tiles. Almost all of it was at the same angle to the edge of the floor and Mattia worked out that it was an angle somewhere between 30 and 45 degrees.

'Take this,' said Alice.

She handed him a piece of glass, reflective on one side and black on the other, pointed like a dagger. Mattia didn't understand. She lifted his chin, just as she had imagined doing the first time they had met.

'You've got to get rid of it. I can't do it on my own,' she said to him.

Mattia looked at the fragment of mirror and then at Alice's right hand, which pointed at the tattoo on her belly.

She anticipated his protest.

'I know you can do it,' she said. 'I never want to see it again. Please, do it for me.'

Mattia rolled the blade in his hand and a shiver ran down his arm.

'But — ' he said.

'Do it for me,' Alice interrupted him, putting a hand to her lips to shut him up and then removing it immediately.

Do it for me, thought Mattia. Those four words stuck in his ear and made him kneel in front of Alice.

His heels touched the wall behind him. He didn't know where to put himself. Uncertain, he touched the skin next to the tattoo to stretch it better. His face had never been so close to a girl's body. The natural thing to do seemed to be to breathe in deeply, to discover its smell.

He approached the flesh with the fragment of mirror. His hand was firm as he opened up a little cut the size of a fingertip. Alice trembled and emitted a cry.

Mattia recoiled and hid the blade behind his back, as though to deny that it had been him.

'I can't do it,' he said.

He looked up. Alice wept silently. Her eyes were closed, clenched in an expression of pain.

'But I don't want to see it any more,' she sobbed.

It was clear to him that she had lost her nerve, and he felt relieved. He stood up and wondered if it would be better to leave.

Alice wiped away a drop of blood that was rolling down her belly. She buttoned up her jeans, while Mattia tried to think of something reassuring to say.

'You'll get used to it. In the end you won't even notice it any more,' he said.

'How's that possible? I'll always have it there, right before my eyes.'

'Exactly,' said Mattia. 'That's exactly why you won't see it any more.'

The Other Room
(1995)

20

Mattia was right: the days had slipped over her skin like a solvent, one after the other, each taking away a very thin layer of pigment from the tattoo; and from both their memories. The outlines, like the circumstances, were still there, black and well delineated, but the colours had merged together until they faded into a dull, uniform tonality, a neutral absence of meaning.

The high-school years had been an open wound that had seemed so deep that it could never heal. They had passed through them in a state of apnoea, he rejecting the world and she feeling rejected by it, and they had noticed that it didn't make a big difference. They had built up a defective and asymmetrical friendship, made up of long absences and much silence, a clean and empty space to which both could come back to breathe when the walls of the school became too close for them to ignore the feeling of suffocation.

Then, over time, the wound of adolescence had healed. The edges of skin had come together in imperceptible but continuous movements. With each fresh abrasion the scab gave way, but then stubbornly reformed, darker and thicker. In the end a new layer of skin, smooth and elastic, had replaced the missing one. From red, the scar had turned white, and ended up merging with all the others.

Now they were lying on Alice's bed, she with her head to one side and he with his head to the other, both with their legs bent unnaturally to avoid contact between any parts of their bodies. Alice thought she could turn around, to end up with her toes against Mattia's back and pretend not to notice. She was sure that he would immediately pull away and decided to spare herself that little disappointment.

Neither of them had suggested putting on any music. Their only plans were to stay there and wait for Sunday afternoon to wear itself out all by itself until it would once again be time to do something necessary, like eating, sleeping or starting yet another week. The yellow light of September came in through the open window, dragging with it the intermittent rustle of the street.

Alice stood up on the bed, making the mattress ripple very slightly under Mattia's head. She held her clenched fists by her sides and stared at him from above. Her hair fell over her face and concealed a serious expression.

'Stay right there,' she said. 'Don't move.'

She stepped over him and jumped down from the bed, her good leg dragging the other one behind it like something that had been attached to her by mistake. Mattia bent his chin over his chest to follow Alice's movements around the room. He saw her opening a cube-shaped box which sat in the middle of the desk, and which he hadn't noticed until that moment.

Alice turned around with one eye closed and one hidden behind an old camera. Mattia started to pull himself up.

'Get down,' she commanded. 'I told you not to move.'

Then she snapped. The Polaroid spat out a thin white tongue and Alice waved it in the air to bring out the colour.

'Where did you get that from?' Mattia asked.

'The cellar. It was my father's. He bought it God knows when and then he never used it.'

Mattia sat up on the bed. Alice dropped the photograph on the carpet and snapped another one.

'Come on, stop,' he protested. 'I look stupid in photographs.'

'You always look stupid.'

She snapped again.

'I feel like being a photographer,' Alice said. 'I've made up my mind.'

'And university?'

Alice shrugged.

'Only my father cares about that,' she said. 'Let him do it himself.'

'You're going to quit?'

'Maybe.'

'You can't wake up one day, decide you want to be a photographer and throw away a year's work. It doesn't work like that,' said Mattia sharply.

'Oh right, I forgot that you were like him,' Alice said ironically. 'You always know what should be done. You knew at the age of five that you wanted to be a mathematician. You're all so boring. Old and boring.'

Then she turned towards the window and snapped a picture at random. She dropped that one on the carpet as well, near the other two, and jumped on it with both feet, as if she were treading grapes.

Mattia thought about a reply of some kind, but nothing came out. He bent over to slip the first photograph out from under Alice's foot. The outline of his arms, crossed behind his head, was gradually emerging from the white. He wondered what extraordinary reaction was happening on that shiny surface and reminded himself to look it up in the encyclopaedia as soon as he got home.

'There's something else I want to show you,' Alice said.

She threw the camera on to the bed, like a little girl who's grown tired of a toy because she's spotted another, more inviting, one, and left the room.

She was gone for a good ten minutes. Mattia started reading the titles of the books, arranged at an angle on the shelf above the desk. They were always the same. He put all the titles together, but no sensible word was produced. He thought he would have liked to identify a logical order in the sequence. She had probably arranged them according to the colour of their spines, perhaps copying the electromagnetic spectrum, from red to violet, or according to height, in decreasing order.

'Da-daaaa,' Alice's voice distracted him.

Mattia turned around and saw her standing in the doorway, gripping the frame as if she was afraid she might fall. She had put on a wedding dress, a dress which was supposed to be dazzlingly white but which time had turned yellow around the hems, as if an illness was slowly devouring it. The years passed in a box had made it dry and stiff. The bodice fell limply over Alice's nonexistent bosom. It wasn't especially low-cut, just enough for one of the straps to slip a few inches below her shoulder. In that position Alice's collarbones looked more pronounced; they broke the soft line of the neck and marked the boundary of a little empty dip, like the basin of a dried-up lake. Mattia wondered what it might be like to follow its outline with the tip of his finger with his eyes closed. The lace with which the sleeves ended was crumpled and on the left arm it was almost flat. The long train continued unseen into the corridor. On her feet, Alice was still wearing her red slippers, which peeked out from under the full skirt, creating a curious dissonance.

'Well? You should say something,' she said without looking at him. With a hand she smoothed the outermost tulle of the skirt. To the touch it struck her as inferior, synthetic.

'Whose is it?' asked Mattia.

'It's mine, isn't it?'

'Come on, really.'

'Whose do you think? It's my mother's.'

Mattia nodded and imagined Fernanda in that dress. He imagined her with the only expression she had ever shown him when, before going home, he appeared in the sitting room where she was watching television: an expression of tenderness and profound commiseration, like the one usually bestowed upon the sick when people visit them in hospital. A ridiculous expression, now that she was the sick one, with an illness that was crumbling its way slowly through the whole of her body.

'Don't stand there gawping like that, come on. Take a picture of me.'

Mattia picked the camera off the bed. He turned it around in his hands to work out which button to press. Alice rocked from one side of the doorway to the other, as if stirred by a breeze that only she was aware of. When Mattia brought the camera to his eyes, she stiffened her back and assumed a serious, almost provocative expression.

'There,' said Mattia.

'Now one of us together.'

He shook his head.

'Come on, don't do your usual pain-in-the-arse routine. And for once I want to see you dressed properly. Not in that mangy sweatshirt that you've been wearing for a month.'

Mattia looked down. The wrists of his blue sweater looked as if they had been devoured by moths. He had a habit of rubbing them with his thumbnail to keep his fingers busy and stop them from scratching the hollow between his index and middle fingers.

'And besides, you don't want to ruin my wedding day, do you?' added Alice with a pout.

She was only messing about, she realized. It was only a joke to pass the time, a little horseplay, a bit of nonsense like so much else. And yet, when she opened the door of the wardrobe and the mirror inside framed her in

122

that white dress alongside Mattia, a moment of panic took her breath away.

'Nothing of any use in here,' she said hastily. 'Come with me.'

Resigned, Mattia followed her. When Alice was like this his legs began to itch and he was gripped by a desire to leave. There was something in her way of behaving, something in the violence with which his friend satisfied her childish whims, that he found unbearable. It felt as if, having tied him to a chair, she had called hundreds of people to show him off like a possession of hers, some kind of funny pet. Most of the time he said nothing and allowed his impatience to emerge through gestures, until Alice tired of his apathy and dropped it, saying you always make me feel like an idiot.

Mattia walked behind the wedding train all the way to Alice's parents' room. He had never been in there. The blinds were almost entirely down and the light entered in parallel lines, so clearly that they seemed to have been drawn on the wooden floor. The air was more dense and tired than in the rest of the house. Leaning against the wall was a double bed, much higher than the one that belonged to Mattia's parents, and two identical bedside tables.

Alice opened one of the wardrobes and ran her finger along her father's suits, all hanging in an orderly fashion, each one protected by its cellophane covering. She took out a black one and threw it on the bed.

'Put that one on,' she ordered Mattia.

'Have you gone mad? Your father will notice.'

'My father never notices anything.'

For a moment she was absorbed, as if reflecting on the words that she had just spoken, or else looking at something through that wall of dark clothes.

'Now I'm going to find you a shirt and tie as well,' she added.

Mattia stood where he was, uncertain what to do. She noticed.

'Will you get a move on? You can't tell me you're ashamed about getting changed here!'

As she said that her empty stomach flipped over. For a moment he felt dishonest. Her words had been a subtle form of blackmail.

Mattia huffed, then sat down on the bed and started undoing his shoes.

Alice went on facing the other way, pretending to choose a shirt that she had already chosen. When she heard the metallic click of the belt she counted up to three and then turned around. Mattia was slipping off his jeans. Underneath he had on a pair of soft grey boxers, not the Y-fronts she had imagined.

Alice thought that she'd already seen him in shorts dozens of times, that underwear didn't make much of a difference, and yet she still felt herself trembling slightly under the four white layers of her wedding dress. He pulled at the edge of his vest to cover himself better and quickly slipped on the elegant trousers. The fabric was soft and light. As it ran over the hairs of his legs it gave them an electric charge, making them stand up like cat's fur.

Alice came over and handed him the shirt. He

124

took it without looking up. He was annoyed and fed up with this pointless play-acting. He was ashamed of showing his thin legs and the sparse hairs on his chest and around his navel. Alice thought he was doing all this to make the scene embarrassing, as usual. Then she thought that, for him, for sure, she was to blame and she felt her throat tightening. She didn't want to, but she looked away and let Mattia take off his vest without her watching him.

'And now?' Mattia called to her.

She turned around. She struggled to breathe when she saw him in her father's clothes. The jacket was a little loose, his shoulders weren't quite wide enough, but she couldn't help thinking that he was incredibly handsome.

'All you need is the tie,' she said to him after a moment.

Mattia took the Bordeaux-coloured tie from Alice's hands and instinctively ran a thumb over the shiny fabric. A shiver ran down his arm and along his spine. He felt that the palm of his hand was as dry as sand. He immediately brought it to his mouth and breathed on it, to moisten it with the condensation of his breath. He couldn't resist the temptation to bite one of the joints of his fingers, trying not to be spotted by Alice, who noticed anyway.

'I don't know how to tie it,' he said, dragging his words.

'Mmm, you really are hopeless.'

The truth was that Alice couldn't wait to show him that she knew how to tie it. Her father had taught her when she was little. In the morning he left the tie on her bed and then, before going out, he passed by her room and asked is my tie ready? Alice ran to him, with the knot already made. Her father lowered his head, holding his hands joined together behind his back, as if he was bowing before a queen. She put the tie around his neck, then tightened it and adjusted it slightly. *Parfait*, he said finally. One morning after the accident, Alice's father had found the tie still on the bed, just as he had left it. From that time onwards he had always made the knot himself and that little ritual had passed away, like so many other things.

Alice prepared the knot, fluttering her skeletal fingers more than necessary. Mattia followed her gestures and they struck him as complicated. He let her adjust the tie around his neck.

'Wow, you look almost respectable. Do you want to see yourself in the mirror?'

'No,' said Mattia. He just wanted to leave, with his own clothes on.

'Photograph,' said Alice, clapping once.

Mattia followed her back into her room. She picked up the camera.

'It hasn't got a self-timer,' she said. 'We'll have to guess.'

She pulled Mattia to her, by the waist. He stiffened and she clicked. The photograph slipped out with a hiss.

Alice fell on to the bed, just like a bride after the lengthy celebrations, and fanned herself with the picture.

He stayed right where he was, feeling on him clothes that weren't his, but with the pleasant

126

sensation of disappearing into them. The light in the room suddenly changed. From yellow, it became blue and uniform, the last whisker of light disappearing behind the building opposite.

'Can I get changed now?'

He said it on purpose, to make her understand that he had had quite enough of that particular game. Alice seemed absorbed in thought; she barely arched an eyebrow.

'There's one last thing,' she said, and got up again. 'The groom carries the bride in his arms over the threshold.'

'Meaning?'

'You've got to take me in your arms. And carry me over there.' Alice pointed to the corridor. 'Then you're free.'

Mattia shook his head. She came over to him and held out her arms like a child.

'Come on, my hero,' she said, teasing him.

Mattia slumped his shoulders even further, defeated. He bent clumsily to pick her up. He had never carried anyone like that. He put one arm behind her knees and one behind her back and, when he pulled her up, he was startled by how light she was.

He stumbled towards the corridor. He felt Alice's breath passing through the very fine weave of the shirt, definitely too close, and heard the train rustling on the floor. When they crossed the threshold, the sound of a prolonged, dry rip froze him where he was.

'Damn,' he said.

He hastily set Alice down. The skirt had got caught on the door-frame. The tear was about six inches long and looked like a mouth open in a grin. They both stopped and stared at it, slightly dazed.

Mattia waited for Alice to say something, to give up and lose her temper with him. He felt as if he ought to apologize, but basically she was the one who had been so insistent on this foolishness. She was asking for trouble.

Alice stared expressionlessly at the tear.

'Who cares?' she said at last. 'It's no use to anyone anyway.'

In and Out of the Water
(1998)

21

Prime numbers are divisible only by 1 and by themselves. They stand in their place in the infinite series of natural numbers, squashed in between two others, like all other numbers, but a step further on than the rest. They are suspicious and solitary, which is why Mattia thought they were wonderful. Sometimes he thought that they had ended up in that sequence by mistake, that they'd been trapped like pearls strung on a necklace. At other times he suspected that they too would rather have been like all the others, just ordinary numbers, but for some reason they weren't capable of it. The second thought struck him mostly at night, in the chaotic interweaving of images that comes before sleep, when the mind is too weak to tell itself lies.

In his first year Mattia had studied the fact that among the prime numbers there are some that are even more special. Mathematicians call them *twin primes*: they are pairs of prime numbers that are close to one another, almost neighbours, but between them there is always an even number that prevents them from really touching. Numbers like 11 and 13, like 17 and 19, 41 and 43. If you have the patience to go on counting, you discover that these pairs gradually become rarer. You encounter increasingly isolated primes, lost in that silent, measured space made only of numbers, and you become aware of the distressing sense that the pairs encountered up until that point were an accidental fact, that their true fate is to remain alone. Then, just when you're about to surrender, when you no longer have any desire to go on counting, you come across another pair of twins, clutching one another tightly. Among mathematicians there is a common conviction that however far you go, there will always be more pairs, even if no one can say where, until they are discovered.

Mattia thought that he and Alice were like that, two twin primes, alone and lost, close but not close enough really to touch one another. He had never told her that. When he imagined confessing these things to her, the thin layer of sweat on his hands evaporated completely and for a good ten minutes he was no longer capable of touching anything.

One winter day he had come home after spending the afternoon at hers, doing nothing the whole time but switch from one television channel to another. Mattia had paid no attention to the words or the images. Alice's right foot, resting against the sitting-room coffee table, invaded his field of vision, penetrating it from the left like the head of a snake. Alice bent and flexed her toes with hypnotic regularity. That repeated movement made something solid and worrying grow in his stomach and he struggled to keep his gaze fixed for as long as possible, so that nothing in the frame would change.

At home he had taken a pile of blank pages from his ring binder, thick enough so that the pen could run softly over them without scratching the stiff surface of the table. He had levelled the edges with his hands, first above and below and then at the sides. He chose the fullest pen from the ones on the desk, removed the cap and slipped it on the end so as not to lose it. Then he began to write in the exact centre of the sheet, without needing to count the squares.

2760889966649. He put the lid back on the pen and set it down next to the paper. Twothousand-sevenhundredandsixtybillioneighthundredand-eightyninemillionninehundredandsixtysixthous-andsixhundredandfortynine, he read out loud. Then again, under his breath, as if to appropriate that tongue-twister to himself. He decided that that number would be his. He was sure that no one else in the world, no one else in the whole history of the world, had ever stopped to consider that number. Probably, until then, no one had ever written it down on a piece of paper, let alone spoken it out loud.

After a moment's hesitation he had gone two lines further down and written 2760889966651. This is hers, he thought. In his head the figures assumed the pale colour of Alice's foot, standing out against the bluish glare of the television.

They could also be two twin primes, Mattia had thought. If they are . . .

He had suddenly stopped at that thought and had begun to search for divisors for the two numbers. With 3 it was easy: it was enough to make the sum of the numbers and see if it was a multiple of 3. 5 was ruled out from the beginning. Perhaps there was a rule for 7 as well, but Mattia couldn't remember it so he started doing

133

the division in a column. 11,13 and so on, in increasingly complicated calculations. As he tried to do it with 37 he became drowsy for the first time and the pen slipped down the page. Reaching 47 he stopped. The vortex that had filled his stomach at Alice's house had dispersed, had diluted into his muscles like the smells in the air and he had no longer been able to notice it. In the room there were only him and a quantity of disordered pages, full of pointless divisions. The clock showed a quarter past three in the morning.

Mattia had picked up the first of the sheets, with the two numbers written in the middle, and felt like an idiot. He had torn it in half and then in half again, until the edges were firm enough to pass like a blade beneath the nail of the ring finger of his left hand.

$$\star \quad \star \quad \star$$

During his four years of university, mathematics had led him into the most remote and fascinating corners of human thought. Mattia copied out the proofs of all the theorems that he encountered in his studies with meticulous ritualism. Even on summer afternoons he kept the blinds lowered and worked in artificial light. He removed from his desk everything that might distract his gaze, to feel really alone with the page. He wrote without stopping. If he found himself hesitating too long over a passage or made a mistake when aligning an expression after the equals sign, he threw the paper to the floor and started from the beginning. Reaching the end of those pages stuffed with symbols, letters and numbers, he wrote the letters *QED* at the end and for a moment he felt he had put a small piece of the world in order. Then he rested against the back of the chair and wove his hands together, without letting them rub against each other.

He slowly lost contact with the page. The symbols, which only a moment before flowed from the movement of his wrist, now seemed distant to him, frozen in a place to which access was refused him. His head, immersed in the darkness of the room, began to crowd with dark and rowdy thoughts and most times Mattia would choose a book, open it at random and begin studying again.

Complex analysis, projective geometry and tensor calculus had not managed to diminish his initial passion for numbers. Mattia liked to count, starting from 1 and proceeding through complicated progressions, which he often invented on the spur of the moment. He allowed himself to be led by numbers and he seemed to know them, one by one. For that reason, when the moment came to choose his dissertation topic, he went with no doubts to the office of Professor Niccoli, professor of discrete calculus, with whom he had never even taken an exam and about whom he knew nothing but his name.

Francesco Niccoli's study was on the third floor of the nineteenth-century building that housed the Faculty of Mathematics. It was a small room, tidy and odourless, dominated by the white of the walls, the shelves, the plastic desk and the cumbersome computer on top of it. Mattia drummed quietly on the door and from inside Niccoli wasn't sure if he was knocking for him or for the office next door. He said come in, hoping not to make a fool of himself.

Mattia opened the door and stepped into the office.

'Hello,' he said.

'Hello,' replied Niccoli.

Mattia's eye was caught by a photograph hanging behind the professor, which showed him, much younger and beardless, holding a silver plate and shaking hands with an important-looking stranger. Mattia narrowed his eyes, but couldn't read what was written on the plate.

'Well, then?' Niccoli urged, studying him with a frown.

'I'd like to write a dissertation on the zeros of the Riemann Zeta Function,' said Mattia, staring over the professor's right shoulder, where a dusting of dandruff looked like a little starry sky.

Niccoli gave a grimace like an ironic smile.

'Excuse me, but who are you?' he asked without concealing his disdain and putting his hands behind his head as if he wanted to enjoy a moment's amusement.

'My name is Mattia Balossino. I've finished my exams and I'd like to graduate within the year.'

'Have you got your record book with you?'

Mattia nodded. He let his rucksack fall from his shoulders, crouched on the floor and rummaged in it. Niccoli stretched out his hands to take the book, but Mattia preferred to set it on the edge of the desk.

For some months the professor had been obliged to hold objects at a distance to get them properly into focus. He quickly ran his eyes over the sequence of 30s and 30s *cum laude*. Not one flaw, not one hesitation or proof that had gone wrong, perhaps on account of a love affair that had ended badly.

He closed the book and looked more carefully at Mattia. He was dressed anonymously and had the posture of someone who doesn't know how to occupy the space of his own body. The professor thought he was another of those who do well in their studies because they are unable to make much headway in life. The ones who, as soon as they find themselves outside the well-trodden paths of the university, always reveal themselves to be fit for nothing.

'Don't you think I should be the one to suggest a topic for you?' he asked, speaking slowly.

Mattia shrugged. His black eyes moved to right and left, following the edge of the desk.

'I'm interested in prime numbers. I want to work on the Riemann Zeta Function,' he replied.

Niccoli sighed. Then he got up and walked over to the white cupboard. As he ran his index finger along the titles of the books he snorted rhythmically. He picked up some typed papers that had been stapled in one corner.

'Fine, fine,' he said, passing them to Mattia. 'You can come back when you've performed the calculations for this article. All of them.'

Mattia picked up the folder and, without reading the title, slipped it into the rucksack that leaned against his leg, open and slack. He mumbled a thank-you and left the office, pulling the door shut behind him.

Niccoli went and sat back down in his chair and thought about how over dinner he would complain to his wife about this new and unexpected annoyance.

22

Alice's father had taken this photography business as the whim of a bored little girl. Nonetheless, for his daughter's twenty-third birthday, he gave her a Canon reflex, with case and tripod, and she had thanked him with a beautiful smile, as impossible to grasp as a gust of icy wind. He had also paid for her to take a course of evening classes, which lasted six months and of which Alice hadn't missed a single lesson. The agreement was clear if implicit: university came before everything else.

Then, at a moment as precise as the line separating light and shade, Fernanda's illness got worse, dragging all three of them into an increasingly tight spiral of new tasks, drawing them towards an inevitable cycle of apathy and mutual indifference. Alice no longer set foot in university and her father pretended not to notice. A feeling of remorse, the origins of which belonged to another time, kept him from imposing his will on his daughter and almost kept him from talking to her at all. Sometimes he thought it wouldn't have taken much, he would only have had to go into her room one evening and tell her ... Tell her what? His wife was disappearing from life like a wet mark drying on a vest and, with her, the thread that still connected him to his daughter was slackening, leaving her free to decide for herself.

What Alice liked about photography were the actions more than the results. She liked opening the back flap of the camera and unrolling the new film by a couple of inches, just enough to catch it in the runner, and thinking that this empty film would soon become something and not knowing what, taking the first few snaps into the void, aiming, focusing, checking her balance, deciding whether to include or exclude pieces of reality as she saw fit, enlarging, distorting.

Every time she heard the click of the shutter, followed by that faint rustle, she remembered when she used to catch grasshoppers in the garden of their house in the mountains when she was a little girl, trapping them between her cupped hands. She thought that it was the same with photographs, but that now she seized time and fixed it on celluloid, capturing it halfway through its jump towards the next moment.

On the course they had taught her that the strap of the camera is wrapped twice around the wrist. That way, if someone tries to steal it they're forced to tear your whole arm off along with it. In the corridor of Our Lady's Hospital, where her mother was being cared for, Alice ran no such risk, but she had become used to carrying her Canon like that anyway.

As she walked she slid along the two-tone wall, brushing it with her right shoulder from time to time to avoid touching anyone. Lunchtime visiting hour had just begun and people were pouring into the hospital like a liquid mass.

Aluminium and plywood doors opened on to the wards, each with its own particular smell.

Oncology smelled of disinfectant and gauze soaked in methylated spirits.

Her mother's room was the second last and she walked in. She was sleeping a sleep that wasn't hers and the gadgets to which she was connected didn't make a sound. The light was faint and drowsy. On the bedside table red flowers were arranged in a vase: Soledad had brought them the previous day.

Alice rested her hands and the camera on the edge of the bed, where the sheet, lifted in the middle by her mother's outline, flattened out again.

She came every day to do nothing. The nurses already took care of everything. Her role was to talk to her mother, she imagined. Lots of people do that, acting as if the patients were capable of listening to their thoughts, able to understand who was standing beside them and conversing inside their own heads, as if illness could open up a different channel of perception between people.

It was not something that Alice believed in, and in that room she felt alone and that was that. Usually she stayed sitting down, waited for half an hour to pass and then left. If she met a doctor she asked for news, which was always the same anyway. Their words and raised eyebrows meant only let's wait for something to go wrong.

That morning, however, she had brought a hairbrush. She took it out of her bag and delicately, making sure not to scratch her face, combed her mother's hair; at least the hair that wasn't squashed against the pillow. She was as inert and submissive as a doll.

141

She arranged her mother's arms outside the sheet, extended and parallel, in a relaxed pose. Another drop of the saline solution in the drip ran down the tube and disappeared into Fernanda's veins.

Alice moved to the end of the bed, with the Canon resting on the aluminium bar. She shut her left eye and pressed the other to the view-finder. She had never photographed her mother before. She pressed the shutter and then leaned a little further forward, without losing the frame.

A rustling sound startled her and the room suddenly filled with light.

'Better?' said a male voice behind her.

Alice turned around. Beside the window a doctor was busying himself with the cord of the Venetian blinds. He was young.

'Yes, thanks,' said Alice, a little intimidated.

The doctor stuck his hands in the pockets of his white coat and went on looking at her, as if waiting for her to continue. She leaned forward and snapped again, more or less randomly, as if to please him.

He must think I'm mad, she said to herself.

Instead the doctor came casually over to her mother's bed. He took a glance at the card, and as he read it he narrowed his eyelids, reducing his eyes to a slit. He went over to the drip and moved a wheel with his thumb. The drops started to come down more quickly and he watched them with satisfaction. Alice thought there was something reassuring about his movements.

The doctor came over to her and grasped the bedrail.

'The nurses are obsessed,' he remarked to himself. 'They want darkness everywhere. As if it wasn't already hard enough in here to tell day from night.'

He turned and smiled.

'Are you the daughter?'

'Yes.'

He nodded, without condescension.

'I'm Dr Rovelli,' he said.

'Fabio,' he added, as if he'd been thinking about it.

Alice shook his hand and introduced herself. For a few seconds they stared at the sleeping Fernanda, without exchanging a word.

Then the doctor tapped twice against the metal of the bed, which sounded hollow, and walked away. As he passed by Alice he leaned slightly towards her ear.

'Don't say it was me,' he whispered, winking and pointing at the light-filled windows.

★ ★ ★

At the end of visiting hours Alice came down the two flights of stairs, crossed the entrance hall and left through the automatic glass doors.

She crossed the courtyard and stopped at the kiosk for a bottle of fizzy water. She was hungry, but she was used to keeping the impulse in check until she had erased it almost entirely. Fizzy drinks were one of her tricks and they were enough to fill her stomach, at least long enough to overcome the critical moment of lunch.

She looked for her wallet in her handbag,

143

hampered slightly by the camera that hung from her wrist.

'I'll get that,' said someone behind her.

Fabio, the doctor whom she had met just half an hour before, stretched out his arm and held out a banknote to the man in the kiosk. He smiled at Alice in a way that stripped her of her will to protest. Instead of the white coat he wore a blue short-sleeved T-shirt and a strong aftershave that she hadn't noticed before.

'And a Coke,' he added, turning to the man.

'Thanks,' said Alice.

She tried to unscrew the bottle, but the top slipped through her fingers without moving.

'May I?' said Fabio.

He took the bottle from her hand and opened it using only his thumb and index finger. Alice thought there was nothing special in the gesture, that she could have done it herself, like anyone else, if only her hands hadn't been so sweaty. And yet she found it strangely fascinating, like a small heroic feat performed specially for her.

Fabio gave her the water and they drank, each from their own bottle, looking at one another stealthily as if studying what to say next. Fabio's hair was short, with chestnut curls that shaded into red where the sun struck them directly. Alice had a sense that he was aware of the way the light played on his hair; that in some way he was aware of everything that he was, and all the things around him.

They moved a few feet away from the kiosk, together, as if they had made a common agreement. Alice didn't know how to say goodbye. She felt in debt, partly because he had given her the water and partly because he had helped her to open it. She wasn't even sure she wanted to go so quickly.

Fabio understood.

'Can I walk you to wherever you're going?' he asked cheekily.

Alice blushed.

'I'm going to the car.'

'To the car, then.'

She didn't say yes or no, but smiled, looking in another direction. Fabio made an obsequious gesture with his hand that meant after you.

They crossed the main road and turned into a smaller one, where the pavement was no longer sheltered by trees.

It was from Alice's shadow, as they walked side by side, that the doctor noticed the asymmetry of her gait. Her right shoulder, weighed down by the camera, acted as a counterpoint to the line of her left leg, which was as hard as a stick. Alice's unsettling grace was heightened in her oblong shadow, making it look one-dimensional, a dark segment branching out into two proportional and equal mechanical prostheses.

'Have you hurt a leg?' he asked.

'What?' said Alice, alarmed.

'I asked you if you'd hurt yourself,' he repeated. 'I saw you were limping.'

Alice felt her good leg contracting too. She tried to correct her walk, leaning on her faulty leg as much as she could until it really hurt. She thought of the cruelty and precision of the word limp.

'I had an accident,' she said. Then, as if by way of apology, she added, 'A long time ago.'

'Car?'

'No, skiing.'

'I love skiing,' Fabio said enthusiastically, sure that he had found an opportunity for a conversation.

'I hate it,' Alice replied crisply.

'Shame.'

'Yes, shame.'

They walked on without saying anything more. The young doctor was surrounded by an aura of tranquillity, a solid and transparent sphere of security. His lips were pursed in a smile even when he wasn't smiling. He looked at ease, as if he met a girl in a hospital room every day and chatted to her as he walked her back to her car. Alice, on the other hand, felt like a piece of wood. Her tendons were on the alert, she was aware of the creaking of her joints, the stiff muscles sticking to her bones.

She pointed to a parked blue Seicento, as if to say that's it, and Fabio spread out his arms. A car passed along the road behind them. From nothing, its noise grew and then faded away again, until it finally disappeared.

'So, are you a photographer?' said the doctor, to gain time as much as anything else.

'Yes,' Alice replied instinctively. She immediately regretted it. For the moment she was a girl who had quit university and was wandering around the streets snapping photographs more or less at random. She wondered whether that was enough to make her a photographer, what was the boundary between being and not being someone.

She bit her thin lip. 'More or less,' she added.

'May I?' the doctor said, opening out his hand for the camera.

'Of course.'

Alice unrolled the strap from her wrist and held it out to him. He turned it around in his hands. He took off the lens cap and aimed the lens first in front of him and then upwards, towards the sky.

'Wow,' he observed. 'It looks professional.'

She blushed and the doctor made as if to give her back the camera.

'You can take a picture if you like,' said Alice.

'No, no, please. I don't know how. You do it.'

'What of?'

Fabio looked around. He turned his head to one side and the other, dubiously. Then he shrugged.

'Of me,' he replied.

Alice looked at him suspiciously.

'Why should I?' she asked him, with a slightly malicious inflection that escaped from her involuntarily.

'Because it means you'll have to see me again, at least to show it to me.'

Alice hesitated for a moment. She looked into Fabio's eyes, carefully for the first time, and couldn't hold their gaze for more than a second. They were blue and shadowless, as clear as the sky behind him, and she felt lost inside them, as if she were naked in a huge empty room.

He's handsome, thought Alice. He's handsome in the way a boy should be handsome.

She aimed the viewfinder at the middle of his face. He smiled, without a hint of embarrassment. He didn't even tilt his head, as people often do in front of the lens. Alice adjusted the focus and then exerted pressure with her index finger. The air was shattered by a click.

23

Mattia presented himself in Niccoli's office a week after their first meeting. The professor recognized him by his knock, a fact that curiously disturbed him. Seeing Mattia come in, he took a deep breath, ready to fly into a fury as soon as the boy said something along the lines of there are things I don't understand or I wanted to ask you if you could explain a few passages to me. If I'm forceful enough, Niccoli thought, I might be able to get rid of him.

Mattia asked his permission and, without looking the professor in the face, set down on the edge of the table the paper that he had been given to study. Niccoli picked it up and lost grip of a little pile of pages numbered and written in beautiful script, appended to the stapled ones. He assembled them and found a properly developed account of the article, each one with its own reference to the text. He quickly flicked through but had no need to examine them thoroughly to work out that they were correct: the order of the pages was enough to reveal their exactness.

He was still a little disappointed; he felt his fit of fury stuck halfway down his throat, like a sneeze that refused to come. He nodded for a long time whilst he studied Mattia's work, trying in vain to suppress a jolt of envy for this boy who seemed so unfit for existence but was doubtless gifted in this subject, as he himself had never really felt.

'Very good,' he said at last, but to himself, without the intention of paying a genuine compliment. Then, with apparent boredom, 'There's a problem raised in the final paragraphs. It concerns the moments of the Zeta Function to — '

'I've done it,' Mattia cut in. 'I think I've solved it.'

Niccoli looked at him with suspicion and then with deliberate disdain.

'Oh, really?'

'In the last page of my notes.'

The professor moistened his index finger with his tongue and flicked through the pages to the end. Frowning, he quickly read Mattia's demonstration, not understanding much of it, but not finding anything to object to either. Then he started from the beginning, more slowly, and this time the reasoning struck him as clear, quite rigorous, in fact, although sullied here and there by amateur pedantry. As he followed the passages his forehead relaxed and he unconsciously began stroking his lower lip. He forgot about Mattia, who was still frozen in the same position as he had been at the beginning, looking at his feet and repeating in his head let it be right, let it be right, as if the rest of his life depended on the professor's verdict. As he said that to himself he didn't imagine, however, that it really would be.

Niccoli rested the pages on the table again, carefully, and leaned into the back of his chair,

150

once again with his hands crossed behind his head, in his preferred position.

'Well, I'd say you're all set,' he said.

* * *

Graduation was fixed for the end of May and Mattia asked his parents not to come. What? was all his mother could say. He shook his head, looking towards the window. The glass rested against a wall of darkness and reflected the image of the three of them around a table with four sides. Mattia saw the reflection of his father taking his mother's arm and giving her a signal to let it go. Then he saw the reflection of her getting up from the table with her hand over her mouth and turning on the tap to wash the dishes, even though they hadn't finished dinner.

Graduation day arrived like any other day and Mattia got up before he heard the alarm. His dreams, which had filled his mind with scribbled sheets of paper during the night, took a few minutes to dissolve. He found no one in the sitting room, just a blue suit, smart and new, laid out beside a perfectly ironed pale pink shirt. On the shirt was a note with the words *To our graduate* and signed Mum and Dad, but in Dad's handwriting alone. Mattia put the clothes on and left the room without looking at himself in the mirror.

He discussed his dissertation, staring the members of the commission straight in the eyes, devoting an equal amount of time to each of them and without a tremble in his voice. Niccoli, sitting in the first row, nodded gravely and peered at the growing amazement on the faces of his colleagues.

When the moment of the announcement came, Mattia arranged himself in a line with the other candidates. They were the only ones standing in the oversized space of the great hall. Mattia felt the eyes of the audience tingle on his back. He tried to distract himself by estimating the volume of the room, taking as his scale the height of the dean, but the tingle climbed up his neck and there it split, gripping his temples. He imagined thousands of little insects pouring into his ears; thousands of hungry moths tunnelling into his brain.

The words that the dean repeated identically for each of the candidates seemed longer each time, and were drowned out by a growing noise in his head, so loud that he couldn't make out his own name when the moment came. Something solid, like an ice cube, obstructed his throat. He shook the dean's hand and it was so dry to the touch that he instinctively sought the metal buckle of the belt that he wasn't wearing. The whole audience rose to its feet with the sound of a rising tide. Niccoli came over and clapped him twice on the shoulder, saying congratulations. Before the applause ended Mattia was out of the hall and walking hastily down the corridor, forgetting to put his toe down first to keep his footsteps from echoing on the way out.

I've done it, I've done it, he silently repeated to himself. But the closer he got to the door the more aware he became of an abyss opening up in his stomach. Outside, the sunlight overwhelmed him, along with the heat and the noise of the traffic. He staggered, as if from fear of falling from the concrete step. There was a group of people on the pavement; Mattia counted sixteen with a single glance. Many of them were holding flowers, almost certainly waiting for their fellow-students. For a moment Mattia wished someone was there for him. He felt the need to abandon his own weight on to someone else's body, as if the contents of his head had suddenly become more than his two legs alone could bear. He looked for his parents, he looked for Alice and Denis, but there were only strangers looking nervously at their watches, fanning themselves with sheets of paper they'd picked up who knows where, smoking, talking loudly and noticing nothing.

He looked at the scroll that he held rolled up in his hand, on which it was written in beautiful cursive script that Mattia Balossino was a graduate, a professional, an adult, that it was time for Mr Balossino, B.Sc., to face up to life, and that this meant he had reached the end of the track that he had blindly followed from the first year of primary school to his degree. He was still only half breathing, as if the air didn't have enough momentum to accomplish the complete cycle.

What now? he wondered out loud.

A short, panting woman said do excuse me and he stepped aside to let her in. He followed her inside, not even she could give him his answer, and walked reluctantly down the corridor and climbed the stairs to the first floor. He stepped into the library and went and sat down at his usual place, beside the window. He set his scroll down on the empty seat beside him and stretched his hands right out on the table. He concentrated on his own breathing, which was still stuck in some backwash between his throat and the bottom of his lungs. It had happened to him before, but never for such a long time.

You can't forget how to do it, he said to himself. It's a thing you can't forget and that's it.

He exhaled all the air and was in a state of apnoea for several seconds. Then he opened his mouth wide and breathed in as hard as he could, so much that the muscles in his chest hurt. This time his breath went all the way to the bottom of his lungs and Mattia thought he could see the molecules of oxygen, round and white, scattering around his arteries and beginning to swirl towards his heart once more.

He stayed in the same position for an indefinite amount of time, without thinking, without noticing the students coming in and out, in an absent-minded state of numbness and agitation.

Then something flashed in front of his eyes, a red patch, and Mattia gave a start. He focused his eyes upon a rose wrapped in cellophane, which someone had slapped rudely on to the desk. Following the stem he recognized Alice's hand with its protruding knuckles, slightly reddened compared to her white fingers, and its rounded nails cut down to the edge of the fingertip.

'You really are a jerk.'

Mattia looked at her as one looks at a hallucination. He felt as if he was approaching this scene from a long way away, from a blurry place that he was already unable to remember well. When he was close enough, he made out on Alice's face a deep and unfamiliar sadness.

'Why didn't you tell me?' she went on. 'You were supposed to let me know. You were supposed to.'

Alice slipped into the seat opposite Mattia, exhausted. She looked outside, towards the street, shaking her head.

'How did you . . . ?' Mattia began.

'Your parents. I found out from your parents.' Alice turned and stared at him, her blue eyes boiling with rage. 'Do you think that's right?'

Mattia hesitated and then shook his head, a dim and distorted outline moving with him over the wrinkled surface of the cellophane.

'I'd always imagined being there. I'd imagined it so many times. While you . . . '

Alice paused, the rest of the sentence trapped between her teeth. Mattia reflected once more on how that moment had suddenly become so real. He tried to remember where he had been until a few seconds before, but without success.

'You just didn't,' Alice finished. 'You just didn't. As ever.'

He felt his head sinking between his shoulders and once again the moths, swarming inside his skull.

'It wasn't important,' he whispered. 'I didn't want — '

'Shut up,' she interrupted him abruptly. From the other desks someone said shhh and the silence of the next few seconds preserved the memory of that hiss.

'You're pale,' said Alice. She looked at Mattia suspiciously. 'Are you OK?'

'I don't know. I feel a bit dizzy.'

Alice got to her feet. She brushed her hair from her forehead, along with a tangle of unpleasant thoughts. Then she bent over Mattia and gave him a kiss on the cheek, silent and light, which in a breath swept away all the insects.

'I'm sure you did brilliantly,' she whispered into his ear. 'I know.'

Mattia felt her hair tickling his neck. He felt the soft hollow of air that separated them filling with her warmth and pressing lightly on his skin, like cotton wool. He became aware of an urge to pull her to him, but his hands remained motionless, as if asleep.

Alice pulled herself up. She picked up his degree certificate from the chair, unrolled it and smiled, reading it under her breath.

'Wow,' she said at last. Her voice assumed a radiant tone. 'We've got to celebrate. Come on, Mr B.Sc., on your feet,' she commanded.

She held out her hand to Mattia. He took it, rather uncertainly at first. He allowed himself to be led out of the library, with the same disarmed trust with which years before he had been dragged into the girls' toilet. Over time the proportions between their hands had changed. Now his fingers completely enwrapped Alice's, like the rough halves of a sea-shell.

'Where are we going?' he asked her.

'For a drive. The sun's out. And you need to catch some of it.'

They left the building and this time Mattia wasn't afraid of the light, the traffic and the people assembled around the entrance.

In the car they kept the windows lowered. Alice drove with both hands on the wheel and sang to 'Pictures Of You', imitating the sound of the words that she didn't know. Mattia felt his muscles gradually relaxing, adapting to the shape of the seat. He felt as if the car was leaving a dark and sticky trail in its wake, consisting of his past and his worries. He gradually began to feel lighter, like a jar being emptied. He closed his eyes and for a second he managed to float on the air that fanned his face and on Alice's voice.

When he opened it again they were on the road leading to his house. He wondered if they might have organized a surprise party for him and prayed that it wasn't so.

'Come on, where are we going?' he asked again.

'Don't you worry,' murmured Alice. 'If you ever take me for a drive you have the right to choose.'

For the first time Mattia was ashamed to be twenty-two and not be able to drive. It was another of the things he had left behind, another obvious step in a boy's life that he had decided not to accomplish, to stay as far as possible from the machinery of life. Like eating popcorn at the cinema, like sitting on the back of a bench, like not respecting your parents' curfew, like playing football with a ball of rolled-up silver foil or standing naked in front of a girl. He thought that from this precise moment things would be different. He decided he would get his licence as soon as possible. He would do it for her, to take her for a drive. Because he was afraid to admit it, but when he was with her it seemed it was worth doing all the normal things that normal people do.

Now that they were close to Mattia's house, Alice turned in another direction. She pulled into the main road and parked the car a hundred yards down, opposite the park.

'*Voilà*,' she said. She unfastened her seat-belt and got out of the car.

Mattia stayed frozen in his seat, his eyes fixed on the park.

'Well? Are you getting out?'

'Not here,' he said.

'Come on, don't be stupid.'

Mattia shook his head.

'Let's go somewhere else,' he said.

Alice looked around.

'What's the problem?' she insisted. 'We're just taking a stroll.'

She came over to the window on Mattia's side. He was stiff, as if someone was sticking a knife in his back. His hand gripped the handle of the door, which was half open. He stared at the trees a hundred metres away. The wide, green leaves covered their knotty skeletons, the fractal structure of the branches. They hid their horrible secret.

He had never been back here. The last time was with the police, that day that his father had told him give your mother your hand and she had pulled hers away and stuck it in her pocket. That day he had still had both his arms bandaged, from his fingers to his elbow, with a thick dressing rolled in so many layers that it took a saw blade to remove it. He had shown the policemen where Michela had been sitting. They had wanted to know the exact spot and had taken pictures, first from far away and then from close up.

From the car, on the way back home, he had seen the diggers sticking their mechanical arms into the river to pull out big piles of wet soil and drop them heavily on the bank. Mattia had noticed that his mother held her breath every time, until each pile disintegrated on the ground. Michela must have been in that slime, but she hadn't been found. She had never been found.

'Let's get away from here. Please,' repeated Mattia. His tone wasn't pleading. Instead he seemed absorbed, annoyed.

Alice got back into the car.

'Sometimes I can't work out whether — '

'That's where I abandoned my twin sister,' he cut in with a flat, almost inhuman voice. He lifted his arm and with his right index finger pointed to the trees in the park. Then he left it there in mid-air, as if he had forgotten.

'Twin sister? What are you talking about? You haven't got a twin sister . . . '

159

Mattia nodded slowly, still staring at the trees.

'She was identical to me. Completely identical to me,' he said.

Then, before Alice had time to ask him, he told her everything. He spilled out the whole story, like a dam collapsing. The worm, the party, the Lego, the river, the bits of glass, the hospital room, the judge, the television appeal, the headshrinkers, everything, as he had never done to anyone. He talked without looking at her, without getting excited. Then he lapsed back into silence. He patted the seat with his right hand, but found only rounded shapes. He had calmed down. He felt remote again, alien to his own body.

Alice touched his chin with a hand and delicately turned his face towards her. What Mattia saw coming towards him was only a shadow. He instinctively closed his eyes and then felt Alice's hot mouth on his, her tears on his cheek, or perhaps they weren't hers, and finally the hands, so light, holding his head tightly and catching hold of all his thoughts and imprisoning them there, in the now missing space between them.

24

Over the past few months they had seen each other often, without ever making a real date but never really by chance. After visiting hours Alice always ended up hanging around Fabio's ward, and he always managed to let her find him. They strolled around the courtyard along an unchanging route that they had decided by mutual agreement, without discussing it. That outside enclosure marked the confines of their story, carving out a region where there was no need to name that clear and mysterious thing that rocked back and forth between them.

Fabio seemed to have a precise knowledge of the dynamics of courtship; he knew how to respect rhythms and moderate phrases as if following a protocol. He guessed at Alice's profound suffering, but he kept out of it, on the edge. The excesses of the world, whatever form they might assume, didn't really concern him. They collided with his equilibrium and common sense and so he preferred to ignore them, simply pretending that they didn't exist. If an obstacle moved across him and blocked his passage, he walked around it, without altering his own pace in the slightest, and soon forgot it. He never had doubts, or hardly ever.

Nonetheless, he knew how to reach an objective, so he was attentive to Alice's moods in a way that was respectful, though slightly pedantic. If she didn't talk, he asked her if something was wrong, but never twice in a row. He was interested in her photographs, in how her mother was and filled the silences with the stories of his own day, with amusing anecdotes picked up around the ward.

Alice allowed herself to be carried away by his self-confidence and gradually abandoned herself to it, as she had abandoned herself to the support of the water when she played dead in the swimming pool as a little girl.

They lived the slow and invisible interpenetration of their universes, like two stars gravitating around a common axis, in ever tighter orbits, whose clear destiny is to coalesce at some point in space and time.

Alice's mother's treatment had been suspended. With a nod of the head, her husband had finally given his consent to let her sink into painless sleep, under the heavy cover of morphine. Alice waited only for it to come to an end and couldn't feel guilty for that. Her mother already lived within her as a memory, settled like a clump of pollen in a corner of her head, where she would stay for the rest of her life, frozen in the same pile of soundless images.

Fabio hadn't planned to ask her and wasn't the type for impulsive gestures, but that afternoon there was something different about Alice. A kind of nervousness emerged out of her way of weaving her fingers together and moving her eyes from one side to the other, always careful not to meet his own. For the first time since meeting her he was hasty and incautious.

'This weekend my parents are going to the seaside,' he said out of nowhere.

Alice seemed not to have heard or let the sentence drop. For some days her head had been buzzing like a wasps' nest. Mattia hadn't called her since graduation day, more than a week previously, and yet it was clear that it was now his turn.

'I thought you could come and have dinner at my place,' Fabio threw in.

His confidence faltered for a moment in the middle of those words, but he immediately shook off his uncertainty. He plunged both hands into the pockets of his white coat and prepared to accept any kind of reply with the same kind of lightness. He knew how to build a shelter for himself even before he needed one.

Alice smiled faintly, slightly panic-stricken.

'I don't know,' she said gently. 'Perhaps it isn't — '

'You're right,' Fabio interrupted her. 'I shouldn't have asked you. Sorry.'

They finished their walk in silence and when they were standing outside Fabio's ward again, he said a prolonged OK, speaking to himself.

Neither of them moved. They exchanged a quick glance and immediately lowered their eyes. Fabio started to laugh.

'We never know how to say goodbye to each other, you and me,' he said.

'Yeah.' Alice smiled at him. She brought a hand to her hair, hooked a lock with her index finger and pulled on it slightly.

Fabio took a resolute step towards her and the

163

gravel of the driveway crunched as it settled beneath his foot. He kissed her on her left cheek, with affectionate arrogance, and then stepped back.

'Well, at least think about it,' he said.

He gave her an open smile, involving his whole mouth, eyes and cheeks. Then he turned around and, walking with his back straight, headed for the entrance.

Now he'll turn around, thought Alice when he was beyond the glass door.

But Fabio turned the corner and disappeared into the corridor.

25

The letter was addressed to Mr Mattia Balossino, B.Sc., and to the touch it was so light and insubstantial that he couldn't believe it contained his whole future. His mother hadn't shown it to him until dinner, perhaps out of embarrassment at having opened it without permission. She hadn't done it on purpose, she hadn't even looked at the name of the addressee: Mattia never got any mail.

'This came,' she said, holding the letter over the dishes.

Mattia glanced quizzically at his father, who nodded at something vague. Before taking the letter he ran the paper napkin over his upper lip, which was already clean. Observing the complicated circular logo, printed in blue next to the address, he had no idea what it might contain. He pressed on both sides of the envelope to take out the folded page inside it. He opened it and began to read, rather impressed by the thought that this letter was specifically for him, Mr Mattia Balossino, B.Sc.

His parents made more noise than necessary with their cutlery and his father repeatedly cleared his throat. After reading it, Mattia refolded the page with the reverse sequence of gestures with which he had opened it, so as to return it to its initial form, and slipped it back into its envelope, which he set down on Michela's chair.

He picked up the fork again, but had a moment of bewilderment at the sight of the sliced courgettes in the dish, as if someone had made them appear there by surprise.

'It sounds like a terrific opportunity,' said Adele.

'Yeah.'

'Are you going to go?'

As she said it, Mattia's mother felt heat flashing in her face. She was aware that it had nothing to do with the fear of losing him. On the contrary, she hoped with all her might that he would accept it, that he would leave this house and the place that he occupied opposite her every evening at dinner, his black head dangling over his plate and that contagious air of tragedy surrounding him.

'I don't know,' Mattia replied to his plate.

'It's a wonderful opportunity,' his mother repeated.

'Yeah.'

Mattia's father broke the silence that followed with random thoughts about the efficiency of the people of northern Europe, about how clean their streets were, putting it all down to the severe climate and the lack of light for much of the year, which limited distractions. He had never been anywhere of the kind, but clearly that was how it was.

When, at the end of dinner, Mattia began stacking up the dishes, collecting them in the same order as he did every evening, his father put a hand on his shoulder and said under his breath go on, I'll finish here. Mattia picked up the envelope from the chair and went to his room.

He sat down on the bed and began turning the letter around in his hands. He folded it backwards and forwards a few times, making the thick paper of the envelope crack. Then he examined the logo beside the address more carefully. A bird of prey, probably an eagle, held its wings open and its head turned on one side so as to show its pointed beak in profile. Its wingtips and claws were inscribed inside a circle, which a printing fault had turned slightly oval. Another circle, larger and concentric with the preceding one, contained the name of the university that was offering Mattia a place. The gothic characters, all those *ks* and *hs* in the name and the *os* with a diagonal line running through them, which in mathematics indicated a null set, made Mattia imagine a tall, dark building, with echoing corridors and very high ceilings, surrounded by lawns with grass cut to a few millimetres from the ground, silent and deserted as a cathedral at the end of the world.

In that unknown and far-off place lay his future as a mathematician. There was a promise of salvation, an uncontaminated place where nothing was yet compromised. Here, on the other hand, there was Alice, just her, and a bog all around her.

It happened as it had on the day of his graduation. Once again his breath was caught halfway down his throat, where it acted as a stopper. He gasped as if the air in his room had suddenly liquefied. The days had already

167

lengthened and the dusk was blue and wearying. Mattia waited for the last remnant of light from outside to go out, meanwhile his mind was already wandering along corridors that he hadn't yet seen, bumping from time to time into Alice, who looked at him without a word and didn't smile at him.

You've just got to decide, he thought. Go or don't go. 1 or 0, like a binary code.

But the more he tried to simplify it, the more confused he seemed to become.

Someone knocked on the door of his room and the sound reached him as if from the bottom of a well.

'Yes?' he said.

The door opened slowly and his father poked his head in.

'Can I come in?' he asked.

'Uh-huh.'

'Why are you here in the dark?'

Without waiting for an answer, Pietro pressed the switch and the 100 watts of the lamp exploded in Mattia's dilated pupils, which contracted with a pleasant pain.

His father sat down on the bed next to him. They had the same way of crossing their legs, with the left calf balanced on the right heel, but neither of them had ever noticed.

'What's the name of that thing you studied?' Pietro asked after a while.

'What thing?'

'That thing in your dissertation. I can't remember what it's called.'

'The Riemann Zeta Function.'

168

'That's the one. The Riemann Zeta Function.'

Mattia rubbed his thumbnail against the nail of his little finger, but the skin there had become so hard and callused that he didn't feel a thing. His nails slipped noisily over each other.

'I wish I'd had your mind,' Pietro went on. 'But I didn't understand a thing about maths. Not really my cup of tea. You have to have a special sort of brain for some things.'

Mattia thought there was nothing nice about having his mind. That he would happily have unscrewed it and replaced it with a different one, or even with a tin of biscuits, provided that it was empty and light. He opened his mouth to reply that feeling special is the worst kind of cage that a person can build, but then he didn't say anything. He thought about the time when his schoolmistress had put him in the middle of the classroom, with everyone else all around looking at him like a rare animal, and it occurred to him that it was as if in all those years he had never moved away from there.

'Did Mum tell you to come?' he asked his father.

The muscles in Pietro's neck stiffened. He sucked in his lips and then nodded.

'Your future is the most important thing,' he said in a vaguely embarrassed voice. 'It's right that you think about yourself now. If you decide to go we'll support you. We haven't got much money, but there's enough if you need it.'

There was another extended silence, in which Mattia thought about Alice and about the share of money that he had stolen from Michela.

'Dad?' he said at last.

'Yes?'

'Could you leave, please? I have to make a phone call.'

Pietro gave a long sigh that also contained a certain amount of relief.

'Of course,' he said.

He got up and before turning around he stretched a hand towards Mattia's face. He was about to touch his cheek, but he stopped a few inches from the unruly tufts of his son's beard. He swerved his caress towards his hair, which he barely touched. After all, it was some time since they had been used to such things.

26

Denis's love for Mattia had burned itself out, like a forgotten candle in an empty room, and had made way for a ravenous discontent. When he was nineteen, Denis found an advertisement for a gay bar on the last page of a local newspaper and tore it out, keeping the scrap of paper in his wallet for two whole months. From time to time he unrolled it and reread the address, even though he already knew it by heart.

All around him, his contemporaries were going out with girls and had got used to sex, so much so that they'd stopped talking about it all the time. Denis felt that his only escape route lay in that piece of newspaper; in that address that had faded from the sweat of his fingertips.

He went there one rainy evening, without really having made his mind up to go. He put on the first thing he dragged out of the wardrobe and went out with a quick shout to his parents in the other room. I'm going to the cinema, he said.

He walked past the bar two or three times, continuing all the way around the block every time. Then he went in with his hands in his pockets and a confidential wink to the bouncer. He sat down at the bar, ordered a lager and sipped it gently, staring at the bottles lined up against the wall, waiting.

A guy came over to him a moment later and Denis decided he'd be OK, even before he looked him properly in the face. The man started talking about himself, or maybe about some film that Denis hadn't seen. He shouted in his ear but Denis didn't listen to a word. He brusquely interrupted him saying let's go to the toilet. The other guy was struck dumb and then he smiled, revealing bad teeth. Denis thought he was horrible, that his eyebrows almost joined up and he was old, too old, but it didn't matter.

In the toilet the guy pulled his T-shirt up over his belly and bent forward to kiss him, but Denis dodged. Instead he knelt down and unbuttoned the other man's trousers. Bloody hell, he said, you're in a hurry. But then he let him get on with it. Denis shut his eyes and tried to finish as quickly as possible.

He didn't get a result with his mouth and felt completely hopeless. Then he used his hands, both of them, insistently. As the guy came he came too, in his pants. He almost ran from the toilet, without giving the stranger time to get his clothes back on. The same old sense of guilt had taken hold of him as soon as he was past the toilet door, and had drenched him like a bucket of icy water.

Outside the bar he wandered about for half an hour in search of a fountain to wash the smell off him.

He had gone back to the bar at various times. Every evening he talked to someone different and he always found an excuse not to give his real name. He hadn't gone off with anyone else. He collected the stories of people like himself, and otherwise he shut up and listened. He slowly discovered that the stories were similar, that there was a process, and that the process involved immersion, putting your whole head under until you touched the bottom and only then coming up for air.

Every one of them had a love that rotted alone in their heart, as his love for Mattia had done. Each of them had been afraid and many of them still were, but not when they were here, amongst others who could understand, protected by the 'scene', as they put it. When he talked to those strangers Denis felt less alone and wondered when his moment would come, the day when he would touch bottom, resurface and finally be able to breathe.

One evening someone had talked to him about 'the lamps'. In their 'scene' that was what they called the little path up behind the cemetery, where the only lights to be seen, faint and trembling, were the lamps from the gravestones whose light filtered between the bars of the big cemetery gate. He had groped his way there, finding it was the right place to empty himself of desire without seeing or being seen, just putting his own body at the disposal of the dark.

It was at the lamps that Denis had touched the depths of the darkness. He had crashed into it with his face, chest and knees, as though diving into shallow water, and afterwards he never went back to the bar, locking himself away, more stubbornly than before, in his own denial.

Then, in his third year at university, he went to Spain. There, far from the probing eyes of his family and friends and all the streets whose names he knew, love found him. Its name was Valerio and was Italian like him; young and scared to death like him. The months they spent together, in a little apartment a few blocks from the Ramblas, had been quick and intense and they removed the useless cloak of suffering, as on the first clear evening after days of pouring rain.

Back in Italy they lost sight of each other, but Denis didn't suffer. With a completely new confidence, which he would never lose, he moved on to other affairs, which seemed to have been waiting for him for all that time, lined up in an orderly fashion just around the corner. The only old friendship he maintained was with Mattia. They spoke only rarely, mostly on the phone, and were capable of sitting in silence for minutes at a time, each lost in his own thoughts, punctuated by the other's reassuring, rhythmical breathing at the other end of the line.

When the call came, Denis was brushing his teeth. At home he always answered after two rings, the time it took to get to the nearest telephone, wherever he happened to be in the apartment.

His mother called Denis it's for you, and he took his time before going to answer. He rinsed his mouth out well, passed the towel over it and glanced once more at his two upper front incisors. Over the past few days he had had a sense that they were overlapping, because of his wisdom teeth pushing in from the sides.

'Hello?'

'Hi.'

Mattia never introduced himself. He knew

that his voice was unmistakable to his friend and anyway he didn't like saying his name.

'So, Mr Graduate, how are you?' Denis said cheerfully. He wasn't upset about the graduation business. He had learned to respect the chasm that Mattia had dug around himself. Years previously he had tried to jump over that chasm, and had fallen into it. Now he contented himself with sitting on the edge, his legs dangling into the void. Mattia's voice no longer stirred anything in his stomach, but he was aware of the idea of him and always would be, as the only true benchmark for everything that had come afterwards.

'Did I disturb you?' asked Mattia.

'No. Did I disturb you?' Denis teased.

'I was the one who called you.'

'Of course, so tell me: I can tell from your voice that something's up.'

Mattia remained silent. Something was up, it was there on the tip of his tongue.

'Well?' Denis pressed. 'And this something would be?'

Mattia exhaled loudly into the receiver and Denis became aware that he was having difficulty breathing. He picked up a pen beside the telephone and started playing with it, passing it between the fingers of his right hand. Then he dropped it and he didn't bend down to pick it up. Mattia still wasn't speaking.

'Shall I start asking questions?' said Denis. 'We could do it so that you — '

'I've been offered a position abroad,' Mattia interrupted. 'At a university. An important one.'

'Wow,' Denis observed, not surprised in the

175

least. 'That sounds fantastic. Are you going?'

'I don't know. Should I?'

Denis pretended to laugh.

'You're asking me that when I haven't even finished university? I'd go like a shot. A change of air always does you good.'

He thought of adding *and what is there to keep you here?* but he didn't say it.

'It's because something happened, the other day,' Mattia ventured. 'The day I graduated.'

'Mmm.'

'Alice was there and . . . '

'And?'

Mattia hesitated for a moment.

'In short, we kissed,' he said at last.

Denis's fingers stiffened around the receiver. He was surprised by his reaction. He was no longer jealous of Alice, there was no point, but at that moment it was as if an undigested bit of the past had come back up his throat. For a moment he saw Mattia and Alice hand in hand in Viola's kitchen, and he felt Giulia Mirandi's invading tongue forcing its way into his mouth like a rolled-up towel.

'Hallelujah,' he remarked, trying to sound happy. 'You two have finally done it.'

'Yeah.'

In the pause that followed both of them wanted to hang up.

'And now you don't know what to do,' Denis struggled to say.

'Yeah.'

'But you and she are now, what would you say . . . ?'

'I don't know. I haven't seen her since.'

'Ah.'

Denis ran the nail of his index finger along the curled wire of the telephone. At the other end Mattia did the same and as always he thought of a DNA helix, missing its twin.

'And yet numbers are everywhere,' said Denis. 'They're always the same, aren't they?'

'Yes.'

'But Alice is only here.'

'Yes.'

'So you've already made your mind up.'

Denis heard his friend's breath easing and becoming more regular.

'Thank you,' said Mattia.

'For what?'

Mattia hung up. Denis spent another few seconds with the receiver pressed to his ear, listening to the silence inside it. Something within him went out, like one last ember that had stayed lit for too long under the ashes.

I said the right thing, he thought.

The engaged tone sounded. Denis hung up and went back into the bathroom to check those wretched wisdom teeth.

27

'¿Qué pasa, mi amorcito?' Soledad asked Alice, tilting her head slightly to catch her eye. Since Fernanda had been in hospital she had eaten at the dinner table with them, because father and daughter facing each other, alone, was unbearable for both of them.

Alice's father had developed the habit of not changing when he came home from work. He had dinner in his jacket and tie, slightly loosened, as if he was passing through. He held a newspaper open on the table and only looked up to make sure that his daughter was gulping down at least the occasional mouthful.

The silence had become part of the meal and disturbed only Sol, who often thought back to the rowdy meals at her mother's house, when she was still very young and could never have imagined she would end up like this.

Alice hadn't even looked at the cutlet and salad on her plate. She took little sips of water, crossing her eyes as she drank and regarding the glass resting on her lips as seriously as if it held some kind of medicine. She shrugged and flashed a swift smile at Sol.

'Sorry,' she said. 'I'm not very hungry.'

Her father nervously turned the page. Before setting the paper back down he gave it an impetuous shake and couldn't help glancing at his daughter's full plate. He didn't comment and started reading again, beginning a random article in the middle, without grasping its meaning.

'Sol?' asked Alice.

'Yes?'

'How did your husband win you? The first time, I mean. What did he do?'

Soledad stopped chewing. Then she started again, more slowly, to gain some time. The first image that ran through her head wasn't of the day she met her husband. Instead she thought back to that morning when she had got up late and wandered barefoot around the house, looking for him. Over the years all the memories of her marriage had become concentrated in those few moments, as if the time spent with her husband had only been the preparation for an ending. That morning she had looked at the previous night's washing-up and the cushions in the wrong place on the sofa. Everything was just as they had left it and the sounds in the air were the same as ever. And yet something, in the way things were arranged and the way the light clung to them, had left her frozen in the middle of the sitting room, dismayed. And then, with disconcerting clarity, she had thought he's gone.

Soledad sighed, feigning her usual nostalgia.

'He brought me home from work on his bicycle. Every day he came with his bicycle,' she said. 'And he gave me some shoes.'

'What?'

'Shoes. White ones, high heels.'

Soledad smiled and indicated the length of the heels with her thumb and index finger.

'They were very pretty,' she said.

179

Alice's father snorted and shuffled in his chair, as if he found all this intolerable. Alice imagined Sol's husband coming out of the shop with the shoebox under his arm. She knew him from the photograph that Sol kept hung over the head of her bed, with a dry little olive branch slipped between the nail and the hook.

For a moment she felt light-headed, but her thoughts immediately turned to Mattia, and stayed there. A week had passed, and he still hadn't called.

I'll go now, she thought.

She slipped a little forkful of salad into her mouth, as if to say to her father look I've eaten. The vinegar stung her lips slightly. She was still chewing as she got up from the table.

'I've got to go out,' she said.

Her father arched his eyebrows.

'And might we know where you're going at this time of day?' he asked.

'Out,' said Alice defiantly. Then she added: 'To a girlfriend's,' to soften the tone.

Her father shook his head, as if to say do what you like. For a moment Alice felt sorry for him, left on his own like that behind his newspaper. She felt a desire to hug him and tell him everything and ask him what she should do, but a moment later the same thought made her shiver. She turned around and headed resolutely for the bathroom.

Her father lowered the newspaper and with two fingers he rubbed his weary eyelids. Sol turned the memory of the high-heeled shoes around in her head for a few seconds, then put it back in its place and got up to clear the things away.

★ ★ ★

On her way to Mattia's house, Alice kept the music turned up but if, when she got there, someone had asked her what she was listening to, she wouldn't have been able to say. All of a sudden she was furious and she was sure that she was about to ruin everything, but she no longer had any choice. That evening, getting up from the table, she had crossed the invisible boundary beyond which things start working by themselves. It was like that time on the skis, when she had moved her centre of gravity too far forward by an insignificant couple of millimetres, just enough to end up face down in the snow.

She had only been to Mattia's house once before. Mattia had disappeared into his room to change and she had had an embarrassed chat with his mother, Mrs Balossino, who had looked at her from the sofa with a vaguely worried air, as if Alice's hair was on fire or something. It hadn't been a comfortable experience.

Alice rang the doorbell and the display beside it lit up red, like a final warning. After a few crackles Mattia's mother answered in a frightened voice.

'Who is it?'

'It's Alice, Mrs Balossini. I'm sorry about the time, but . . . is Mattia there?'

From the other end she heard a thoughtful silence. Alice pulled her hair over her right

181

shoulder, having the disagreeable impression of being observed through the lens of the entry-phone. The door opened with an electrical click. Before coming in, Alice smiled at the camera to say thank you.

In the empty hallway her footsteps echoed with the rhythm of a heartbeat. Her bad leg seemed to have lost all its life, as if her heart had forgotten to pump blood into it.

The door to the apartment was half open, but there was no one to welcome her. Alice pushed it and said, 'Hello?' Mattia emerged from the sitting room and stopped at least two metres away from her.

'Hi,' he said, without moving his arms.

'Hi.'

They stood looking at each other for a few seconds, as if they didn't know each other at all. Mattia had crossed his big toe over his second one, inside his slipper, and by squashing one over the other and against the floor he hoped he could break them.

'Sorry if I'm — '

'Won't you come in?' Mattia broke in automatically.

Alice turned to close the door and the round brass handle slipped from her sweaty palm. The door slammed, shaking the frame, and a shiver of impatience ran through Mattia.

What's she doing here? he thought

It was as if the Alice he had been talking to Denis about only a few minutes before wasn't the same one who had just dropped by without warning. He tried to clear his mind of that

182

ridiculous thought, but the irritation remained in his mouth like a kind of nausea.

He thought of the word hunted. Then he thought about when his father used to drag him on to the carpet and imprison him between his enormous arms. He tickled him on his tummy and on his sides and he exploded with laughter, he laughed so hard that he couldn't breathe.

Alice followed him into the sitting room. Mattia's parents stood waiting, like a little welcoming committee.

'Good evening,' she said, shrinking back.

'Hi, Alice,' replied Adele, without moving.

Pietro, on the other hand, came over and unexpectedly stroked her hair.

'You're getting prettier and prettier,' he said. 'How's your mother?'

Adele, behind her husband's back, kept up a paralysed smile and bit her lip for not having asked the question herself.

Alice blushed.

'Same as usual,' she said, so as not to appear over-dramatic. 'She's getting by.'

'Say hello from us,' said Pietro.

All four of them stood in silence. Mattia's father seemed to stare right through Alice and she tried to distribute her weight uniformly on her legs, so as not to look crippled. She realized that her mother would never meet Mattia's parents and she was a bit sorry about that, but she was even sorrier to be the only one thinking anything of the kind.

'You two go on,' Pietro said at last.

Alice passed beside him with her head lowered

after smiling once more at Adele. Mattia had already reached his room.

'Shall I close it?' asked Alice once she was inside, pointing to the door. All her courage had deserted her.

'Uh-huh.'

Mattia sat down on the bed, with his hands crossed on his knees. Alice looked around the room. The things that filled it seemed not to have been touched by anyone; they looked like articles that had been carefully and calculatedly displayed in a shop window. There was nothing useless, not a photograph on the wall or a cuddly toy left over from childhood, nothing that gave off that smell of familiarity and affection that teenagers' rooms usually have. With all the chaos that she had in her body and her head, Alice felt out of place.

'You've got a lovely room,' she said, without really meaning it.

'Thanks,' said Mattia.

There was an enormous list of things to say floating over their heads and both of them tried to ignore it by looking at the floor.

Alice slid her back along the wardrobe and sat down on the ground with her working knee against her chest. She forced a smile.

'So, how does it feel to have graduated?'

Mattia shrugged and smiled very slightly.

'Exactly the same as before.'

'You really don't know how to be happy, do you?'

'Apparently not.'

Alice let an affectionate mmm slip between

her closed lips and thought that this embarrassment between them made no sense and yet it was there, solid and ineradicable.

'But things have been happening to you lately,' she said.

'Yes.'

Alice thought about whether to say it or not. Then she said it, without a drop of saliva in her mouth.

'Something nice, no?'

Mattia drew in his legs.

Here we go, he thought.

'Yes, actually,' he said.

He knew exactly what he was supposed to do. He was supposed to get up and go and sit next to her. He was supposed to smile, look into her eyes and kiss her. All that. It was just mechanical, a banal sequence of vectors that would bring his mouth to hers. He could do it even if at that moment he didn't feel like it; he could trust the precision of his movements.

He made as if to get up, but somehow the mattress kept him where he was, like a sticky morass.

Once again Alice acted in his place.

'Can I come over there?' she asked.

He nodded and, even though there was no need, moved slightly to one side.

Alice pulled herself to her feet, with the help of her hands.

On the bed, in the space that Mattia had left free, there was a piece of paper, typed and folded in three like an accordion. Alice picked it up to move it and noticed that it was written in English.

'What is it?' she asked.

'I got it today. It's a letter from a university.'

Alice read the name of the city, written in bold in the top left-hand corner, and the letters dimmed under her eyes.

'What does it say?'

'I've been offered a grant.'

Alice felt dizzy and panic turned her face white.

'Wow,' she lied. 'For how long?'

'Four years.'

She gulped. She was still standing up.

'And are you going?' she asked under her breath.

'I don't know yet,' said Mattia, almost apologizing. 'What do you think?'

Alice remained silent, with the sheet of paper in her hands and her gaze lost somewhere on the wall.

'What do you think?' Mattia repeated, as if she really hadn't heard him.

'What do I think about what?' Alice's voice had suddenly hardened, so much that Mattia gave a start. For some reason she thought about her mother in hospital, dazed with drugs. She looked expressionlessly at the sheet of paper and wanted to tear it up.

Instead she put it back down on the bed, where she had been about to sit down.

'It would be important for my career,' Mattia said by way of self-justification.

Alice nodded seriously, with her chin thrust out as if she had a golf ball in her mouth.

'Fine. So what are you waiting for? Off you go.

It seems to me that there's nothing to keep you here,' she said between clenched teeth.

Mattia felt the veins in his neck swelling. Perhaps he was about to cry. Since that afternoon in the park he had always felt the tears there, like a lump that was hard to swallow. Maybe this day his tear ducts, clogged for so long, had finally opened and all that accumulated stuff had begun to force its way out.

'But if I went away,' he began in a slightly quivering voice, 'would you . . . ?' He stopped.

'Me?' Alice stared at him from above, like a stain on the bed-cover. 'I'd imagined the next four years differently,' she said. 'I'm twenty-three and my mother's about to die. I . . . ' She shook her head. 'But none of that matters to you. Just think of your career.'

It was the first time she had used her mother's illness to hit out at someone, and all in all she didn't regret it. She saw Mattia shrinking in front of her eyes.

He didn't reply and ran through in his mind the instructions for breathing.

'But don't you worry,' Alice went on. 'I've found someone it does matter to. In fact that's what I came here to tell you.' She paused, her mind blank. Once again things were taking a course of their own; once again she was tumbling down the slope and forgetting to stick in her ski-poles to brake. 'His name's Fabio, he's a doctor. I didn't want you to . . . You know.'

She uttered the phrase like a little actress, in a voice that wasn't hers. She felt the words scratching her tongue like sand. As she uttered

187

them, she studied Mattia's expression, to pick up a hint of disappointment that she could cling to, but his eyes were too dark for her to make out any spark in them. She was sure none of it mattered to him and her stomach crumpled like a plastic bag.

'I'll be off,' she said quietly, exhausted.

Mattia nodded, looking towards the closed window to eliminate Alice completely from his field of vision. That name, Fabio, had plunged into his head like a splinter and he just wanted Alice to leave.

He saw that outside the evening was clear and a warm wind was about to blow through. The opaque pollen of the poplars, swarming under the beam from the streetlights, looked like big legless insects.

Alice opened the door and he got to his feet. He walked her to the front door, following her at a small distance behind. She distractedly checked in her bag that she had everything, to gain another moment. Then she murmured OK and left.

Before the lift doors closed, Alice and Mattia exchanged a goodbye that meant nothing at all.

28

Mattia's parents were watching television. His mother's knees were curled up under her nightdress; his father's legs were stretched out, crossed on the low table in front of the sofa, the remote control resting on one thigh. Alice hadn't responded to their goodbye, she didn't even seem to have noticed that they were there.

Mattia spoke from behind the back of the sofa.

'I've decided to accept,' he said.

Adele brought a hand to her cheek and, bewildered, sought her husband's eyes. Mattia's father turned slightly and looked at his son as one looks at a son who has grown up.

'Fine,' he said.

Mattia went back to his room. He picked up the sheet of paper from the bed and sat down at the desk. He perceived the universe expanding; he could feel it accelerating under his feet and for a moment he hoped that its stretching fabric would burst and let him come crashing down.

He groped around for the light switch and turned it on. He chose the longest of the four pencils lined up side by side, dangerously close to the edge of the desk. From the second drawer he took the sharpener and bent down to sharpen it into the waste-paper basket. He blew away the thin sawdust that was left on the end of the pencil. There was already a blank sheet in front of him.

He put his left hand on the paper, its back facing upwards and the fingers open. Over it he ran the very sharp graphite tip. He lingered for a second, ready to plunge it into the confluence of the two big veins at the base of his middle finger. Then, slowly, he removed it, and took a deep breath.

On the sheet he wrote *For the kind attention of the Dean*.

29

Fabio was waiting for her by the front door, with the lights of the landing, the door and the sitting room all lit. As he took from her hands the plastic bag holding the tub of ice cream, he linked his fingers with hers and kissed her on one cheek, as if it was the most natural thing in the world. He said that dress really suits you and he meant it, and then he went back to the stove to get on with cooking dinner, but without taking his eyes off her.

The stereo was playing music that Alice didn't recognize, but it wasn't there to be listened to, just to complete a perfect scenario; there was nothing casual about it. Two candles were lit, the wine was already open and the table was tidily set for two, with the blades of the knives turned inwards, which meant that the guest was welcome, as her mother had taught her when she was little. There was a white tablecloth with no wrinkles and the napkins were folded in a triangle with the edges perfectly aligned.

Alice sat down at the table and counted the empty plates stacked on top of each other to work out how much there was to eat. That evening, before coming out, she had spent a long time locked in the bathroom staring at the towels that Soledad changed every Friday. In the marbled-topped chest of drawers she had found her mother's make-up and used it. She had made herself up in the semi-darkness, and before running the lipstick over her lips, she had sniffed the tip. The smell hadn't reminded her of anything.

She had granted herself the ritual of trying on four different dresses, even though it was obvious from the outset, if not from the previous day, that she had already decided on the one she had worn to the confirmation of the Ronconis' son, the one that her father had said was the most inappropriate because it left her back uncovered to below the ribs and her arms completely bare.

Still barefoot and wearing the little blue dress whose neckline against her pale skin looked like a smile of satisfaction, Alice had gone down to Sol in the kitchen and asked her apprehensively for an opinion. You look wonderful, Sol had said. She kissed her on the forehead and Alice had been worried about smudging her make-up.

In the kitchen Fabio moved with great agility and at the same time with the excessive care of someone who knows he's being watched. Alice sipped the white wine that he had poured and the alcohol produced little explosions in her stomach, which had been empty for at least twenty hours. The heat spread along her arteries, then rose slowly to her head and swept away the thought of Mattia, like the evening tide when it takes over the beach again.

Sitting at the table, Alice carefully assessed Fabio's silhouette, the clear line that separated his chestnut hair from his neck, his pelvis, which was not especially slender, and his shoulders, somewhat inflated under his shirt. She found herself thinking of how it would feel to be safely trapped in his arms, with no possibility of choice.

She had accepted his invitation because she had told Mattia about him and because — she was sure of it now — what she could find here was more like love than anything else she would ever have.

Fabio opened the fridge and cut from a stick of butter a slice which Alice thought was at least 80 or 90 grams. He threw it into the pan to thicken the risotto and it disintegrated, giving up all its saturated and animal fats. He turned off the flame and stirred the risotto with a wooden spoon for another few minutes.

'There we are,' he said.

He dried his hands on a dishcloth hanging over a chair and turned towards the table, holding the frying pan.

Alice darted a terrified glance at the contents.

'Hardly anything for me,' she said, gesturing a pinch with her fingers, just before he poured a hypercalorific ladleful on to her plate.

'You don't like it?'

'It's not that,' lied Alice. 'It's just that I'm allergic to mushrooms. But I'll try it.'

Fabio looked disappointed and stood there with the frying pan in mid-air. He actually lost a little colour from his face.

'Damn, I'm really sorry. I had no idea.'

'It doesn't matter. Really.' Alice smiled at him.

'If you want I can — ' he went on.

Alice hushed him by taking his hand. Fabio looked at her as a child looks at a present.

'I can try it, though,' said Alice.

Fabio resolutely shook his head.

'Absolutely not. What if it makes you ill?'

He took the pan away and Alice couldn't help smiling. For a good half-hour they sat talking over the empty plates and Fabio had to open another bottle of white.

Alice had the pleasant sensation of losing part of herself with each sip. She was aware of the insubstantiality of her own body and at the same time of the massive bulk of Fabio's, sitting in front of her with his elbows resting on the table and his shirt-sleeves rolled halfway up his forearms. The thought of Mattia, so incessant over the past few weeks, vibrated faintly in the air like a slightly slackened violin-string, a dissonant note lost in the middle of an orchestra.

'Well, we can console ourselves with the main course,' said Fabio.

Alice thought she was going to faint. She had hoped it was going to end there. Instead Fabio rose from the table and took from the oven a baking-tin with two tomatoes, two aubergines and two yellow peppers, stuffed with something that looked like mince mixed with breadcrumbs. The composition of colours was cheerful, but Alice immediately thought of the exorbitant dimensions of those vegetables and imagined them, completely whole as they were now, in the middle of her stomach, like rocks at the bottom of a pond.

'You choose,' Fabio said invitingly.

Alice bit her lip. Then she timidly pointed at the tomato and he transferred it on to her plate, using a knife and fork as pincers.

'And?'

'That's enough,' said Alice.

'Impossible. You haven't eaten a thing. And with all that you've drunk!'

Alice looked at him and for a moment she hated him deeply, as much as she hated her father, her mother, Sol and anyone else who had ever counted the things on her plate.

'That one,' she said, giving in, pointing at the aubergine.

Fabio served himself one of each vegetable and before attacking them he looked at them with satisfaction. Alice tried the stuffing, slipping in the very tip of her fork. Apart from the meat she immediately recognized eggs, ricotta and parmesan and hastily calculated that a whole day of fasting wouldn't be enough to compensate.

'How is it?' Fabio asked, smiling, with his mouth half full.

'Delicious,' she replied.

She summoned up the courage to bite into a mouthful of aubergine. She gulped back her nausea and went on, one bite after another without saying a word. She finished the whole aubergine, and as soon as she had set her fork down next to her plate, she was assailed by a sudden urge to vomit. Fabio was talking and pouring more wine. Alice nodded and with each movement she felt the aubergine dancing up and down in her stomach.

Fabio had already shovelled everything down, while on Alice's plate there still lay the tomato, red and filled with that nauseating mixture. If

195

she cut it into tiny pieces and hid it in her napkin he would notice immediately because there was nothing to hide her apart from the candles, which had already burned halfway down.

Then, like a blessing, the second bottle of wine was finished and Fabio struggled from the table to get a third. He held his head in his hands and said out loud to her stop it please stop. Alice laughed. Fabio looked in the fridge and opened all the cupboards, but he couldn't find another bottle.

'I think my parents must have taken them,' he said. 'I'll have to go to the cellar.'

He exploded with laughter for no reason and Alice laughed with him, even though it hurt her stomach.

'Don't you move from there,' he commanded, pointing a finger at his forehead.

'OK,' Alice replied and the idea came to her straight away.

As soon as Fabio was outside, she picked up the greasy tomato with two fingers and carried it to the bathroom, holding it at arm's length to avoid the smell. She locked herself in, lifted the seat and the toilet smiled at her as if saying let me do it.

Alice studied the tomato. It was big, perhaps it needed to be cut up into little pieces, but it was also soft and she said to herself who cares and threw it in as it was. It dropped in with a plop and a splash of water nearly soaked her blue dress. The tomato settled on the bottom and disappeared halfway down the outlet.

She pressed the flush and the water went

down like healing rain but, instead of disappearing down the hole, it started filling the bowl and a less than reassuring gurgle rose from the bottom.

Alice drew back in horror and her bad leg wobbled so much that she almost ended up on the floor. She watched the water level rise and rise and then suddenly stop.

The sound of the siphon went off. The bowl was full to the brim. The surface of the transparent water quivered slightly and there at the bottom, motionless, was the tomato, trapped in the same spot as before.

Alice stood and looked at it for at least a minute, frozen with panic and at the same time strangely curious. She was reawakened by the sound of the key turning in the front door. She took the toilet brush and plunged it into the water, her face contorted into a grimace of disgust. The tomato just wouldn't move.

'What do I do now?' she whispered to herself.

Then, almost unconsciously, she pressed the flush again and this time the water began to spill out and spread over the floor in a thin layer, until it licked at Alice's elegant shoes. She tried to lift the flush again, but the water kept flowing and pouring out and, if Alice hadn't put the rug over it, it would have reached the door and from there the other room.

After a few seconds the water stopped again. The tomato was still down there, intact. The lake on the floor had stopped spreading. Mattia had once explained to her that there's a precise point at which water stops spreading, when the surface tension has become strong enough to hold it together, like a film.

Alice looked at the mess she had made. She closed the lid of the toilet, as if surrendering to disaster, and sat down on it. She brought her hands to her closed eyes and began to cry. She cried for Mattia, for her mother, for her father, for all that water, but mostly for herself. Under her breath she called Mattia, as if seeking his help, but his name remained on her lips, sticky and insubstantial.

Fabio knocked at the toilet door and she didn't move.

'Alice, everything OK?'

Alice could see his outline through the frosted glass of the door. She sniffed quietly and cleared her throat to disguise her tears.

'Sure,' she said. 'I'll be there in a minute.'

She looked around, lost, as if she really didn't know how she'd ended up in that bathroom. The toilet bowl dripped on the floor in at least three different places and Alice hoped, for a moment, that she could drown in those few millimetres of water.

Getting Things in Focus
(2003)

30

She had turned up at Marcello Crozza's studio at ten o'clock one morning and, feigning a determination that had cost her three walks around the block, had said I want to learn the trades could you take me on as an apprentice? Crozza, who had been sitting by the automatic developer, had nodded. Then he had turned around and, looking her straight in the eyes, had said I can't pay you. He hadn't wanted to say forget it, because he'd done the same thing himself many years before and the memory of the courage it had taken him was all that was left of his passion for photography. In spite of all his disappointments, he wouldn't have denied anyone that sensation.

What was more, they were holiday photographs. Families of three or four people, by the sea or in tourist destinations, hugging in the middle of St Mark's Square or under the Eiffel Tower, with their feet cut off and always in the same pose. Photographs taken with automatic cameras, over-exposed or out of focus. Alice didn't even look at them any more: she developed them and then slipped them all into the paper envelope with the yellow and red Kodak logo.

It was just a matter of being in the shop, receiving rolls of twenty-four or thirty-six shots, shut away in their little plastic containers, of marking the customer's name on the slip and telling them they'll be ready tomorrow, of printing out receipts and saying thank you, goodbye.

Sometimes, on Saturdays, there were weddings. Crozza picked her up from home at a quarter to nine, always in the same suit and without his tie, because in the end he was the photographer, not a guest.

In church they had to set up the two lights, and on one of the first occasions Alice had dropped one and it had smashed on the steps of the altar and she had looked at Crozza in terror. He had pulled a face as if one of the pieces of glass had got stuck in his leg, but then he had said it doesn't matter, just clear it up.

He was fond of her and didn't know why. Perhaps because he had no children, or because since Alice had been working there he was able to go to the bar at eleven o'clock and check his lottery numbers and when he came back to the shop she smiled at him and asked him so, are we rich? Perhaps because she had that bad leg and lacked a mother as he lacked a wife and all lacks are pretty much the same. Or because he was sure that she would get tired of him quickly and in the evening he would pull down the shutter on his own again and set off for home where there was no one, with his head empty and yet so very heavy.

Instead, after a year and a half, Alice was still there. Now that she had the keys she arrived before him in the morning and Crozza found her on the pavement in front of the shop, chatting with the lady from the grocer's next door, with whom he had never exchanged more than a 'Good morning'. He paid her off the books, five hundred euros a month. If they did weddings together he would drop her outside the door of the Della Rocca household and, with the engine of his Lancia still running, take out his wallet and hand her an extra fifty, saying see you Monday.

Sometimes she brought him her own snap-shots and asked his opinion, even though it was clear to both of them that he had nothing more to teach her. They sat down at the desk and Crozza looked at the photographs, holding them up to the light, and gave her some advice about exposure time, or how best to use the shutter. He let her use his Nikon whenever she wanted and, secretly, he had decided he would give it to her as a present the day she left.

'We're getting married on Saturday,' said Crozza. It was his way of saying they had a job.

Alice was putting on her denim jacket. Fabio would be there to pick her up at any moment.

'OK,' she said. 'Where?'

'At the Gran Madre. Then there's a reception in a private villa in the hills. Rich folk's stuff,' commented Crozza with a touch of disdain, immediately regretting it because he knew that Alice came from there too.

'OK,' she murmured. 'Do you know who they are?'

'They sent the invitation. I've put it over there somewhere,' said Crozza, pointing to the desk under the cash register.

Alice looked in her bag for an elastic band and tied up her hair. Crozza watched from across the shop. Once he had masturbated thinking about her, kneeling in the gloom after they'd lowered the shutters, but then he had felt so dreadful that he hadn't eaten and the next day he had sent her home saying you've got the day off today, I don't want anyone under my feet.

Alice rummaged among the sheets of paper stacked under the desk, more to fill the time while waiting than out of genuine interest. She found the envelope with the invitation, stiff and imposingly large. She opened it and the name leaped off the page in a gilded cursive, full of flourishes.

Ferruccio Carlo Bai and Maria Luisa Turletti Bai are delighted to announce the marriage of their daughter Viola . . .

Her eyes darkened before she went any further. A metallic taste flooded her mouth. She swallowed and it was like gulping down that fruit gum from the changing room all over again. She closed the envelope and thoughtfully waved it in the air for a moment.

'Can I go alone?' she ventured at last, her back still turned to Crozza.

He shut the drawer of the cash register with a rattle and a ding.

'What?' he asked.

Alice turned around and her eyes were wide open and bright with something and Crozza couldn't help smiling they were so beautiful.

'I've cracked it now, haven't I?' said Alice, walking over to him. 'I can do it. Otherwise I'll never be able to manage on my own.'

Crozza looked at her suspiciously. She rested her elbows on the desk, right in front of him, and pushed herself forward. She was only a few inches from his nose and that gleam in her eyes begged him to say yes and not to ask for explanations.

'I don't know if — '

'Please,' Alice broke in.

Crozza stroked his earlobe and was forced to look away.

'All right then,' he gave in. He didn't understand why he felt like saying it under his breath. 'But don't screw it up.'

'I promise I can do it,' Alice said, making her translucent lips disappear into a smile.

Then she pushed herself forward on her elbows and gave him a kiss, which tickled Crozza's three-day beard.

'Go on, go on,' he said, dismissing her with his hand.

Alice laughed and the sound of it scattered through the air as she left with her unique, sinuous, rhythmic gait.

That evening Crozza stayed a little longer than usual in the shop, doing nothing. He looked at the things around him and noticed that they had more presence, as they had done many years before when people had come to him to have their picture taken.

He took the camera out of the bag, where Alice always put it back after giving all the lenses and mechanisms a good clean. He screwed on the lens and aimed it at the first object that came

205

into view, the umbrella stand by the entrance. He enlarged part of the rounded edge until it looked like something else, like the crater of an extinct volcano. But then he didn't take the picture.

He put the camera away, picked up his jacket, turned out the lights and left. He closed the shutters with the padlock and headed in the opposite direction to his usual one. He couldn't take a stupid smile off his face and he really had no desire to go home.

★　★　★

The church was decorated with two enormous bouquets of lilies and marguerites, arranged on either side of the altar, and with dozens of miniature copies of the same bouquet at the end of each pew. Alice set up the lights and arranged the reflector panel. Then she sat and waited in the first row. A lady was running the vacuum cleaner over the red carpet that Viola would walk down in an hour's time. Alice thought about when she and Viola used to sit on the railings and talk. She couldn't remember what they had talked about, only that she had looked at her rapt from a place just behind her eyes, a place full of jumbled thoughts that she had kept to herself even then.

Over the next half-hour all the pews filled up and people accumulated at the back, where they stood fanning themselves with the order of service.

Alice went outside and waited on the cobbles

for the bride's car to arrive. High in the sky the sun warmed her hands and its rays seemed to pass right through them. As a little girl she had liked looking at her palms against the light, the red peeking through her closed fingers. Once she had shown it to her father and he had kissed her fingertips, pretending to eat them.

Viola arrived in a gleaming grey Porsche, and the driver had to help her out and pick up her cumbersome train. Alice madly snapped away, more to hide her face behind the camera more than anything else. Then, when the bride passed by, she lowered it deliberately and smiled at her.

They looked at each other for only a moment and Viola caught her breath. Alice couldn't study her expression, because the bride had already passed her and was entering the church on her father's arm. For some reason Alice had always imagined him taller.

She was careful not to lose so much as a moment. She took various close-ups of the happy couple and their families. She immortalized the exchange of rings, the reading of the promises, the communion, the kiss and the signing of the register. She was the only one moving in the whole church. It seemed to Alice that Viola's shoulders stiffened slightly when she was near her. She increased the exposure time still further, to obtain that blurry quality which, according to Crozza, suggested eternity.

As the couple left the church, Alice walked ahead of them, limping backwards, bending slightly so as not to alter her height with a low perspective. Through the lens she became aware that Viola was looking at her with a frightened half-smile, as if she was the only one who could see a ghost. Alice exploded the flash in her face at regular intervals, about fifteen times, until the bride was forced to narrow her eyes.

She watched them getting into the car and Viola darted her a glance from behind the window. She was sure she would immediately start talking to her husband about her, about how strange it was that she had been there. She would describe her as the class anorexic, the cripple, someone she had never hung out with. She wouldn't mention the sweet, the party and everything else. Alice smiled at the thought that it might be their first half-truth as a married couple, the first of the tiny cracks that would eventually converge into a gaping hole.

'Miss, the couple are waiting on the river-bank for the photographs,' said a voice behind her.

Alice turned around and recognized one of the witnesses.

'Certainly. I'll be right there,' she replied.

She quickly went into the church to dismantle her equipment. She was still putting the various pieces of the camera in the rectangular case when she heard someone calling to her.

'Alice?'

She turned around, already sure who had been speaking.

'Yes?'

Standing in front of her were Giada Savarino and Giulia Mirandi.

'Hi,' said Giada ostentatiously, approaching Alice to kiss her on both cheeks.

Giulia stayed where she was, staring at her feet as she had done at school.

Alice barely brushed Giada's cheek with her own pursed lips.

'What on earth are you doing here?' shrieked Giada.

Alice thought it was a stupid question and couldn't help smiling.

'I'm taking photographs,' she replied.

Giada responded with a smile, showing the same dimples she had had at seventeen.

It was strange to find them here, still alive, with their shared bits of past that suddenly counted for nothing.

'Hi, Giulia,' Alice forced herself to say.

Giulia smiled at her and struggled to speak.

'We heard about your mother,' she said. 'We're really sorry.'

Giada nodded, repeatedly, to show her agreement.

'Yeah,' replied Alice. 'Thanks.'

She started hastily putting things away. Giada and Giulia looked at each other.

'We'll let you get on with your work,' Giada said, touching her shoulder. 'You're very busy.'

'OK.'

They turned around and walked towards the exit, the crisp click of their heels echoing off the walls of the now empty church.

★ ★ ★

The couple were waiting in the shade of a big tree standing some feet apart. Alice parked next to their Porsche and got out with the shoulder bag. It was hot and she felt her hair sticking to the back of her neck.

'Hi,' she said, walking over.

'Alice,' said Viola. 'I didn't think — '

'Neither did I,' Alice cut in.

They pretended to hug, as if they didn't want to dirty their clothes. Viola was even more beautiful than she had been at school. Over the years the features of her face had become sweeter, the outlines were softer and her eyes had lost that imperceptible vibration that made them so terrible. She still had that perfect body.

'This is Carlo,' said Viola.

Alice shook his hand and felt how smooth it was.

'Shall we start?' she asked, cutting her short.

Viola nodded and sought her husband's eyes, but he didn't notice.

'Where shall we put ourselves?' she asked.

Alice looked around. The sun was at its zenith and she would have to use the flash to eliminate all the shadows from the faces. She pointed to a bench in full sunlight on the river-bank.

'Sit down there,' she said.

She took longer than usual to set up the camera. She pretended to busy herself with the flash, mounted one lens and then swapped it for another one. Viola's husband fanned himself with his tie, while she tried to use her finger to stop the little drops of sweat trickling down her forehead.

Alice left them to stew for a bit as she pretended to find the right distance to take the picture.

Then she started giving them brusque orders. She said put your arms around each other, smile, now serious, take her by the hand, rest her head on your shoulder, whisper in her ear, look at each other, closer, towards the river, take your jacket off. Crozza had taught her that you mustn't let your subjects breathe, you mustn't give them time to think, because it takes only a minute for the spontaneity to evaporate.

Viola obeyed, two or three times asking apprehensively is that all right?

'OK, now let's go into the field,' said Alice.

'More?' asked Viola, startled. The red of her flushed cheeks was starting to show through her foundation. The black line of the pencil surrounding her eyes was already slightly smudged, the edges were getting jagged, making her look tired and slightly shabby.

'You pretend to run away and let him chase you across the field,' Alice explained.

'What? You want me to run?'

'Yes, run.'

'But . . . ' Viola began to protest. She looked at her husband and he shrugged.

She snorted, then lifted up her skirt and began running. Her heels sank a few millimetres into the ground, and raised up little clumps that dirtied the inside of her white dress. Her husband ran after her.

'You're going too slowly,' he said.

Viola turned around all of a sudden with a look that reduced him to ashes, a look that Alice remembered all too well. She let them run after each other for two or three minutes, until Viola freed herself clumsily from her husband's clutches, saying that's enough.

Her hair had come undone on one side and a lock fell down her cheek.

'Yes,' said Alice. 'Just a few more shots.'

She took them to the ice-cream stand and bought two lemon iced lollies, which she paid for.

'Hold these,' she said, holding them out to the couple.

They unwrapped them suspiciously. Viola was careful not to get the sticky syrup all over her hands.

They had to pretend to eat them, arms crossed, and then each offer their own to the other. Viola's smile was becoming increasingly tense.

When Alice told her to hold on to the street lamp and use it as a pivot to spin around, Viola exploded.

'This is ridiculous,' she said.

Her husband looked at her, slightly intimidated, and then looked at Alice, as if to apologize. She smiled.

'It's part of the classic album,' she explained. 'That's what you asked for. But we can skip that sequence.'

She forced herself to sound sincere. She felt her tattoo pulsating, as if it wanted to jump out of her skin. Viola stared at her furiously and Alice held her gaze until her eyes stung.

'Have we finished?' said Viola.

Alice nodded.

'Let's go then,' she said to her husband.

Before letting himself be dragged away, he came over to Alice and shook her hand politely once more.

'Thanks,' he said.

'My pleasure.'

Alice watched them climb back up the slight slope to the car park. Around her there were the usual sounds of Saturday, the laughter of children on the swings and the voices of the mothers looking after them. There was music in the distance and the rush of cars on the road, like a carpet of sound.

She wanted to tell Mattia, because he would have understood. But now he was far away. She thought that Crozza would be furious, but he would forgive her in the end. She was sure of it.

She smiled. She opened the back of the camera, took out the film and unrolled it completely under the white light of the sun.

What Remains
(2007)

31

His father phoned on Wednesday evenings, between eight and a quarter past. They had rarely seen each other over the last nine years and it had been a long time since the last visit, but the phone call in Mattia's two-room apartment had become a ritual. In the long pauses between words the same old silence arose between the two of them: there were no televisions or radios on, never any guests rattling their cutlery to disturb it.

Mattia could imagine his mother listening to the phone call from her armchair without changing her expression, with both arms on the arm-rests, as when he and Michela were at primary school and she sat there listening to them reciting poetry by heart and Mattia always knew it while Michela said nothing, incapable of doing anything.

Every Wednesday, after hanging up, Mattia found himself wondering whether the orange floral pattern on the cover of that armchair was still the same or whether they'd replaced it, since it had been threadbare even back then. He wondered whether his parents had grown old. Of course they'd grown old, he heard it in his father's voice, which was slower and wearier, more like an attack of breathlessness.

His mother came to the phone infrequently and her questions were a matter of form, always the same. Is it cold, have you had your dinner yet, how are your classes going? We have dinner at seven over here, Mattia had explained the first few times. Now he merely said yes.

'Hello?' he said, speaking in Italian. '*Pronto?*'

There was no reason to answer it in English. Only about ten people had his home number and none of them would have dreamed of trying to get in touch with him at that time of day.

'It's Dad.'

The delay in his reply was only just perceptible. Mattia would have had to fetch a stop-watch to measure it and calculate how much the signal deviated from the straight line of over 600 kilometres long that connected him and his father, but he forgot every time.

'Hi. Are you well?' said Mattia.

'Yes. And you?'

'Fine . . . And Mum?'

'She's right here.'

The first silence always fell at that point, like a mouthful of air after swimming a length underwater.

Mattia scraped his index finger along the scratch in the pale wood of the round table, a few inches from the middle. He couldn't even remember whether he had scratched it or whether it had been the old tenants. Just under the enamelled surface it was compressed chipboard, which got under his fingernail without hurting him. Each Wednesday he dug that furrow a few fractions of a millimetre deeper, and sooner or later he would break through to the other side.

'So you saw the sunrise?' his father asked.

Mattia smiled. It was a joke they had between them, perhaps the only one. About a year before, somewhere in a newspaper, Pietro had read that watching the dawn over the North Sea is an unforgettable experience and in the evening he had read his son the cutting down the phone. You absolutely have to go, he had advised. Since that day he asked him from time to time so have you seen it? Mattia always answered no. His alarm was set to seventeen minutes past eight and the shortest way to the university didn't pass along the seafront.

'No, no dawn yet,' he replied.

'Well, it's not going anywhere,' said Pietro.

They had already run out of things to say, but they lingered there for a few seconds, with the receivers pressed to their ears. They both breathed in a little of the affection that still survived between them, diluted along hundreds of miles of coaxial cables and nourished by something whose name they didn't know and which perhaps, if they thought too carefully about it, no longer existed.

'I'll say goodbye, then,' Pietro said at last.

'Sure.'

'And try to keep well.'

'OK. Say hi to Mum.'

They hung up.

For Mattia it was the end of the day. He walked around the table. He looked distractedly at the papers stacked up on one side, and the work he had brought back from the office. He was still stuck on that passage. Wherever they

219

took the proof from, he and Alberto always ended up banging their heads against it sooner or later. He knew that the solution lay behind that final obstacle, and that once past it getting to the end would be easy, like letting himself roll down a grassy slope with his eyes closed.

But he was too tired to go back to work. He went into the kitchen and filled a pan with water from the tap. He put it on the stove and lit the gas. He spent so much time on his own that a normal person would have gone crazy in a month.

He sat down on the folding plastic chair, without completely relaxing. He looked up towards the unlit bulb in the middle of the ceiling. It had blown just a month after he'd arrived, and he had never replaced it. He ate with the light turned on in the other room.

If he had simply upped and left the apartment that very evening and not come back, no one would have found any sign of his presence, apart from those incomprehensible pages stacked on the table. Mattia had put nothing of himself into the place. He had kept the anonymous pale oak furniture and the yellowed wallpaper that had been stuck to the walls since the building was constructed.

He got to his feet. He poured boiling water into a cup and immersed a tea-bag in it. He watched the water turning dark. The methane flame was still lit and in the gloom it was violently blue. He lowered the heat until it was almost out and the hiss faded. He put his hand to the ring, from above. The heat exerted a faint pressure on his devastated palm. Mattia brought it down, slowly, and closed it around the flame.

* * *

He had spent hundreds and then thousands of identical days at university, and consumed innumerable canteen lunches in the little low building at the end of the campus, but even now he remembered the very first day when he had walked in and copied the sequence of gestures of the other people. He had joined the queue and, taking small footsteps, had reached the pile of plastic, imitation-wood trays. He had picked one up, set the paper napkin on it, and helped himself to cutlery and a glass. Then, once he was in front of the uniformed woman who served up the portions, he had pointed to one of the three aluminium tubs, at random, without knowing what was in them. The cook had asked him something, in her own language or perhaps in English, and he hadn't understood. He had pointed to the tub again and she had repeated the question, exactly the same as before. Mattia shook his head. I don't understand, he had said in English in a loud and nervy voice. She had raised her eyes to the sky and waved the empty plate in the air. She's asking you if you want sauce on that muck, said the young man next to him in Italian. Mattia had spun round, disoriented, and shook his head. The young man had turned towards the dinner lady and simply said no. She had smiled at him and finally filled Mattia's dish and handed it to him. The young

221

man had chosen the same and had brought it up to his nose and sniffed it with disgust. This stuff is revolting, he had observed.

You've just got here, then? he had asked him after a while, still staring at the liquid purée on the plate. Mattia had said yes and the young man had nodded with a frown, as if it was a serious matter. After paying, Mattia froze in front of the cash register, with the tray gripped in his hands. He had looked around for an empty table, somewhere he could avoid feeling people's eyes on him eating alone. He had just taken a step towards the back of the room when the young man from before had overtaken him and said come on, over here.

Alberto Torcia had already been there for four years, with a permanent researcher's post and a special grant awarded by the European Union for the quality of his most recent publications. He too had escaped from something, but Mattia had never asked him what. Neither of them, after so many years, could have said whether the other was a friend or just a colleague, in spite of the fact that they shared an office and had lunch together every day.

★   ★   ★

It was Tuesday. Alberto sat down opposite Mattia and, through the full glass of water that he brought to his lips, glimpsed the new mark, pale and perfectly circular, that he had on his palm. He didn't ask any questions, he merely gave him a crooked glance to let him know that he had

222

understood. Gilardi and Montanari, sitting at the same table with them, were sniggering over something they had found on the internet.

Mattia drained his glass in one gulp, then cleared his throat.

'Yesterday evening an idea came to me about the discontinuity that — '

'Please, Mattia,' Alberto interrupted him, dropping his fork and flopping back in his seat. His gestures were always very exaggerated. 'At least have pity on me when I'm eating.'

Mattia looked at the table. The slice of meat on his plate was cut into identical little squares and he separated them with his fork, leaving between them a regular grill of white lines.

'Why don't you do something else with your evenings?' Alberto went on more quietly, as if he didn't want the other two to hear him. As he spoke he drew little circles in the air with his knife.

Mattia said nothing and didn't look at him. He brought a little square of meat to his mouth, chosen from the ones on the edge whose fringed borders disturbed the geometry of the composition.

'If only you'd come and have a drink with us every now and again,' Alberto continued.

'No,' Mattia said brusquely.

'But — ' Alberto protested.

'Anyway, you know.'

Alberto shook his head and frowned, defeated. After all this time he still insisted on keeping to himself. Since they had known one another he had only managed to drag him out of the house about ten times.

223

He turned to the other two, breaking into their conversation.

'Have you seen her over there?' he asked, pointing to a girl sitting two tables away with an elderly gentleman. As far as Mattia knew, the man taught in the geology faculty. 'If only I wasn't married, Christ, what I could do to a woman like that.'

The others hesitated for a moment, because it had nothing to do with what they were talking about, but then they let it go and joined in, speculating about what such a babe was doing with an old buffer like that.

Mattia cut all the little squares of meat along the diagonal. Then he reassembled the triangles so as to form a larger one. The meat was already cold and tough. He took a piece of it and swallowed it almost whole. The rest he left where it was.

Outside the canteen Alberto lit a cigarette, to give Gilardi and Montanari time to move away. He waited for Mattia who was following a rectilinear crack along the floor and thinking about something that had nothing to do with being there.

'What were you saying about discontinuity?' he said.

'It doesn't matter.'

'Come on, don't be a dick.'

Mattia looked at his colleague. The tip of the cigarette between his lips was the only colour that brightened that entirely grey day, the same as the one before and doubtless the same as the one that would follow.

'We can't get away from it,' said Mattia. 'We've convinced ourselves that it exists. But perhaps I've found a way to get something interesting out of it.'

Alberto came closer. He didn't interrupt Mattia until he had finished delivering his explanation, because he knew that Mattia didn't talk much, but when he did it was worth shutting up and listening.

32

The *weight of consequences* had collapsed on
her all at once one evening a few years before,
when Fabio, as he pushed inside her, had
whispered I want to have a baby. His face was so
close to Alice's that she had felt his breath sliding
along her cheeks and dispersing among the
sheets.

She had pulled him to her, guiding his head
into the hollow between her neck and shoulder.
Once, before they were married, he had told her
it was the perfect fit, that his head was made to
slip into that space.

So what do you think? Fabio had asked her,
his voice muffled by the pillow. Alice hadn't
replied, but had held him a bit tighter. She
hadn't had the breath to speak.

She'd heard him closing the drawer with the
condoms in it and had bent her right knee a little
more to make room for him. Rhythmically she
stroked his hair, her eyes wide open.

That secret had crept after her since her
school days, but it had never taken hold of
her mind for more than a few seconds. Alice had
set it aside, like something she would think about
later on. Now, all of a sudden, there it was, like
an abyss cut into the black ceiling of the room,
monstrous and irrepressible. Alice wanted to
say to Fabio stop for a moment, wait, there's
something I haven't told you, but he moved with

disarming trust and he certainly wouldn't have understood.

She felt him come inside her, for the first time, and imagined that sticky liquid full of promise that he was going to deposit in her dry body, where it too would dry.

She didn't want a baby, or rather she hadn't really thought about it. The question didn't arise and that was that. Her menstrual cycle had stopped around about the last time she had eaten a whole chocolate pudding. The truth was that Fabio wanted a baby and she had to give him one. Had to, because when they made love he didn't ask her to turn the light on, he hadn't done that since the first time at his house. Because when it was over he lay on top of her and the weight of his body cancelled out all her fears and he didn't speak, just breathed, and anyway he was there. She had to, because she didn't love him, but his love was enough for both of them, to keep them safe.

From then on sex had assumed a new guise. It bore within itself a precise purpose, which had soon led them to abandon everything that wasn't strictly necessary.

For weeks and then months nothing had happened. Fabio had himself examined and his sperm count was good. In the evening he told Alice, being very careful to do it as he held her tightly in his arms. He immediately added you don't have to worry, it's not your fault. She pulled away and went into the other room before bursting into tears, and Fabio hated himself because in fact he thought — in fact he knew

227

— that it was his wife's fault.

Alice started feeling spied on. She kept an imaginary count of days, drawing little lines on the calendar beside the phone. She bought tampons and then threw them away unused. On the right days she pushed Fabio away in the dark, telling him we can't today.

He kept the same count, without telling her. Alice's secret crept slimily and transparently between them, forcing them further and further apart. Every time he hinted at doctors, treatment or the cause of the problem, Alice's face darkened and he was sure that it wouldn't be long before she found a pretext for an argument, any random nonsense.

Exhaustion slowly defeated them. They stopped talking about it and, along with the conversations, sex too had grown less frequent, until it was reduced to a laborious Friday night ritual. They took turns to wash, before and after doing it. Fabio would come back from the bathroom, the skin of his face still gleaming with soap and wearing fresh underwear. In the meantime Alice would already have slipped on her T-shirt and would ask can I go now? When she came back into the room she would find him already asleep, or at least with his eyes closed, facing the wall and with his whole body on his side of the bed.

★ ★ ★

There was nothing very different about that Friday, at least at first. Alice joined him in bed just after one, having spent the whole evening

228

shut up in the darkroom that Fabio had given her as a third anniversary present. He lowered the magazine he was reading and watched his wife's bare feet walk towards him, sticking to the wooden floor.

Alice slipped between the sheets and pressed herself against his side. Fabio let the magazine fall to the floor and turned out the bedside light. He did everything he could not to make it look like a habit, a duty, but the truth was clear to both of them.

They followed a series of movements that had become consolidated into a routine over time, and which made everything simpler, then Fabio entered her, with the help of his fingers.

Alice wasn't sure that he was really crying, because she held her head tilted to one side to avoid contact with his skin, but she noticed that there was something different in his way of moving. He was thrusting more violently, more urgently than usual, then he suddenly stopped, breathed heavily and started again, as though fighting between the desire to penetrate more deeply and the desire to slip away from her and from the room. She heard him sniffing as he panted.

When he finished he quickly withdrew, got out of bed and went and shut himself in the bathroom, without even turning on the light.

He stayed there for longer than usual. Alice moved towards the middle of the bed, where the sheets were still cool. She put a hand on her stomach, in which nothing was happening, and, for the first time, she thought she no longer had anyone to blame, that all these mistakes were hers alone.

Fabio crossed the room in the semi-darkness, climbed into bed and turned over so that he had his back to her. It was Alice's turn to go, but she didn't move. She felt that something was about to happen, the air was full of it.

It took him another minute, or perhaps two, before he spoke.

'Alice,' he said.

'Yes?'

He hesitated again.

'I can't do this any more,' he said softly.

Alice felt his words gripping her belly, like climbing plants sprouting suddenly from the bed. She didn't reply. She let him go on.

'I know what it is,' Fabio went on. His voice grew clearer. As it struck the walls it assumed a slight metallic echo. 'You don't want to let me in, you don't even want me to speak. But like this . . .'

He stopped. Alice's eyes were open. They were accustomed to the dark. She followed the outlines of the furniture: the armchair, the wardrobe, the chest of drawers and on top of it the mirror that didn't reflect anything. All those objects were there, motionless and terribly insistent.

Alice thought of her parents' room. She thought they were similar, that all bedrooms in the world were similar. She wondered what she was afraid of, losing him or losing those things: the curtains, the paintings, the carpet, all that security folded carefully away in the drawers.

'You barely ate two courgettes this evening,' Fabio went on.

'I wasn't hungry,' she replied automatically.

Here we go, she thought.

'The same yesterday. You didn't even touch the meat. You cut it up in little pieces and then hid it in your napkin. Do you really think I'm that stupid?'

Alice clenched the sheets. How could she have thought he would never notice? She saw before her eyes the hundreds, thousands of times in which the same scene had been repeated before her husband's eyes. She felt furious about all the things he must have thought in silence.

'I expect you also know what I ate the evening before and the evening before that,' she said.

'Tell me what it is,' he said, loudly this time. 'Tell me what it is that you find so repellent about food.'

She thought of her father bringing his face down to the plate when he ate soup, the sound he made, how he sucked the spoon rather than simply putting it in his mouth. She thought with disgust of the chewed-up pulp between her husband's teeth, every time he sat in front of her for dinner. She thought of Viola's fruit gum, with all those hairs stuck to it and its synthetic strawberry flavour. Then she thought about herself, without her T-shirt, reflected in the big mirror in her old house and the scar that made her leg something slightly apart, something detached from her torso and useless. She thought of the balance, so fragile, of her own silhouette, the thin strip of shadow that her ribs cast over her belly and which she was prepared to defend at all costs.

'What do you want? Do you want me to start stuffing myself? To deform myself to have your baby?' She spoke as if the baby was already there, somewhere in the universe. She called it *your* baby on purpose. 'I can have treatment if you're so keen on the idea. I can take hormones, medicine, all the junk necessary to let you have this child of yours. Maybe then you'll stop spying on me.'

'That isn't the point,' Fabio shot back. He had suddenly regained all his irritating self-confidence.

Alice moved towards the edge of the bed to get away from his threatening body. He rolled on to his back. His eyes were open and his face was tense, as if he was trying to see something beyond the darkness.

'It isn't?'

'You should think about all the risks, particularly in your condition.'

In your condition, Alice silently repeated to herself. She instinctively tried to bend her weak knee, to demonstrate to herself that she was in full control, but it barely moved.

'Poor Fabio,' she said. 'With that wife of his, crippled and . . . '

She couldn't finish her sentence. That last word that was already trembling in the air stayed in her throat.

'There's a part of the brain,' he began, ignoring her, as though an explanation might make everything simpler, 'probably the hypothalamus, which controls the body mass index. If that index falls too low, gonadotropin production is inhibited. The mechanism is blocked, periods stop. But they're just the initial symptoms. Other things happen, more serious things. The density of minerals in the bones diminishes and osteoporosis ensues. The bones crumble like wafers.'

He talked like a doctor, listing causes and effects in a monotonous voice, as if knowing the name of an illness was the same as curing it. Alice reflected that her bones had already crumbled once, and that these things didn't interest her.

'Raising that index is enough for everything to return to normal,' Fabio added. 'It's a slow process, but we still have time.'

Alice lifted herself up on her elbows. She wanted to leave the room.

'Fantastic. I suppose you've had all this ready for a while,' she remarked. 'That's all there is to it. Easy as that.'

Fabio sat up as well. He took her arm, but she broke away. He stared into her eyes through the gloom.

'It's not only about you any more,' he said.

Alice shook her head.

'Yes it is,' she said. 'Perhaps that's what I really want, haven't you thought of that? I want to feel my bones crumbling, I want to block the mechanism. As you said yourself.'

Fabio thumped the mattress, making it shake.

'So now what do you want to do?' she said provocatively.

Fabio sucked in air through his teeth. The

233

compressed violence in his lungs froze his arms.

'You're just selfish. You're spoilt and selfish.'

He threw himself on the bed and turned his back to her again. All of a sudden things seemed to return to their place in the shadow. There was silence again, but it was an imprecise silence. Alice noticed something like a faint whirring sound, like the rustle of old films in the cinema. She listened, trying to work out where it was coming from.

Then she saw the outline of her husband bobbing slightly up and down. She became aware of his suppressed sobs, like a rhythmical vibration of the mattress. His body asked her to stretch out a hand and touch him, to stroke his neck and his hair, but she left it there. She got up from the bed and walked towards the bathroom, slamming the door behind her.

33

After lunch Alberto and Mattia had gone down to the basement, where nothing ever changed and you measured the passing of time only by the heaviness of your eyes as they struggled with the white light of the fluorescent bulbs on the ceiling. They had slipped into an empty classroom and Alberto had sat down on the teacher's desk. His body was massive, not exactly fat, but to Mattia it seemed as if it was constantly expanding.

'Fire away,' said Alberto. 'Tell me everything from the start.'

Mattia picked up a piece of chalk and broke it in half. A thin white dust rested on the tips of his leather shoes, the same ones he had worn on the day of his graduation.

'Let's consider things in two dimensions,' he said.

He started to write in his fine hand. He started at the top left corner and filled the first two blackboards. On the third he copied out the results that he would be using later. It was as if he had performed this calculation hundreds of times, when in fact it was the first time he had pulled it out of his head. He turned towards Alberto every now and again, and nodded at him seriously, while his mind scampered after the chalk.

Reaching the end, after a good half-hour,

Mattia wrote *QED* next to the framed result, just as he had done when he was a boy. The chalk had dried the skin of his hand, but he didn't even notice. His legs were trembling slightly.

For about ten seconds they stayed there in quiet contemplation. Then Alberto clapped his hands and the noise echoed through the silence like a whiplash. He got down off the desk and almost fell on the floor, because his legs had gone to sleep from dangling like that. He put a hand on Mattia's shoulder and Mattia found it both heavy and reassuring.

'No bullshit this time,' he said. 'You're having dinner with me tonight; we've got something to celebrate.'

Mattia smiled faintly.

'OK,' he said.

They cleaned the blackboard together. They took care that nothing legible was left, that no one would be able to make out so much as a shadow of what had been written on it. No one would really have understood it, but they were already jealous of the result, as one is of a beautiful secret.

They left the classroom and Mattia turned out the lights. Then they went upstairs, one behind the other, each savouring the little glory of that moment.

★   ★   ★

Alberto's house was in a residential area exactly like the one where Mattia lived, but on the other side of the city. Mattia took the journey in a half-empty bus, with his forehead resting against the window. The contact between that cold surface and his skin brought him relief, it made him think of the bandage that his mother used to put on Michela's head, nothing but a damp cloth handkerchief, but enough to calm her in the evening when she had those attacks that made her tremble all over and grind her teeth. Michela wanted her brother to wear a bandage too, she said so to her mother with her eyes, and he would lie down on the bed and stay there, waiting for his sister to finish writhing.

He had put on his black jacket and shirt. He had had a shower and shaved. In an off-licence he had never been into before he had bought a bottle of red wine, choosing the one with the most elegant label. The lady had wrapped it up in a sheet of tissue paper and then put it in a silver-coloured bag. Mattia rocked it back and forth like a pendulum, as he waited for someone to open the door. With his foot he arranged the doormat in front of the door so that the perimeter coincided precisely with the lines of the paving.

Alberto's wife came to the door. She ignored both Mattia's outstretched hand and the bag with the bottle. Instead she drew him to her and kissed him on the cheek.

'I don't know what you two have been up to, but I've never seen Alberto as happy as he is tonight,' she whispered. 'Come in.'

Mattia resisted the temptation to rub his ear against his shoulder to get rid of the itch.

'Alberto, Mattia's here,' she called into

another room, or towards the floor above.

Instead of Alberto his son Philip appeared from the hall. Mattia knew him from the photograph that his father kept on his desk, in which Philip was still only a few months old and round and impersonal like all newborn babies. It had never occurred to him that he might have grown. Some of his parents' features were forcibly making their way across his face: Alberto's long chin, his mother's not-quite-open eyelids. Mattia thought about the cruel mechanism of growth, the soft cartilages subject to imperceptible but inexorable changes and, just for a moment, about Michela and her features, frozen for ever since that day in the park.

Philip came over, pedalling his tricycle like a boy possessed. When he noticed Mattia, he braked suddenly and stared at him in astonishment, as if he had been caught doing something forbidden. Alberto's wife picked him up, lifting him from the tricycle.

'Here's the horrid little monster,' she said, burying her nose in his cheek.

Mattia gave him a forced smile. Children made him uneasy.

'Let's go in. Nadia's here already,' Alberto's wife went on.

'Nadia?' said Mattia.

Alberto's wife looked at him, confused.

'Yes, Nadia,' she said. 'Didn't Albi tell you?'

'No.'

There was a moment of embarrassment. Mattia didn't know a Nadia. He wondered what was going on and feared that he knew.

'Anyway she's in there. Come on.'

As they walked towards the kitchen, Philip studied Mattia suspiciously, hiding behind his mother's back, his index and middle fingers in his mouth and his knuckles gleaming with saliva. Mattia was forced to look elsewhere. He remembered the time he had followed Alice down a longer hall than this one. He looked at Philip's scribbles hanging from the walls instead of paintings and was careful not to trample on his toys scattered on the floor. The whole house, its very walls, was impregnated with a smell of vitality that he was unused to. He thought about his own apartment, where it was so easy to decide simply not to exist. He already regretted accepting the invitation to dinner.

In the kitchen Alberto greeted him, shaking his hand affectionately, and he responded automatically. The woman sitting at the table stood up and held out her hand.

'This is Nadia,' Alberto said. 'And this is our next Fields Medal.'

'Nice to meet you,' said Mattia, embarrassed.

Nadia smiled at him. She made as if to lean forward, perhaps to kiss him on the cheeks, but Mattia's motionlessness held her back.

'A pleasure,' she said, and nothing more.

For a few seconds he remained absorbed by one of the big earrings that hung from her ears: a gold circle at least five centimetres in diameter, which when she moved began swinging in a complicated motion that Mattia tried to decompose into the three Cartesian axes. The size of the earring and its contrast with Nadia's very black hair made him think of something shameless, almost obscene, that frightened and aroused him at the same time.

They sat down at the table and Alberto poured red wine for everyone. He grandly toasted the article they would soon write and obliged Mattia to explain to Nadia, in simple terms, what it was about. She joined in with an uncertain smile, which betrayed thoughts of a different kind and made him lose the thread of the conversation more than once.

'It sounds interesting,' she observed finally, and Mattia looked down.

'It's much more than interesting,' said Alberto, waving his hands around as if imitating the shape of a helicoid, which Mattia imagined as if it was real.

Alberto's wife came in holding a soup tureen, from which emanated a strong smell of cumin. The conversation turned to food, a more neutral territory. A tension that they hadn't previously been aware of dissipated. Everyone, apart from Mattia, expressed nostalgia for some kind of delicacy that they couldn't get here in northern Europe. Alberto talked about the ravioli his mother used to make. His wife remembered the seafood salad they used to eat together in their university days, in that restaurant facing the beach. Nadia described the cannoli full of fresh ricotta and dotted with tiny chips of dark black chocolate from the *pasticceria* in the little village that she came from. As she described them she kept her eyes closed and sucked in her lips as if she could still taste a little of that flavour. She caught her lower lip with her teeth for a moment and then let it go. Mattia stared at that detail without realizing it. He thought there was something exaggerated about Nadia's femininity, in the fluidity with which she rolled her hands around, and the southern inflection with which she pronounced her labial consonants, almost doubling them when there was no need. It was as if she possessed a dark power, which depressed him and at the same time made his cheeks burn.

'You just need the courage to go back,' Nadia concluded.

All four of them remained in silence for a few seconds, as if each of them was thinking about what it was that kept them so far from home. Philip banged his toys against one another a few feet away from the table.

Alberto was able to keep a tottering conversation alive all through dinner, often embarking on long monologues, his hands waving above an increasingly untidy table.

After dessert, his wife got up to collect the plates. Nadia made as if to help her, but she told her to stay where she was and disappeared into the kitchen.

They sat in silence. Lost in thought, Mattia ran an index finger along the serrated part of the knife blade.

'I'll just go and see what she's up to in there,' said Alberto, getting up as well. From behind Nadia's back he darted a glance at Mattia, which meant do your best.

He and Nadia were left on their own with Philip. They looked up at the same time, because there was nothing else to look at, and they both laughed with embarrassment.

'What about you?' Nadia said to him after a while. 'Why did you choose to stay here?'

She studied him with her eyes half closed, as if trying to guess his secret. She had long, thick eyelashes and Mattia thought they were too still to be real.

He finished lining up the crumbs with his index finger. He shrugged.

'I don't know,' he said. 'It's as if there's more oxygen here.'

She nodded reflectively, as if she had understood. From the kitchen came the voices of Alberto and his wife talking about ordinary things, about the tap that was leaking again and who would put Philip to bed, things which at that moment seemed tremendously important to Mattia.

Silence fell again and he forced himself to think of something to say, something that seemed normal. Nadia entered his field of vision wherever he looked, an awkward presence. The pale colour of her low-cut top distracted him, even as he was staring at his empty glass. Under the table, hidden by the tablecloth, were their legs and he imagined them down there, in the dark, forced into a strained intimacy.

Philip came over and put a toy car in front of him, right on his napkin. Mattia looked at the miniature Maserati, then looked at Philip, who observed him in turn, waiting for him to decide to do something.

Rather hesitantly he picked up the toy car and

242

made it go back and forth on the tablecloth. He felt Nadia's dense gaze upon him, assessing his embarrassment. With his mouth he imitated a shy vroom. Then he stopped. Philip stared at him in silence, slightly annoyed. He stretched out his arm, took the car back and returned to his toys.

Mattia poured himself some more wine and drained it in one go. Then he realized that he should have offered some to Nadia first and asked her would you like some? She said no no, drawing in her hands and hunching her shoulders, as people usually do when they're cold.

Alberto came back into the room and made a kind of grunt. He rubbed his face hard with his hands.

'Sleepy time,' he said to the child. He lifted him up by the collar of his polo shirt as if he was a doll.

Philip followed him without protest. As he left he glanced back at his toys piled up on the floor as if he had hidden something in the middle of them.

'Maybe it's time for me to go too,' said Nadia, not quite turning towards Mattia.

'Yeah, perhaps it's time,' he said.

They both contracted their leg muscles as if to get up, but it was a false departure. They stayed where they were and looked at each other again. Nadia smiled and Mattia felt pierced by her gaze, stripped to the bone as if he could no longer hide anything.

They got up, almost at the same time. They put their chairs next to the table and Mattia

243

noticed that she too had the foresight to lift hers off the ground.

Alberto found them standing there, not knowing how to move.

'What's happening?' he said. 'Are you off already?'

'It's late, you must be tired,' Nadia replied for both of them.

Alberto looked at Mattia with a smile of complicity.

'I'll call you a taxi,' he said.

'I'll take the bus,' Mattia said quickly.

Alberto gave him a sidelong look.

'At this time of night? Come on,' he said. 'And anyway Nadia's place is on the way.'

34

The taxi slipped along the deserted avenues on the edge of town, between identical buildings without balconies. Few windows were still lit. The March days ended early and people adapted their body clocks to the night.

'The cities are darker here,' said Nadia, as if thinking out loud.

They sat at opposite ends of the back seat. Mattia stared at the changing numbers on the taximeter, and watched the red segments going out and lighting up to compose the various figures.

She thought about the ridiculous space of solitude that separated them and tried to find the courage to occupy it with her body. Her apartment was only a few blocks away and time, like the road, was being consumed in a great hurry. It wasn't just the time of that particular evening, it was the time of possibilities, her nearly thirty-five years. Over the past year, since breaking up with Martin, she had begun to notice the foreignness of the place, to suffer from the chill that dried her skin and never really left her, even in the summer. And yet she couldn't make up her mind to leave. She depended on the place now; she had grown attached to it with the obstinacy with which people only become attached to things that hurt them.

She reflected that if anything was going to be

resolved, it would be resolved in that car. Afterwards she would no longer have the strength. She would finally abandon herself, without remorse, to her translations, to the books whose pages she dissected by day and night, to earn her living and fill the holes dug by time.

She found him fascinating. He was strange, even stranger than the other colleagues that Alberto had introduced her to, to no avail. The subject they studied seemed only to attract sinister characters, or to make them so over the years. She could have asked Mattia which of the two he was, to ask something funny, but she didn't feel like it. And yet, 'strange' conveyed the idea. And disturbing. But there was something in his eyes, a kind of shining molecule drowning in those dark pupils, which, Nadia was sure, no woman had ever been able to capture.

She was taken with the idea of trying to seduce him. She had pulled her hair to one side to turn her bare neck to him and she ran her fingers back and forth along the seams of the bag that she held on her lap. But she didn't dare to go any further and she didn't want to turn round. If he was looking elsewhere, she didn't want to find out.

Mattia coughed quietly into his clenched fist, to warm it up. He noticed Nadia's urgency, but couldn't make up his mind. And even if he did decide, he thought, he wouldn't know what to do. Once Denis, talking about himself, had told him that all overtures were the same, like openings in chess. You don't have to come up with anything, there's no point, because you're both after the same thing anyway. Then the game starts finding its own way and it's only at that point that you move on to strategy.

But I don't even know the openings, he thought.

What he did was to rest his left hand in the middle of the seat, like the end of a rope thrown into the sea. He kept it there, even though the synthetic fabric made him shiver.

Nadia understood and in silence, without any abrupt movements, she slid towards the middle. She lifted his arm, taking it by the wrist as if she knew what he was thinking, and put it around her neck. She rested her head against his chest and closed her eyes.

She was wearing strong perfume and it nestled in her hair; it stuck to Mattia's clothes and forced its way into his nostrils.

The taxi pulled up on the left, in front of Nadia's house, with its engine running.

'Seventeen thirty,' said the taxi driver.

She got up and they both thought how much trouble it would be finding themselves like this again, breaking an old equilibrium and rebuilding a different one. They wondered if they'd still be able to do it.

Mattia rummaged in his pockets and found his wallet. He held out a twenty and said no change, thanks. She opened the door.

Now, follow her, Mattia thought, although he didn't move.

Nadia was already on the pavement. The taxi driver watched Mattia in the rear-view mirror, waiting for instructions. The squares on the taxi-meter were all illuminated and flashing *00.00*.

'Come on,' said Nadia and he obeyed.

The taxi set off again and they climbed to the top of a steep flight of stairs, with the steps covered in blue carpet and so narrow that Mattia had to walk with his feet at an angle.

Nadia's apartment was clean and very well kept, as only the home of a woman living on her own can be. In the middle of a circular table there was a wicker basket full of dry petals, which had stopped giving off any perfume a long time ago. The walls were painted in strong colours, orange, blue and yolk-yellow, so unusual here in the north that there was something disrespectful about them.

Mattia asked may I come in? and watched Nadia taking off her coat and laying it on a chair with the confidence of someone moving in her own space.

'I'm going to get something to drink,' she said.

He waited in the middle of the sitting room, his ravaged hands hidden in his pockets. Nadia came back a few moments later with two glasses half full of red wine. She was laughing at a thought of her own.

'I'm not used to all this any more. It hasn't happened to me for a long time,' she confessed.

'That's fine,' replied Mattia, rather than say that it had never happened to him.

They sipped the wine in silence, looking cautiously around. Each time their eyes met they smiled faintly, like two children.

Nadia kept her legs folded on the sofa, so that she could get closer to him. The scene was set. All that was required was an action, a wrench, cold-blooded, instant and brutal as beginnings always are.

She thought about it for another moment. Then she set her glass down on the floor, behind the sofa so as not to risk knocking it with her foot, and stretched out resolutely towards Mattia. She kissed him. With her feet she slipped off her high heels, which fell resoundingly to the floor. She climbed astride him, not leaving him the breath to say no.

She took his glass from him and guided his hands to her hips. Mattia's tongue was rigid. She began rolling hers around his, insistently, to force it to move, until he began to do the same, in the opposite direction.

With a certain awkwardness they rolled on to one side and Mattia ended up underneath. One of his legs was under the sofa and one was sticking out, blocked by her weight. He thought of the circular movement of his own tongue, its periodic motion, but soon he lost concentration, as if Nadia's face squashed against his own had managed to obstruct the complicated mechanism of his thought, like that time with Alice.

He slid his hands under Nadia's top and contact with her skin didn't repel him. They took off their clothes slowly, without pulling apart or opening their eyes. There was too much light in the room and any interruption would have made them stop.

As he busied himself with the fastening of her bra Mattia thought it happens. In the end it happens, in some way you didn't know before.

35

Fabio had got up early. He had switched off the alarm clock so that Alice wouldn't hear it and had left the room, forcing himself not to look at his wife, lying on her side of the bed, with one arm out of the sheet and her hand stretched out as if she was dreaming about clutching on to something.

He had fallen asleep out of exhaustion and passed through a sequence of nightmares that gradually became more and more gloomy. Now he felt the need to do things with his hands, to get himself dirty, to sweat and wear out his muscles. He weighed up the idea of going to hospital to do an extra shift, but his parents were due to come for lunch, as they did every second Saturday of the month. Twice he picked up the phone with the intention of calling them and telling them not to come, that Alice didn't feel well, but then they would have phoned to find out what was wrong, and he would have had to talk to his wife, again, and things would have got even worse.

In the kitchen he took off his T-shirt. He drank some milk from the fridge. He could pretend nothing was wrong, behave as if nothing had happened the previous night and carry on like that, as he had always done, but at the bottom of his throat he felt a completely new sense of nausea. The skin of his face was taut with the tears that had dried on his cheeks. He splashed his face with water at the sink and dried himself with the tea-towel hanging next to it.

He looked out of the window. The sky was overcast, but the sun would come out shortly. At this time of year it was always like that. On such a day he could have taken his son out on the bike, followed the track that ran along the canal and reached the park. There they would have drunk from the fountain and sat on the grass for about half an hour. Then they would have come back, on the road this time. They would have stopped for a moment at the pastry shop and bought a tray of cakes for lunch.

He didn't ask for much. Only for a normal life; the one that he had always deserved.

He went down to the garage, still in his underwear. From the top shelf he took down the box of tools and its heaviness brought him a moment of relief. He took out a cross-cut screwdriver, a size nine and a size twelve spanner, and started dismantling the bike, piece by piece, methodically.

First he smeared grease over the gears, then he polished the frame with a rag drenched in methylated spirits. With his fingernail he scraped away the spots of mud that were stuck to it and also cleaned thoroughly between the pedals, in the cracks that his fingers couldn't enter. He put the various pieces back together again and checked the brake cables, adjusting them so that they were perfectly balanced. He pumped up both tyres, testing their pressure with the palm of his hand.

He took a step backwards, wiped his hands on his thighs and observed his work with a weary sense of detachment. He knocked the bike to the ground with a kick. It folded in on itself, like an animal. One pedal started spinning in mid-air and Fabio listened to its hypnotic swish, until silence fell once more.

He was about to leave the garage, but then he turned back. He lifted the bike and put it back in its place. He couldn't help checking to see if it was damaged. He wondered why he wasn't capable of leaving everything in a mess, giving vent to the rage that flooded his brain, cursing and smashing things. Why he preferred everything to seem as if it was in its proper place even when it wasn't.

He turned out the light and climbed the stairs.

Alice was sitting at the kitchen table. She was sipping tea thoughtfully. There was nothing in front of her but the sweetener container. She raised her eyes and looked him up and down.

'Why didn't you wake me up?'

Fabio shrugged. He went over to the tap and turned on the water as far as it would go.

'You were fast asleep,' he replied.

He poured washing-up liquid on to his hands and rubbed them hard under the water to remove the black streaks of grease.

'I'll be late with lunch,' she said.

Fabio shrugged again.

'We could just forget about lunch,' he said.

'What's this, a new development?'

He rubbed his hands together even harder.

'I don't know. It's just an idea.'

'It's a new idea.'

'Yeah, you're right. It's an idiotic idea,' Fabio shot back through clenched teeth.

He turned off the tap and left the kitchen, as if in a hurry. Shortly afterwards Alice heard the thunder of water in the shower. She put the cup in the sink and went back to the bedroom to get dressed.

On Fabio's side the sheets were crumpled, full of wrinkles flattened by the weight of his body. The pillow was folded in half, as if he had kept his head underneath it, and the blankets were piled up at the end of the bed, kicked away by his feet. There was a faint smell of sweat, as there was every morning, and Alice threw the window open to let in some fresh air.

The pieces of furniture that had seemed to her to have a soul, a breath of their own, the night before, were nothing but the usual pieces of furniture in her room, as scentless as her tepid resignation.

She made the bed, stretching the sheets out properly and tucking the corners under the mattress. She turned down the top sheet so that it was halfway down the pillows as Sol had taught her and got dressed. From the bathroom came the buzz of Fabio's electric razor, which for some time she had associated with drowsy weekend mornings.

She wondered whether the previous night's conversation had been different from the others or whether it would be resolved as always. Would Fabio, just out of the shower and still not wearing his T-shirt, hug her from behind and keep his head pressed against her hair, for a long time, long enough to allow the rancour to evaporate? There was no other possible solution, for the time being.

Alice tried to imagine what would happen otherwise. She was engrossed in the sight of the curtains swelling slightly in the draught. She became aware of a sharp sense of abandonment, like a presentiment, not unlike what she had felt in that snow-filled ditch and then in Mattia's room and which she felt every time, even now, looking at her mother's made-up bed. She brought her index finger to the pointed bone of her pelvis, running it along the sharp outline that she was not prepared to give up, and when the buzz of the razor stopped she shook her head and went back into the kitchen, with the more solid and imminent worry of lunch.

She chopped up the onion and cut off a little chunk of butter, which she set aside in a small dish. All those things that Fabio had taught her. She was accustomed to dealing with food with ascetic detachment, following simple sequences of actions, the end result of which would not concern her.

She liberated the asparagus stalks from the red elastic band that kept them together, held them under the cold water and laid them out on a chopping board. She set a pan full of water on the ring.

She was alerted to the presence of Fabio in the room by a series of small approaching noises. She froze, waiting for contact with his body.

Instead he sat down on the sofa and started

254

distractedly flicking through a magazine.

'Fabio,' she called to him, not really knowing what to say.

He didn't reply. He turned a page, making more noise than necessary. He gripped one corner between his fingers, uncertain whether to tear it or not.

'Fabio,' she repeated at the same volume, but turning round.

'What is it?'

'Can you get me the rice, please? It's in the top cupboard. I can't reach.'

It was just an excuse, they both knew that. It was just a way of saying come here.

Fabio threw the magazine on the table and it struck an ashtray carved from half a coconut, which began to spin on its axis. He sat there for a few seconds with his hands resting on his knees, as if he was thinking about it. Then he suddenly rose to his feet and walked over to the sink.

'Where?' he asked angrily, taking care not to look at Alice.

'There.' She pointed.

Fabio pulled a chair over to the fridge, making it squeak on the ceramic tiles. He climbed up on it with bare feet. Alice looked at them as if she didn't know them. She found his feet attractive, but in a vaguely frightening way.

He picked up the cardboard box of rice. It was already open. He shook it. Then he smiled in a way that Alice found sinister. He tilted the box and the rice started spilling on to the floor, like thin white rain.

'What are you doing?' said Alice.

Fabio smiled.

'There's your rice,' he replied.

He shook the rice harder and the grains scattered all around the kitchen. Alice came over.

'Stop it,' she said, but he ignored her. Alice repeated it more loudly.

'Like at our wedding, remember? Our bloody wedding,' shouted Fabio.

She gripped him by a calf to make him stop and he poured the rice over her head. A few grains stayed stuck in her smooth hair. She looked up at him and said again stop it.

A grain hit her in the eye, hurting her, and with her eyes closed Alice delivered a slap to Fabio's shin. He reacted by shaking his leg hard and hitting her with a kick just below her left shoulder. His wife's bad knee did what it could to keep her upright, bending first forwards and then backwards, like a crooked hinge, and then made her fall to the ground.

There was no rice left in the box. Fabio stayed standing on the chair, bewildered, with the box upside down in his hand, looking at his wife on the floor, curled up like a cat. A violent shock of comprehension flashed through his brain.

He got down.

'Alice, did you hurt yourself?' he said. 'Let me see.'

He put a hand on her head to look into her face, but she squirmed away.

'Leave me alone!' she yelled.

'Darling, I'm sorry,' he pleaded. 'You've — '

'Go away!' shouted Alice, with a vocal power

that neither of them could have suspected she owned.

Fabio pulled away. His hands trembled. He took two steps back, then stammered an OK. He ran towards the bedroom and came out wearing a T-shirt and a pair of shoes. He left the house without turning to look at his wife, who hadn't moved.

36

Alice pushed her hair behind her ears. The cupboard door was still open above her head, the chair in front of her. She hadn't hurt herself. She didn't want to cry. She couldn't think about what had just happened.

She started picking up the grains of rice scattered over the floor. The first few she picked up one by one. Then she started bringing them together in the palm of her hand.

She got up and threw a handful into the pan, in which the water was already boiling. She stood and looked at them, carried chaotically up and down by convective motions. Mattia had called them that, once. She turned out the flame and went and sat on the sofa.

She wouldn't put anything away. She would wait for her inlaws to arrive and find it like that. She would tell them how Fabio had behaved.

But no one arrived. He must have warned them already. Or he had gone to their house and was telling them his version, saying that Alice's belly was as dry as a dried-up lake and that he was fed up with going on like this.

The house was plunged into silence and the light seemed unable to find a place for itself. Alice picked up the telephone receiver and dialled her father's number.

'Hello?' answered Soledad.

'Hi, Sol.'

'Hi, *mi amorcito*. How's my baby?' said the housekeeper with her usual concern.

'So so,' said Alice.

'Why? *¿Qué pasó?*'

Alice remained silent for a few seconds.

'Is Dad there?' she asked.

'He's asleep. Shall I go and wake him up?'

Alice thought of her father, in the big bedroom that he now shared only with his thoughts, with the lowered blinds drawing lines of light on his sleeping body. The rancour that had always divided them had been absorbed by time; Alice could hardly remember it. What oppressed her most about that house, her father's serious, penetrating glance, was what she missed most now. He wouldn't say anything, he hardly ever spoke. Stroking her cheek, he would ask Sol to change the sheets in her room and that would be that. After her mother's death something had altered in him: it was as if he had slowed down. Paradoxically, since Fabio had entered Alice's life, her father had become more protective. He no longer talked about himself, he let her do the talking, losing himself in his daughter's conversation, carried along by the timbre rather than the words, and responded with thoughtful murmurs.

His moments of absence had begun about a year before, when one evening he had confused Soledad with Fernanda. He had pulled her to him to kiss her, as if she really was his wife, and Sol had been forced to give him a gentle slap on the cheek to which he had reacted with the whining resentment of a child. The next day he

259

hadn't remembered a thing, but the vague sense of there being something wrong, an interruption in the cadenced rhythm of time, had led him to ask Sol what had happened. She had tried not to reply, to change the subject, but he hadn't let it go. When the housekeeper had told the truth he had grown gloomy, had nodded and, turning round, had said I'm sorry, in a low voice. Then he had closed himself away in his study and stayed there until dinnertime, without sleeping or doing anything. He had sat down at his desk, with his hands resting on the walnut surface, and had tried in vain to reconstruct that missing segment in the ribbon of his memory.

Episodes such as this were repeated with ever greater frequency and all three of them, Alice, her father and Sol, tried to pretend nothing was wrong, waiting for the moment when it would no longer be possible.

'Alice?' Sol urged. 'So shall I go and wake him up?'

'No no,' Alice said quickly. 'Don't wake him. It's nothing.'

'Really?'

'Yes. Let him rest.'

She hung up and lay down on the sofa. She tried to keep her eyes open, directing them at the plastered ceiling. She wanted to be there at the moment when she noticed a new, uncontrollable change. She wanted to be witness to the umpteenth little disaster, memorize its trajectory, but after a few minutes her breathing became more regular and Alice fell asleep.

37

Mattia was startled to find that he still had instincts, buried beneath the dense network of thoughts and abstractions that had woven itself around him. He was startled by the violence with which these instincts emerged and confidently guided his gestures.

The return to reality was painful. Nadia's foreign body had settled on his own. Contact with her sweat on one side and the crumpled fabric of the sofa and their squashed clothes on the other was suffocating. She was breathing slowly. Mattia thought that if the ratio between the periods of their breath was an irrational number, there was no way of combining them to find a regularity.

He tried to take in some air by stretching over Nadia's head, but it was saturated with heavy condensation. He suddenly wanted to cover himself up. He twisted one leg because he felt his member, flaccid and cold, against her leg. He clumsily hurt her with his knee. Nadia gave a start and raised her head. She had already gone to sleep.

'Sorry,' said Mattia.

'Doesn't matter.'

She kissed him and her breath was too hot. He remained motionless, waiting for her to stop.

'Shall we go into the bedroom?' she said.

Mattia nodded. He would have liked to go

261

back to his apartment, his comfortable void, but he knew it wasn't the right thing to do.

They both became aware of how embarrassing and unnatural the moment was, as they slipped beneath the sheets from opposite sides of the bed. Nadia smiled as if to say everything's fine. In the darkness she huddled up against his shoulder. She gave him another kiss and quickly fell asleep.

Mattia too closed his eyes, but was forced to open them again immediately, because a jumble of terrible memories lay in wait for him, piled up beneath his eyelids. Once again he had difficulty breathing. He reached his left hand under the bed and began rubbing his thumb against the iron netting, at the pointed juncture where two meshes met. In the darkness he brought his finger to his mouth and sucked it. The taste of blood calmed him for a few seconds.

He gradually became aware of the unfamiliar sounds of Nadia's apartment: the faint hum of the fridge, the heating that rustled for a few seconds and then stopped with a click of the boiler, and a clock, in the other room, that sounded to him as if it was going too slowly. He wanted to move his legs, to get up and out of there. Nadia was still in the middle of the bed, depriving him of the space he needed to turn around. Her hair stung his neck and her breathing dried the skin of his chest. Mattia thought that he wouldn't manage to close his eyes. It was late already, perhaps after two. He had a lesson the next day and was bound to make mistakes at the blackboard, he would look a complete idiot in front of all the students. At his own place, on the other hand, he would have been able to sleep, at least for the few remaining hours.

If I'm quiet about it she won't notice, he thought.

He remained motionless for more than a minute, thinking. The sounds were becoming more and more noticeable. Another sharp rattle from the boiler made him stiffen and he decided to leave.

With little movements he managed to free the arm that was underneath Nadia's head. In her sleep she noticed the lack and moved to try to find him. Mattia drew himself upright. He rested first one foot on the floor and then the other. When he got up the bed squeaked slightly as it settled.

He turned to look at her in the semi-darkness and vaguely remembered the moment when he had turned his back on Michela in the park.

He walked barefoot to the sitting room. He picked up his clothes from the sofa and his shoes from the floor. He opened the door, as always, without a sound, and when he was in the corridor, still clutching his trousers, he finally managed to breathe deeply.

38

On the Saturday evening of the rice incident, Fabio had called her on her mobile. Alice had wondered why he hadn't tried before on the home phone and then thought that perhaps it was because the home phone was an object that related to both of them and he didn't like the fact that there was something they shared at that moment any more than she did. It had been a short call, in spite of the drawn-out silences. He had said for tonight I'm staying here, like a decision that had already been taken, and she had replied as far as I'm concerned you can stay there tomorrow as well and as long as you like. Then, once these tiresome details had been worked out, Fabio had added Alice, I'm sorry and she had hung up without saying me too.

She hadn't answered the telephone again. Fabio's insistent calls soon abated, and she, in an attack of self-commiseration, had said to herself you see? Walking barefoot through the flat she had picked up at random a few things of her husband's, documents and a few items of clothing, and put them in a box, which she had then dumped in the hall.

One evening she had come back from work and had found it wasn't there. Fabio had obviously been, though he had not taken much else away with him. The furniture was all in place and the wardrobe still full of his clothes, but on

264

the sitting-room shelves there were now gaps among the books, black spaces that bore witness to the start of the break-up. Alice had stopped to look at them and for the first time her detachment had assumed the concrete outlines of a hard fact, the massive consistence of a solid form.

With a certain relief she yielded to it. She felt as if she had always done everything for someone else, but now there was just her and she could just stop, surrender and that was that. She had more time for the same things, but she was aware of an inertia in her actions, a weariness, as if she was moving through a viscous liquid. She finally gave up performing even the easiest tasks. Her dirty clothes piled up in the bathroom and she, lying on the sofa for hours, knew that they were there, that it wouldn't take much effort to pick them up, but none of her muscles considered this a sufficient motive.

She invented a case of the flu so as not to go to work. She slept much more than necessary, even in broad daylight. She didn't even lower the blinds; she had only to close her eyes to be unaware of the light, to cancel out the objects that surrounded her and forget her hateful body, getting weaker and weaker but still tenaciously attached to her thoughts. The weight of consequences was always there, like a stranger sleeping on top of her. It watched over her even when Alice plunged into sleep, a heavy sleep saturated with dreams, which was coming more and more to resemble an addiction. If her throat was dry, Alice imagined she was suffocating. If one of her arms grew itchy after spending too long under the pillow, it was because an Alsatian was eating it. If her feet were cold because they had ended up outside the blankets, Alice found herself once more at the bottom of the crevasse, immersed in snow up to her neck. But she wasn't afraid, or hardly ever. Paralysis allowed her to move only her tongue and she stretched it out to taste the snow. It was sweet and Alice would have liked to eat it all, but she couldn't turn her head. And then there she was, waiting for the cold to rise up her legs, to fill her belly and spread from there to her veins, freezing her blood.

Her waking life was infested with thoughts that were only partly structured. Alice got up when she couldn't do anything else and the confusion of half-sleep slowly faded away, leaving milky residues in her head, like interrupted memories, which mixed with the others and seemed no less true. She wandered through the silent flat like the ghost of herself, unhurriedly following her own lucidity. I'm going mad, she thought sometimes. But she didn't mind. In fact, it made her smile, because at last she was the one making the choices.

In the evening she ate lettuce leaves, fishing them straight from the plastic bag. They were crunchy and made of nothing. They tasted only of water. She didn't eat them to fill up her stomach, but just to stand in for the ritual of dinner and somehow occupy that time, which she didn't know what else to do with. She ate lettuce until the flimsy stuff made her feel ill.

She emptied herself of Fabio and of herself, of all the useless efforts she had made to get where she was and find nothing there. With detached curiosity she observed the rebirth of her weaknesses, her obsessions. This time she would let them decide, since she hadn't been able to do anything anyway. Against certain parts of yourself you remain powerless, she said to herself, as she regressed pleasurably to the time when she was a girl. The time when Mattia had left and a short time afterwards her mother, too, on two journeys that were different but equally remote from her. Mattia. That was it. She thought of him often. Again. He was like another of her illnesses, from which she didn't really want to recover. You can fall ill with just a memory and she had fallen ill that afternoon in the car, by the park, when she had covered his face with her own to prevent him from looking on the site where that horror had taken place.

No matter how hard she tried, in all those years spent with Fabio she couldn't extract so much as one image that crushed her heart so powerfully, that had the same impetuous violence in its colours and which she could still feel on her skin and in the roots of her hair and between her legs. There had been that one time at dinner with Riccardo and his wife, when they'd laughed and drunk a lot. She'd been helping Alessandro to wash the dishes and had cut the tip of her thumb on a glass that had shattered in her hands. And as she dropped it she had said ouch, not loudly — she had barely whispered it — but Fabio had heard and come running. He had examined her thumb under the light; leaning forward he had brought it to his lips and sucked a little of the blood, to make it stop, as if it had been his. With her thumb in his mouth he had looked up at her, with those disarming eyes that Alice couldn't resist. Then he had closed the wound in his hand and kissed Alice on the mouth. She had tasted in his saliva the taste of her own blood and imagined that it had circulated all the way around her husband's body and come back to her, cleaned, as though through dialysis.

There had been that time and there had been an infinite number of others, which Alice no longer remembered, because the love of those we don't love in return settles on the surface and from there quickly evaporates. What was left now was a faint red patch, almost invisible on her drawn skin, the spot where Fabio had struck her with a kick.

Sometimes, particularly in the evening, she thought of his words. *I can't do this any more.* She stroked her belly and tried to imagine what it would have been like to have someone in there, drowning in her cold liquid. *Tell me what it is.* But there was nothing to explain. There was no reason, or not only one. There was no beginning. There was her and that was that and she didn't want anyone in her belly.

Perhaps I should tell him that, she thought.

Then she picked up her mobile and ran through the contact list till she got to F. She rubbed the keyboard with her thumb, as if hoping to activate the call by mistake. Then she pressed the red button. To see Fabio, talk to him, rebuild: it all seemed like an inhuman effort and she preferred to stay there, watching the furniture in the sitting room being covered with a layer of dust that was getting thicker by the day.

39

He hardly ever looked at the students. When he met their clear eyes directed at the blackboard and him, he felt as if he were undressed. Mattia wrote out his calculations and commented on them precisely, as if he was explaining them to himself as well as to everyone else. The classroom was too big for the dozen fourth-year students who took his course in algebraic topology. They arranged themselves in the first three rows, more or less always in the same places and leaving an empty row between one and the next, as he himself had done in his university days, but in none of the students could he spot anything that reminded him of himself.

In the silence he heard the door at the back of the classroom closing but he didn't turn round until the end of his demonstration. He turned a page in his notes, which he didn't really need, realigned the pages and only then noticed a new figure in the topmost margin of his field of vision. He looked up and spotted Nadia. She had taken a seat in the back row; she was dressed in white. She sat with her legs crossed and didn't greet him.

He almost lost his thread, said I'm sorry and tried to find the passage in his notes, but was unable to concentrate. A barely perceptible murmur ran through the students; the teacher had never once hesitated since the beginning of the course.

He started over and reached the end, writing quickly and bending his writing more and more towards the bottom as it shrank towards the right-hand edge of the blackboard. He crammed the last two passages into a top corner because he had run out of space. Some of the students leaned forward to make out the exponents and subscripts that had been jumbled up with the formulae around them. There was still a quarter of an hour to go before the end of the lesson when Mattia said OK, I'll see you tomorrow.

He set down the chalk and watched the students getting up, slightly puzzled, giving him a little wave before leaving the classroom. Nadia was still sitting there, in the same position, and no one seemed to notice her.

They were left on their own. They seemed very far apart. Nadia rose to her feet at the same moment as he moved to head towards her. They met more or less halfway across the lecture theatre and stayed a good metre apart.

'Hi,' said Mattia. 'I didn't think — '

'Listen,' she broke in, looking resolutely into his eyes. 'We don't even know each other. I'm sorry I just turned up like this.'

'No, don't — ' he tried to say, but Nadia didn't let him speak.

'I woke up and you had gone, you could at least have . . . '

She stopped for a second. Mattia was forced to lower his gaze because his eyes stung, as if he hadn't blinked for more than a minute.

'But it doesn't matter,' Nadia went on. 'I'm not running after anybody. I'm not up to it any more.'

She held out a piece of paper and he took it.

'That's my number. But if you decide to use it do it soon.'

They both looked at the floor. Nadia was about to lean forward, and wobbled slightly on her heels, but then suddenly turned round.

'Bye,' she said.

Mattia cleared his throat rather than replying. He thought it took her a long time to get to the door. Not enough time to make a decision, to articulate a thought.

Nadia stopped in the doorway.

'I don't know what's wrong with you,' she said. 'But whatever it is, I think I like it.'

Then she left. Mattia looked at the piece of paper, on which there was a name and a sequence of numbers, mostly odd numbers. He picked up his papers from the desk, but waited for the hour to finish before leaving.

★ ★ ★

In the office Alberto was on the telephone and holding the receiver pinched between his chin and his cheek, to be free to gesticulate with both arms. He raised an eyebrow to greet Mattia.

When he hung up he leaned back into his chair and stretched his legs. He gave him a complicit smile.

'So?' he asked. 'Were we up late last night?'

Mattia deliberately avoided his gaze. He shrugged. Alberto got up and went and stood behind Mattia's chair, massaging his shoulders like a trainer with his boxer. Mattia didn't like to be touched.

'I understand, you don't feel like talking about it. All right then, let's change the subject. I've jotted down a draft for the article. Feel like casting your eye over it?'

Mattia nodded. He drummed gently with his index finger on the 0 of the computer, waiting for Alberto to take his hands off his shoulders. Some images from the previous night, always the same ones, ran through his head like faint flashes of light.

Alberto went back to his desk and slumped heavily on to his chair. He started looking for the article amidst a shapeless pile of papers.

'Ah,' he said. 'This came for you.'

He threw an envelope on to Mattia's desk. Mattia looked at it without touching it. His name and the address of the university were written in thick blue ink, which must have passed through to the other side of the paper. The *M* of Mattia started with a straight line, then, slightly detached from it, a soft, concave curve set off, continuing into the right-hand vertical. The two *ts* were held together by a single horizontal line and all the letters were slightly sloped, piled up as if they had fallen on top of one another. There was a mistake in the address, a *c* too many before the *sh*. He would have needed only one of those letters, or nothing but the asymmetry between the two pot-bellied loops of the *B* in Balossino, to recognize Alice's handwriting straight away.

He gulped and reached around for the letter-opener, which was in its place in the second drawer down. He turned it nervously around in his fingers and slipped it into the flap of the envelope. His hands were trembling and he gripped harder on the handle to control himself.

Alberto watched him from the other side of the desk, pretending to be unable to find the papers that were already in front of him. The tremble in Mattia's fingers was apparent even from that distance, but the piece of paper was hidden in the palm of his hand and Alberto couldn't see it.

He watched his colleague as he closed his eyes and stayed like that for a good few seconds, before opening them again and looking around, as if lost and suddenly far away.

'Who's it from?' Alberto ventured.

Mattia looked at him with a kind of resentment, as if he didn't actually recognize him. Then he got up, ignoring the question.

'I've got to go,' he said.

'What?'

'I've got to go. I think . . . to Italy.'

Alberto got up as well, as if to stop him.

'What are you talking about? What's happened?'

He instinctively walked over to him and tried once more to peer at the piece of paper, but Mattia kept it hidden between his hand and the rough fabric of his jumper, at waist-height, like something secret. Three of the four white corners showed beyond his fingers, giving a clue to its rectangular shape and nothing more.

'Nothing. I don't know,' Mattia shot back, with one arm already in the sleeve of his windcheater. 'But I've got to go.'

'And what about the article?'

'I'll look at it when I get back. You just go ahead.'

Then he left, without giving Alberto time to protest.

40

The day Alice went back to work she turned up almost an hour late. She had switched off the alarm clock without even waking up and as she got ready to go out she had had to stop often, because every movement put an unbearable strain on her body.

Crozza didn't tell her off. He needed only to look at her face to understand. Alice's cheeks were hollow and her eyes, although they looked as if they were popping too far out of her head, looked absent, veiled by an ominous sense of indifference.

'Sorry I'm late,' she said as she walked in, without really meaning it.

Crozza turned the page of his newspaper and couldn't help glancing at the clock.

'There are pictures to be developed by eleven,' he said. 'The usual crap.'

He cleared his throat and lifted the newspaper higher. He followed Alice's movements from the corner of his eye. He watched her putting her bag in the usual place, taking off her jacket and sitting down at the machine. She moved slowly and with excessive precision, which betrayed her efforts to make everything look as if it was all right. Crozza watched her sitting lost in thought for a few seconds, with her chin resting on her hand, and at last, after brushing her hair back behind her ears, deciding to begin.

He calmly assessed her excessive thinness, hidden beneath her high-collared cotton jumper and in her far from skin-tight trousers, but apparent in her hands and even more in the outline of her face. He felt a furious sense of powerlessness, because he played no part in Alice's life, but by God she did in his, like a daughter whose name he hadn't been able to choose.

They worked until lunchtime without speaking. They only exchanged indispensable nods of the head. After all the years they had spent in there every gesture seemed automatic and they moved with agility, sharing out the space fairly. The old Nikon was in its place under the counter, in its black case, and they both sometimes wondered if it still worked.

'Lunch. Let's go — ' the photographer said hesitantly.

'I've got something to do at lunchtime,' Alice interrupted. 'Sorry.'

He nodded thoughtfully.

'If you don't feel well, you can go home for the afternoon,' he said. 'There isn't much to do, as you can see.'

Alice looked at him in alarm. She pretended to rearrange the things on the counter: a pair of scissors, an envelope for photographs, a pen and a roll of film cut into four equal segments. All she was doing was swapping them around.

'No, why? I — '

'How long is it since you've seen each other?' the photographer interrupted.

Alice gave a slight jump. She stuck one hand into her bag, as if to protect it.

'Three weeks. More or less.'

Crozza nodded, then shrugged.

'Let's go,' he said.

'But . . . '

'Come on, let's go,' he repeated, more firmly.

Alice thought for a moment. Then she decided to follow him. They locked up the shop. The handle hanging from the door jangled in the shadow and then stopped. Alice and Crozza set off towards the photographer's car. He walked slowly, without showing it, out of respect for her laborious gait.

The old Lancia started only at the second attempt and Crozza muttered a curse between his teeth.

They drove down the avenue almost as far as the bridge, and then the photographer took a road off to the right and switched on the indicator before turning again towards the hospital. Alice suddenly froze.

'But where . . . ?' she tried to say.

He pulled up outside a building with its shutters half closed, by the entrance to the Accident and Emergency department.

'It's none of my business,' he said, without looking at Alice, 'but you've got to go in there. To Fabio, or some other doctor.'

Alice stared at him. Her initial puzzlement had made way for fury. The road was silent. Everyone was hidden away at home or in a bar for lunch. The leaves of the plane trees fluttered soundlessly.

'I haven't seen you like this since . . . ' The photographer hesitated. 'Since I've known you.'

Alice weighed up that *like this* in her head. It sounded ominous and she glanced at herself in the mirror, but it only showed the side of the car. She shook her head, then released the lock and got out of the car. She slammed the door and without turning round she resolutely walked in the opposite direction to the hospital.

She walked quickly, more quickly than she really could, to get away from that place and Crozza's damned cheek, but after about a hundred metres she had to stop. She was out of breath and with each step she took her leg hurt more and more, pulsating as if asking her for mercy. The bone seemed to penetrate the living flesh, as if it had left its proper place again. Alice moved all her weight to the right and just managed to keep her balance, leaning one hand against the rough wall beside her.

She waited for the pain to pass, for her leg once more to become inert as usual and her breathing to become an unconscious action again. Her heart pumped blood slowly, without conviction, but she could hear it even in her ears.

You've got to go to Fabio. Or some other doctor, Crozza's voice went on repeating.

And then? she thought.

She turned back, towards the hospital, walking with difficulty and without any precise intention. Her body chose the way as if by instinct and the passers-by she met on the pavement stepped aside, because Alice was staggering a little, although she wasn't aware of it. Some of them stopped, unsure whether to offer to help, but then walked on.

Alice stepped into the courtyard of Our Lady's Hospital and didn't think back to the time when she had walked along the same little avenue with Fabio. She felt as if she didn't have a past, as if she had found herself in that place without knowing where she had come from. She was tired, with that tiredness that only emptiness brings.

She climbed the steps holding on to the hand rail and stopped in front of the doorway. She wanted only to get there, to activate the sliding doors of the department and wait for a few minutes, just long enough to collect her strength and leave. It was a way of giving chance a little push, only that, to find herself where Fabio was and see what happened. She wouldn't do what Crozza said, she wouldn't listen to anyone, and she wouldn't admit even to herself that she really hoped she would find him.

Nothing happened. The automatic doors opened and when Alice took a step back they closed again.

What did you expect? she wondered.

She thought about sitting down for a few seconds, hoping it would pass. Her body was asking her something, every nerve was screaming it, but she didn't want to listen.

She was about to turn round, when she heard the electric swish of the doors again. She looked up at the sound, convinced that this time she would really find her husband standing in front of her.

The door was wide open, but Fabio wasn't there. Instead, on the other side of the doorway, a girl was standing. It was she who had activated the sensor, but she didn't come out. She stood right where she was, smoothing her skirt with her hands. At last she imitated Alice: she took a step back and the door closed again.

Alice studied her, curious about her gesture. She noticed that she wasn't as young as all that. She might have been the same age as Alice, more or less. She kept her torso bent slightly forward and her shoulders thrown back, very narrowly, as if there wasn't enough room around them.

Alice thought there was something familiar about her, perhaps in her facial expression, but she couldn't place her. Her thoughts closed in on themselves; they spun in the void.

Then the girl did it again. She stepped forward, put her feet together and a few seconds later stepped back.

It was then that she looked up and smiled at Alice from the other side of the glass.

A shiver ran down Alice's spine, vertebra by vertebra, before losing itself in her blind leg. She held her breath.

She knew someone else who smiled like that, merely arching their upper lip, barely revealing the two incisors, and leaving the rest of the mouth motionless.

It can't be, she thought.

She approached to see better and the doors remained wide open. The girl looked disappointed and stared quizzically at her. Alice understood and stepped back to let her go on with her game. The other girl continued as if nothing was wrong.

She had the same dark hair, thick and wavy at the bottom, that Alice had managed to touch only a very few times. Her cheekbones protruded slightly and hid her black eyes, but as she looked at her Alice remembered the same expression that had kept her awake until late at night: the same opaque gleam as she had seen in Mattia's eyes.

It's her, she thought, and a feeling very like terror gripped her throat.

She instinctively fumbled for the camera in her bag, but she hadn't brought so much as a stupid instamatic.

She went on looking at the girl, not knowing what else to do. She turned her head towards her and her vision dimmed from time to time, as if her crystalline lens couldn't find the right curvature. With her dry lips she pronounced the word Michela, but not enough air came from her mouth.

The girl never seemed to tire of this. She played with the automatic door like a little girl. Now she was taking small jumps, back and forth, as if to catch the doors out.

An old lady walked over from inside the building. A big rectangular yellow envelope protruded from her bag, perhaps a radiological report. Without saying a word, she took the girl by the arm and led her outside.

The girl didn't resist. When she passed by Alice, she turned for a moment to look at the sliding doors, almost as if thanking them for amusing her. She was so close that Alice was aware of the displacement of air produced by her body. By holding out a hand she could have touched her, but it was as though she was paralysed.

She watched the two women as they walked slowly away.

Now people were coming in and out. The doors were constantly opening and closing, in a hypnotic rhythm that filled Alice's head.

As if suddenly coming to, she called Michela, this time out loud.

The girl didn't turn round and neither did the old lady who was with her. They didn't alter their pace by one iota, as if the name meant nothing to them.

Alice thought she should follow them, look at the girl from closer up, talk to her, understand. She put her right foot on the first step and drew her other leg back, but it remained frozen where it was, fast asleep. She found herself toppling in. With her hand she sought the hand rail, but didn't find it.

She collapsed like a broken branch and slipped down the two remaining steps.

From the ground she just had time to see the women disappearing around the corner. Then she felt the air becoming saturated with moisture and sounds growing rounder and further away.

41

Mattia had taken the three flights of stairs at a run. Between the first and the second he had bumped into one of his students, who had tried to stop him to ask something. He had overtaken him saying sorry, I've got to go, and in trying to avoid him he had almost stumbled. Having reached the entrance hall he had suddenly slowed down, to compose himself, but still walked quickly. The dark marble of the floor gleamed, reflecting things and people like a stretch of water. Mattia had given a nod of greeting to the porter and gone outside.

The cold air had taken him by surprise and he had wondered what are you doing?

Now he was sitting on the low wall in front of the entrance and wondering why on earth he had reacted like that, as if all he had been doing for all those years was waiting for a signal to go back.

He looked again at the photograph that Alice had sent him. The two of them were together, by her parents' bed, dressed up as a bridal couple with those clothes that smelled of mothballs. Mattia looked resigned, while she was smiling. One of her arms was around his waist. The other held the camera and was partially out of the frame, as if she was now holding it towards him, as an adult, to stroke him.

On the back Alice had written only one line and below it her signature.

You've got to come here.
Alice

Mattia tried to find an explanation for the message and even more for his own muddled reaction. He imagined coming out of the Arrivals zone of the airport and finding Alice and Fabio waiting for him, on the other side of the barrier. Greeting her, kissing her on the cheeks, and then shaking her husband's hand by way of introduction. They would pretend to argue about who should take the suitcase to the car and on the way they would try in vain to tell each other how life had been, as if it could really be summed up. Mattia in the back seat, them in the front: three strangers pretending to have something in common and scratching the surface of things, just to avoid silence.

It's pointless, he said to himself.

That lucid thought brought him some relief, as if he was taking control of himself again after a moment's puzzlement. He tapped the photograph with his finger, already intending to put it away and go back to Alberto, to get on with their work.

While he was still lost in his thoughts, Kirsten Gorbahn, a post-doc from Dresden with whom he had recently written some articles, came over to peer at the photograph.

'Your wife?' she asked him cheerfully, pointing at Alice.

Mattia twisted his neck to look up at Kirsten. He was about to hide the photograph, but then he thought it would be rude. Kirsten had that

285

oblong face, as if someone had pulled it very hard by the chin. In two years spent studying in Rome she had learned a little Italian, which she pronounced with all the os closed.

'Hi,' Mattia said uncertainly. 'No, she isn't my wife. She's just . . . a friend.'

Kirsten chuckled, amused by who knows what, and took a sip of coffee from the polystyrene cup that she was holding in her hands.

'She's cute,' she remarked.

Mattia looked her up and down, slightly uneasily, and then looked back at the photograph. Yes, she really was.

42

When Alice woke up, a nurse was taking her pulse. She still had her shoes on, and was lying at a slight angle on top of a white sheet on a trolley by the entrance. She immediately thought of Fabio, who might have seen her in that terrible state, and suddenly sat up.

'I'm fine,' she said.

'Lie down,' the nurse ordered her. 'We're about to do a check-up.'

'There's no need. Really, I'm fine,' Alice insisted, overcoming the resistance of the nurse, who tried to keep her where she was. Fabio wasn't there.

'You fainted, young lady. You have to see a doctor.'

But Alice was already on her feet. She checked that she still had her bag.

'It's nothing. Believe me.'

The nurse raised her eyes to the sky but didn't stand in her way. Alice glanced around, lost, as if looking for someone. Then she said thank you and left in a hurry.

She hadn't hurt herself when she fell. She seemed only to have banged her right knee. She felt the rhythmical pulsation of the bruise under her jeans. Her hands were a little scratched and dusty, as if she had dragged them along the gravel in the courtyard. She blew on them to clean them.

She walked over to the reception desk and bent down to the round hole in the glass. The lady on the other side looked up at her.

'Hello,' said Alice. She had no idea how to explain herself. She didn't even know how long she had been unconscious for.

'A little while ago . . . ' she said, 'I was standing there . . . '

She pointed to the spot where she had been, but the lady didn't move her head.

'There was a woman, by the entrance. I didn't feel well. I fainted. Then . . . You see, I need to find out the name of that person.'

The receptionist looked at her, bewildered, from behind the counter.

'I'm sorry?' she asked with a grimace.

'It sounds strange, I know,' Alice insisted. 'But you've got to help me. Perhaps you could give me the names of the patients who had appointments in this department today. Or examinations. Just the ladies, those are the only ones I need.'

The lady looked at her. Then she smiled coldly.

'We aren't authorized to give out that kind of information,' she replied.

'It's very important. Please. It's really very important.'

The receptionist tapped with a pen on the register in front of her.

'I'm sorry. It really isn't possible,' she replied irritably.

Alice snorted. She was about to pull away from the counter, but then she approached again.

'I'm Dr Rovelli's wife,' she said.

The lady sat up straighter in her chair. She

arched her eyebrow and tapped the register with her pen again.

'I understand,' she said. 'If you like I'll let your husband know you're here.'

She picked up the receiver but Alice stopped her with a gesture of her hand.

'No,' she said, without controlling the tone of her voice. 'There's no need.'

'Are you sure?'

'Yes, thanks. Just leave it.'

★ ★ ★

She set off towards home. All the way there she couldn't think about anything else. Her mind was becoming clear again, but all the images that passed through it were obliterated by that girl's face. The details were already blurring, plunging fast into the midst of an ocean of other memories of no importance, but that inexplicable sense of familiarity remained. And that smile, the same as Mattia's, mixed with her own intermittent reflection on the glass.

Perhaps Michela was alive and she had seen her. It was madness, and yet Alice really couldn't help believing it. It was as if her brain desperately needed that one thought. As if she was clutching at it to stay alive.

She began to think, to formulate hypotheses. She tried to reconstruct how things might have been. Perhaps the old lady had kidnapped Michela, had found her in the park and taken her away, because she had a violent desire for a little girl but couldn't have children. Her womb was defective or else she was unwilling to make a bit of room in it.

Just like me, thought Alice.

She had kidnapped her and then brought her up in a house a long way from there, with a different name, as if she was her own.

But in that case, why come back? Why risk being discovered after all those years? Perhaps she was being devoured by guilt. Or else she just wanted to tempt fate, as she herself had done outside the door of the oncology department.

On the other hand, perhaps the old woman had nothing to do with it. She had met Michela a long time later and knew nothing about her origins, her real family, just as Michela remembered nothing about herself.

Alice thought of Mattia, pointing from inside her car at the trees in front of him, and every detail fell into place, his ashen, absent face with its hint of death. *She was completely identical to me*, he had said.

Suddenly it seemed to her that everything was consistent, that the girl really was Michela, the vanished twin, and that every detail was in place: the blank expanse of her forehead, the length of her fingers, her circumspect way of moving them. And more than anything that childish game of hers, that more than anything.

But just a second later, she realized she was confused. All those details collapsed into a vague sense of weariness, orchestrated by the hunger that had clenched at her temples for days, and Alice feared losing her senses all over again.

At home, she left the door half open with the

keys still in it. She went into the kitchen and opened the cupboard without even taking her jacket off. She found some tuna and ate it straight from the tin without draining off the oil. The smell made her feel sick. She threw the empty tin into the sink and picked up a tin of peas. With her fork she fished them from the cloudy water and ate half of them, without breathing. They tasted of sand and the shining skin stayed stuck to her teeth. Then she pulled out the box of biscuits that had been open in the cupboard since the day Fabio had left. She ate five, one after the other, barely chewing them. They scratched her throat as she swallowed them, like bits of glass. She only stopped when the cramps in her stomach were so strong that she had to sit down on the floor to endure the pain.

When it had passed, she stood up and walked to the dark-room, limping without restraint, as she did when she was on her own. She took one of the boxes from the second shelf. The word *Snapshots* was written on the side in indelible red pen. She spilled the contents on to the table. With her fingers she spread out the various photographs. Some of them were stuck together. Alice quickly inspected them and at last found the one she was looking for.

She studied it for a long time. Mattia was young, and so was she. His head was tilted to one side. It was hard to study his expression and check the resemblance. A lot of time had passed. Perhaps too much.

That fixed image brought others to the surface

and Alice's mind stitched them together to recreate movement, fragments of sounds, scraps of sensations. She was filled with searing but pleasurable nostalgia.

If she had been able to choose a starting point, she would have chosen that one: she and Mattia in a silent room with their private intimacies, hesitant about touching each other but their outlines fitting precisely together.

She had to let him know. If she only saw him she would understand. If his sister was alive, Mattia had the right to know.

For the first time, she became aware of all the space that separated them, the ludicrous distance. She was sure that he was still there, where she had written to him several times, many years before. If he had moved, she would have been aware of it somehow. Because she and Mattia were united by an elastic and invisible thread, buried under a pile of trivia, a thread that could exist only between two people like themselves: two people who had acknowledged their own solitude, each within the other.

She felt around under the pile of photographs and found a pen. She sat down to write, careful not to smudge the ink with her hand. At last she blew on it to dry it. She looked for an envelope, slipped the photograph inside and sealed it.

Perhaps he'll come, she thought.

A pleasant apprehension gripped her bones and made her smile, as if at that very moment time had begun again.

43

Before seeking the runway, the plane on which
Mattia was travelling crossed the green patch of
the hill, passed the basilica and flew twice over
the centre of the city in a circular trajectory.
Mattia took the bridge, the older one, as his
point of reference and from there followed the
road to his parents' house. It was still the same
colour as when he had left it.

He recognized the park nearby, bounded by
the two main roads that flowed together into a
broad curve bisected by the river. On so clear an
afternoon you could see everything from up
there: no one could have disappeared into
nothingness.

He leaned further forward, to look at what
the plane was leaving behind it. He followed the
winding road that climbed part of the way up
the hill and found the house of the Della Rocca
family, with its white façade and its windows all
attached to one another, like an imposing block
of ice. A little further on there was his old school,
with the green fire escapes, their surfaces, he
remembered, cold and rough to the touch.

The place where he had spent the first half of
his life, the half that was over now, was like an
enormous sculpture made of coloured cubes and
inanimate shapes.

From the airport he took a taxi. His father had
insisted that he wanted to come and collect him,

293

but he had said no, I'll come on my own, in that tone that his parents knew well and which was pointless to resist.

After the taxi had driven off, he stood on the pavement on the other side of the street, looking at his old house. The bag that he carried over his shoulder wasn't very heavy. It contained clean clothes for two or three days at the most.

He found the entrance to the apartment block open and climbed to his floor. He rang the bell and heard no sound from inside. Then his father opened the door and, before they were able to say anything, they smiled at each other, each contemplating the passing of time in the changes that had occurred in the other.

Pietro Balossino was old. It wasn't just the white hair and the thick veins that stood out too much on the back of his hands. He was old in the way he stood in front of his son, his whole body trembling almost imperceptibly, and leaned on the door handle, as if his legs were no longer enough on their own.

They hugged, rather awkwardly. Mattia's bag rolled off his shoulder and slipped between them. He let it fall to the floor. Their bodies were still the same temperature. Pietro Balossino touched his son's hair and remembered too many things. Feeling them all at the same time gave him a pain in his chest.

Mattia looked at his father to ask where's Mum? and he understood.

'Your mother's resting,' he said. 'She didn't feel very well. It must be the heat these past few days.'

Mattia nodded.

'Are you hungry?'

'No. I'd just like a little water.'

'I'll go and get you some.'

His father quickly disappeared into the kitchen, as if looking for an excuse to get away. Mattia thought that that was all that was left, that parental affection resolves itself into small solicitudes, the concerns that his parents listed on the telephone every Wednesday: food, heat and cold, tiredness, sometimes money. Everything else lay as if submerged at unreachable depths, in a mass of subjects never addressed, excuses to be made and received and memories to be corrected, which would remain unchanged.

He walked down the corridor to his bedroom. He was sure he would find everything as he had left it, as if that space was immune to the erosion of time, as if all the years of his absence constituted only a parenthesis in that place. He felt an alienating sense of disappointment when he saw that everything was different, like the horrible feeling of ceasing to exist. The walls that had once been pale blue had been covered with cream-coloured wallpaper, which made the room look lighter. Where his bed had been was the sofa that had been in the sitting room for years. His desk was still at the window, but on it there was no longer anything of his, just a pile of newspapers and a sewing machine. There were no photographs, neither of him nor of Michela.

He stood in the doorway as if he had needed permission to enter. His father came over with the glass of water and seemed to read his thoughts.

'Your mother wanted to learn to sew,' he said, as if by way of justification. 'But she soon got fed up with it.'

Mattia drank the water down in one go. He rested his bag against the wall, where it wasn't in the way.

'I have to go now,' he said.

'Already? But you've only just got here.'

'There's someone I have to see.'

He walked past his father, avoiding his eye and sliding his back against the wall. Their bodies were too similar and bulky and adult to be so close to one another. He took the glass through to the kitchen, rinsed it and set it upside down on the draining board.

'I'll be back this evening,' he said.

He nodded goodbye to his father, who was standing in the middle of the sitting room, at the same spot where in another life he was hugging his mother, talking about him. It wasn't true that Alice was waiting for him, he didn't even know where to find her, but he had to get out of there as quickly as possible.

44

During the first year they had written to one another. It was Alice who had started it, as with all the other things that concerned them. She had sent him a photograph of a cake with the rather clumsy inscription *Happy Birthday* made out of strawberries cut in half. She had signed the back only with an *A* followed by a full stop and nothing else. She had made the cake for Mattia's birthday, and then she had thrown it whole into the dustbin. Mattia had replied in a letter of four closely written pages, in which he told her how hard it was to start over in a new place without knowing the language, and in which he apologized for leaving. Or at least that was how it seemed to Alice. He hadn't asked her anything about Fabio, either in that letter or in the ones that followed, and she hadn't talked about him. Both of them, however, were aware of his strange and menacing presence, just beyond the edge of the page. Partly for that reason they had soon begun to reply to each other's letters coldly and at increasingly large intervals, until their correspondence had faded away entirely.

After a few years Mattia had received another card. It was an invitation to Alice and Fabio's wedding. He had stuck it on the fridge with a piece of tape, as if once it was there it would inevitably remind him of something. Each morning and each evening he found himself standing in front of it and each time it seemed to hurt him a little less. A week before the ceremony he had managed to send a telegram that said *Thanks for invitation must decline due to work commitments. Best wishes, Mattia Balossino.* In a shop in the city centre he had spent a whole morning choosing a crystal vase that he had then sent to the couple at their new address.

It was not to this address that he went when he came out of his parents' house. Instead he headed for the hill, to the Della Roccas' house, where he and Alice had spent their afternoons together. He was sure he wouldn't find her there, but he wanted to pretend that nothing had changed.

He hesitated for a long time before pressing the buzzer. A woman replied, probably Soledad.

'Who is it?'

'I'm looking for Alice,' he said.

'Alice doesn't live here any more.'

Yes, it was Soledad. He recognized her Spanish inflection, still quite marked.

'Who is looking for her?' asked the house-keeper.

'It's Mattia.'

There was an extended silence. Sol tried to remember.

'I can give you her new address.'

'That's OK. I've got it, thanks,' he said.

'Goodbye then,' said Sol, after another, shorter silence.

Mattia walked off without turning to look up. He was sure that Sol would be standing at one of the windows watching him, recognizing him only now and wondering what had become of him in all those years and what it was he had come back in search of now. The truth was that even he didn't know.

45

Alice hadn't expected him so soon. She had sent the card only five days before and it was possible that Mattia hadn't even read it yet. At any rate she was sure that he would call first, that they would arrange to meet, perhaps in a bar, where she would prepare him calmly for the news.

Her days were filled with waiting for some kind of signal. At work she was distracted but cheerful and Crozza hadn't dared to ask her why, but in his heart he felt he deserved some credit for it. The void left by Fabio's departure had made way for an almost adolescent frenzy. Alice assembled and dismantled the image of the moment when she and Mattia would meet; she ran through the details of it; she studied the scene from different angles. She wore away at the thought until it seemed not so much a projection as a memory.

She had also been to the local library. She had had to get a card, because she had never set foot in it before that day. She had looked for the newspapers that mentioned Michela's disappearance. Reading them had upset her, as if all that horror was happening again, not far from where she was. Her confidence had wavered at the sight of a photograph of Michela on the front page, in which she looked lost and stared at a point above the lens, perhaps the forehead of whoever was taking the picture. That image had instantly undermined the memory of the girl at the hospital, superimposing itself over her too precisely to seem believable. For the first time Alice had wondered if it mightn't all be a mistake, a hallucination that had lasted too long. Then she had covered the photograph with one hand and gone on reading, resolutely dispelling that doubt.

Michela's body had never been found. Not so much as an item of clothing, not a trace. The child had vanished and for months the line of a kidnapping had been pursued, fruitlessly in the end. No suspects had been named. The news had moved to the inside pages before finally disappearing altogether.

When the bell rang, Alice was drying her hair. She opened the door distractedly, without even asking who's there, as she arranged the towel on her head. She was barefoot and the first thing Mattia saw of her was her bare feet, the second toe slightly longer than the big one, as if pushing its way forward, and the fourth bent underneath, hidden away. They were details that he knew, which had survived in his mind longer than words and situations.

'Hi,' he said, looking up.

Alice took a step back and instinctively closed both sides of her dressing-gown, as if her heart might burst out of her chest. Then she focused on Mattia; she realized that he was really there. She hugged him, pressing her inadequate weight against him. He circled her waist with his right arm, but kept his fingers raised, as if out of caution.

'I'll be right there. I'll just be a moment,' she said, rushing her words. She went back inside and closed the door, leaving him outside. She needed a few minutes on her own to get dressed and put on her make-up and dry her eyes before he noticed.

Mattia sat down on the step outside the front door with his back to the door. He studied the little garden, the almost perfect symmetry of the low hedge that ran along both sides of the path and the undulating shape that broke off halfway through a sine curve. When he heard the click of the lock he turned round and for a moment everything seemed as it had been when he had been the one waiting outside for Alice and she coming out, well dressed and smiling, then together they walked down the street without having decided where they were going.

Alice bent forward and kissed him on the cheek. To sit down next to him she had to hold on to his shoulder, because of her stiff leg. He moved aside. They had nothing to rest their backs against, so they both sat leaning slightly forward.

'You were quick,' said Alice.

'Your card arrived yesterday morning.'

'So that place isn't all that far away.'

Mattia looked at the ground. Alice took his right hand and opened it on the palm side. He didn't resist, because with her he had no need to be ashamed of the marks.

There were new ones, you could make them out as darker lines in the middle of that tangle of white scars. None of them seemed all that recent, apart from one circular halo, like a burn. Alice followed its outline with the tip of her index finger and he was barely aware of her touch through all the layers of hardened skin. He calmly let her look, because his hand told much more than he could in words.

'It seemed important,' said Mattia.

'It is.'

He turned to look at her, to ask her to go on.

'Not yet,' said Alice. 'First let's get away from here.'

Mattia got up before she did, then held out his hand to help her, as they had always done. They walked towards the street. It was difficult to talk and think at the same time, as if the two actions cancelled one another out.

'Here,' said Alice.

She turned off the alarm of a dark green station wagon and Mattia thought it was too big for her alone.

'Do you want to drive?' Alice asked him with a smile.

'I don't know how.'

'Are you joking?'

He shrugged. They looked at each other over the roof of the car. The sun sparkled on the bodywork between them.

'I don't need to drive there,' he said by way of justification.

Alice tapped her chin with the key, thoughtfully.

'Then I know where we've got to go,' she said, shaking herself as she had done when she announced her ideas as a little girl.

They got into the car. There was nothing on the dashboard in front of Mattia, apart from two compact discs, one resting on the other with their spines towards him: Mussorgsky's *Pictures at an Exhibition* and a collection of Schubert sonatas.

'Are you a fan of classical music now?'

Alice darted a quick glance at the discs. She wrinkled up her nose.

'No way. They're his. They put me to sleep and that's it.'

Mattia wriggled against the seat-belt. It scratched his shoulder because it was set for someone shorter, probably Alice, who sat there while her husband was driving. They listened to classical music together. He tried to imagine it, then he allowed himself to be distracted by the words printed on the wing-mirror: *Objects in the mirror are closer than they appear.*

'It's Fabio, isn't it?' he asked. He already knew the answer, but he wanted to untie that knot, dissolve that awkward, silent presence that seemed to be studying them from the back seat. He knew that otherwise the dialogue between them would stall right there, like a boat run aground on the rocks.

Alice nodded, as if it was an effort. If she explained everything all at once, about the baby, the quarrel and the rice that was still stuck in the corners of the kitchen, he would think that was the reason she had called him. He wouldn't believe the story about Michela, he would think of her as a woman having a crisis with her husband, trying to re-establish old relationships

304

to keep from feeling so alone. For a moment she wondered whether that wasn't actually the case.

'Have you got any children?'

'No, none.'

'But why — '

'Leave it,' Alice cut in.

Mattia fell silent, but didn't apologize.

'What about you?' she asked after a while. She had hesitated to ask, for fear of the reply. Then her voice had come out all by itself, almost startling her.

'No,' Mattia replied.

'You don't have children?'

'I haven't got . . . ' He wanted to say anyone. 'I'm not married.'

Alice nodded.

'Still playing hard to get then?' she said, turning to smile at him.

Mattia shook his head with embarrassment, and understood what she meant.

They had reached a large, deserted car park near the truck terminal, surrounded by big, interconnecting Portakabins. Three stacks of wooden pallets wrapped up in polythene lay beside a grey wall, next to a lowered shutter. Further up, on the roof, there was a neon sign which must have shone bright orange at night.

Alice stopped the car in the middle of the car park and turned off the engine.

'Your turn,' she said, opening the door.

'What?'

'Now you drive.'

'No, no,' said Mattia. 'Forget it.'

She stared at him carefully, with her eyes half

closed and her lips pursed as if she was only now rediscovering a kind of affection that she had forgotten about.

'So you haven't changed that much,' she said. It wasn't a reproach; in fact she seemed relieved.

'Neither have you,' he said.

She shrugged.

'OK then,' he said. 'Let's give it a go.'

Alice laughed. They got out of the car to switch seats and Mattia walked with his arms dangling exaggeratedly to demonstrate his total resignation. For the first time each of them found themselves in the role of the other, each showing the other what they thought was their true profile.

'I don't know where to start,' said Mattia, with his arms raised on the steering wheel, as if he really didn't know where to put them.

'Nothing at all? You've never driven, not even once?'

'Practically never.'

'So we're in a bit of a fix.'

Alice leaned over him. For a moment Mattia stared at her hair falling vertically towards the centre of the earth. Under the T-shirt that lifted slightly over her belly he recognized the upper edge of the tattoo, which he had observed close up a long time ago.

'You're so thin,' he said without thinking, as if he was thinking out loud.

Alice suddenly jerked her head round to look at him, but then she pretended nothing was wrong.

'No,' she said, shrugging. 'No different from usual.'

She pulled back a little and pointed to the three pedals.

'Right then. Clutch, brake and accelerator. Left foot only for the clutch and right foot for the other two.'

Mattia nodded, still somewhat distracted by the proximity of her body and the invisible smell of bubble-bath that she had left behind.

'You know the gears, right? And anyway they're written down here. First, second, third. And I have a feeling that'll do for now,' Alice went on. 'When you change gears, hold down the clutch and then slowly release it. And to get started: hold down the clutch and then release it while giving it a bit of accelerator. Ready?'

'And if I'm not?' he replied.

He tried to concentrate. He felt as nervous as if he were about to sit an exam. Over time he had become convinced that he no longer knew how to do anything outside of his element, the ordered and transfinite sets of mathematics. As normal people aged they acquired self-confidence, while he was losing it, as if his was a limited reserve.

He assessed the space that separated them from the pallets stacked at the end. About fifty metres, at least. Even if he set off at top speed he would have time to brake. He held the key turned too long, making the starting motor screech. He delicately released the clutch, but didn't press hard enough on the accelerator and the engine stalled with a gulp. Alice laughed.

'Almost. A bit more decisive this time though.'

Mattia took a deep breath. Then he tried

again. The car set off with a jerk and Alice told him clutch and into second. Mattia changed gear and accelerated again. They drove straight on until they were almost ten metres from the wall of the factory, when he decided to turn the steering wheel. They did a 180-degree turn that threw them both to one side and returned to the point they had started from.

Alice clapped her hands.

'You see?' she said.

He turned the car again. Performed the same move. It was as if he only knew how to follow that narrow, oval trajectory, although he had a vast square all to himself.

'Keep straight on,' said Alice. 'Turn on to the road.'

'Are you mad?'

'Come on, there's no one there. And besides, you've learned how to do it.'

Mattia adjusted the steering wheel. He felt his hands sweating in contact with the plastic and adrenalin stirring his muscles as it hadn't done for ages. For a moment he thought he was driving a car, the whole thing, with its pistons and greased mechanisms, and that he had Alice, so close, to tell him what to do. It was what he had imagined so often. Not really quite the same, in fact, but for once he resolved to pay no attention to the imperfections.

'OK,' he said.

He steered the car towards the car-park exit. Having reached the turning into the street he leaned towards the windscreen and looked in both directions. He delicately turned the steering wheel and couldn't help following its movements with his whole torso, as children do when they pretend to drive.

He was on the road. The sun, already low in the sky, was behind him and shone into his eyes from the rear-view mirror. The arrow of the speedometer showed that he was going at 30 kilometres an hour and the whole car vibrated with the hot breath of a domesticated animal.

'Am I doing OK?' he asked.

'Brilliantly. Now you can change into third.'

The road went on for another hundred metres or so and Mattia looked straight ahead. Alice took advantage of the fact to observe him calmly from close up. He was no longer the Mattia from the photograph. The skin of his face was no longer an even texture, smooth and elastic: now the first wrinkles, still very shallow, furrowed his brow. He had shaved, but new stubble was already emerging from his cheeks, dotting them with black. His physical presence was over-whelming; he no longer seemed to have any cracks through which one could invade his space, as she had often liked to do when she was a girl. Or else it was that she no longer felt she had the right to do so. That she was no longer capable of it.

She tried to find a resemblance to the girl from the hospital, but now that Mattia was there, her memory had become even more confused. All those details that seemed to coincide were no longer as clear as they had been. The colour of the girl's hair was lighter, perhaps. And she didn't remember the dimples at the sides of her mouth, or those eyebrows, so thick at the outer ends. For the first time she was really worried that she had made a mistake.

How will I explain it to him? she wondered.

Mattia cleared his throat, as if the silence had gone on for too long or as if he had noticed that Alice was staring at him. She looked elsewhere, towards the hill.

'You remember the first time I came to pick you up in the car?' she said. 'I'd had my licence for less than an hour.'

'Yeah. And out of all the possible guinea pigs you chose me.'

Alice thought that it wasn't true. She hadn't chosen him over all the others. The truth was that she hadn't thought about anyone else.

'You spent the whole time clutching on to the handle. You kept saying go slowly, go slowly.'

She cried out with the shrill voice of a little girl. Mattia remembered that he had gone against his will. That afternoon he had been supposed to be studying for his mathematical analysis exam, but in the end he had given in, because it seemed so damned important to Alice. For the whole afternoon he had felt stupid, as we all feel stupid when we think of the time we waste wishing we were somewhere else.

'We drove around for half an hour in search of two free parking spaces because you couldn't get into a single one,' he said, to banish those thoughts.

'It was just an excuse to keep you with me,' Alice replied. 'But you never understood anything.'

They both laughed, to stifle the ghosts let loose by the phrase.

'Where do I go?' asked Mattia, becoming serious.

'Turn here.'

'OK. But then that's enough. I'll let you have your seat back.'

He changed from third to second without Alice having to tell him, and took the bend well. He turned into a shady street, narrower than the other one and without the line down the middle, squashed between two rows of identical, windowless buildings.

'I'll stop here,' he said.

They had more or less got there when an articulated lorry emerged from around the corner, heading straight towards them and taking up most of the road.

Mattia gripped the wheel tightly. He didn't know how to move his foot instinctively on to the brake, so he accelerated instead. With her good leg Alice tried to find a pedal that wasn't there. The lorry didn't slow down. It moved slightly further to its own side.

'I can't get through,' said Mattia. 'I can't get through.'

'Brake,' said Alice, trying to seem calm.

Mattia couldn't think. The lorry was a few metres away and only now did it show any sign of slowing down. He felt his foot contracting on the accelerator and thought about how he could pass it on one side. He remembered when on his bike he would come down the ramp of the cycle track and at the end he had to slow down

311

abruptly to get between the posts that stopped the cars getting through. But Michela didn't slow down, she passed between them on her bike with stabilizers, but not once did she brush them with the handlebars.

He turned the steering wheel to the right and seemed to be heading straight for the wall.

'Brake,' Alice repeated. 'The middle pedal.'

He pressed it down hard, with both feet. The car jerked violently forward and came to a standstill just a few centimetres from the wall.

With the recoil Mattia struck his head against the left-hand window. The seat-belt kept him steady where he was. Alice rocked forwards like a bending twig, but held on tight to the door handle. The lorry passed them by, indifferently, joined in two long, red, articulated segments.

★ ★ ★

They sat in silence for a few seconds, as though contemplating an extraordinary event. Then Alice started laughing. Mattia's eyes stung and the nerves in his neck pulsed as if they had all been suddenly inflated and were about to explode.

'Did you hurt yourself?' Alice asked. It was as if she couldn't stop laughing.

Mattia was terrified. He didn't reply. She tried to become serious again.

'Let me see,' she said.

She freed herself from her seat-belt and stretched over him as he stared at the wall directly in front of them. He was thinking about

312

the word anelastic. About how the kinetic energy now making his legs tremble would have been unleashed all at once in the impact.

At last he took his feet off the brake and the car, its engine off, slipped backwards slightly, down the almost imperceptible slope of the road. Alice pulled on the handbrake.

'You're fine,' she said, brushing Mattia's forehead.

He closed his eyes and nodded. He concentrated to keep from crying.

'Let's go home and you can lie down for a bit,' she said, as if the home was theirs.

'I have to go back to my parents' house,' protested Mattia, but without much conviction.

'I'll take you back later. Now you need to rest.'

'I have to — '

'Shut up.'

They got out of the car to swap seats. The darkness had taken over the whole of the sky, apart from a thin, useless strip running along the horizon.

They didn't say another word for the rest of the journey. Mattia trapped his head in his right hand. He covered his eyes and pressed his temples with his thumb and middle finger. He read and reread the words on the wing-mirror: *Objects in the mirror are closer than they appear.* He thought about the article he had left Alberto to write. He was bound to mess it up; Mattia had to get back as soon as possible. And then there were lessons to prepare, his silent apartment.

Alice turned to look at him, worried, taking

313

her eyes off the road from time to time. She was doing all she could to drive gently. She wondered if it would be better to put on some music, but she didn't know what he would like. Basically she didn't know anything about him at all.

Outside the house she went to help him out of the car, but Mattia got out by himself. He swayed on his feet as she opened the door. Alice moved quickly, but carefully. She felt responsible, as if it was all the unexpected consequence of a bad joke.

She threw the cushions on the floor to make room on the sofa. She said to Mattia lie down here and he obeyed. Then she went into the kitchen to make him some tea or camomile or anything that she could hold in her hands when she came back into the sitting room.

As she waited for the water to boil she started tidying up, frantically. Every now and again she turned to glance at the sitting room, but all she could see was the back of the sofa, its bright, uniform blue.

Soon Mattia would ask her why she had summoned him there and there would be no escape for her. But now she was no longer sure of anything. She had seen a girl who looked like him. So? The world is full of people who look like each other. Full of stupid and meaningless coincidences. She hadn't even spoken to her. And she wouldn't have known how to find her again anyway. Thinking about it now, with Mattia in the other room, the whole thing seemed ridiculous and cruel.

The only certainty was that he had come back

and that she didn't want him to go away again.

She washed the dishes that were already clean in the sink and emptied the pot full of water sitting on the stove. A handful of rice had been lying on the bottom of it for weeks. Seen through the water, the grains looked bigger.

Alice poured the boiling water into a cup and dipped a tea-bag in it. It coloured with a dark gush. She put in two lavish spoonfuls of sugar and came back. Mattia's hand had slipped from his closed eyes to his throat. The skin of his face had relaxed and his expression was neutral. His chest moved regularly up and down and he was breathing only through his nose.

Alice set the cup down on the glass table and, without taking her eyes off him, sat down in the armchair next to him. Mattia's breathing restored her calm. It was the only sound.

She slowly began to feel that her thoughts were regaining coherence. At last they slowed down, after dashing madly towards some vague destination. She found herself back in her own sitting room as if she had been dropped in it from another dimension.

Before her was a man whom she had once known and who was now someone else. Perhaps he really did look like the girl in the hospital. But they weren't identical, they certainly weren't that. And the Mattia who was sleeping on her sofa was no longer the boy she had seen disappearing through the doors of the lift, that evening when a hot, unquiet wind came down from the mountains. He was not the Mattia who had taken root in her head and prevented her

315

from moving on to everything else.

No, what she had in front of her was a grown-up person who had built a life around a terrifying abyss, on a terrain that had already collapsed, and who had succeeded, far away from here, amongst people Alice didn't know. She had been prepared to destroy all that, to disinter a buried horror, for a simple suspicion, as slender as the memory of a memory.

But now that Mattia was there in front of her, with his eyes closed over thoughts to which she had no access, everything suddenly seemed clearer: she had looked for him because she needed to, because since the night she had left him on that landing, her life had rolled into a hole and hadn't moved from there. Mattia was at the end of that tangle that she carried within herself, twisted by the years. If there was still some chance of untying it, some way of loosening it, then it was by pulling that end that she now gripped between her fingers.

She felt that something was being resolved, like a long wait coming to an end. She sensed it in her limbs, even in her bad leg which was never normally aware of anything. Getting up was a natural gesture. She didn't even wonder if it was appropriate or not, if it was really her right to do so. It was only time, sliding and dragging itself after more time. Only obvious gestures that knew nothing of the future and the past.

She bent over Mattia and kissed him on the lips. She wasn't afraid of waking him, she kissed him as you kiss a waking person, lingering over his closed lips, compressing them as if to leave a mark on them. He gave a start, but didn't open his eyes. He parted his lips and went along with her. He was awake.

It was different from the first time. Their facial muscles were stronger now, more conscious, and they sought an aggression that had something to do with the precise roles of a man and a woman. Alice stayed bent over him, without getting on to the sofa, as if she had forgotten the rest of her own body.

The kiss lasted a long time, whole minutes, long enough for reality to find a fissure between their clamped mouths and slip inside, forcing them both to analyse what was happening.

They pulled apart. Mattia gave a quick smile, automatically, and Alice brought a finger to her damp lips, as if to check that it had really happened. There was a decision to be made and it had to be made without a word. They looked at each other, but they had already lost their synchronicity and their eyes didn't meet.

Mattia stood up, uncertainly.

'I'm just off for a minute . . . ' he said, pointing to the corridor.

'Sure. It's the door at the end.'

He left the room. He still had his shoes on and the sound of his footsteps seemed to be slipping away underground.

★ ★ ★

He locked himself in the bathroom. He rested his hands on the basin. He felt stunned, foggy. In the place where he had taken the bump he

317

noticed a little swelling, slowly spreading.

He turned on the tap and put his wrists under the cold water, as his father had done when he wanted to staunch the blood gushing from Mattia's hands. He looked at the water and thought about Michela, as he did every time. It was a painless thought, like thinking about going to sleep or breathing. His sister had slipped into the current, dissolved slowly in the river and through the river she had come back inside him. Her molecules were scattered around his body.

He felt his circulation returning. Now he had to think, about that kiss and about what it was that he had come in search of after all that time. About why he had been prepared to receive Alice's lips and about why he had then felt the need to pull away and hide in here.

She was in the other room waiting for him. Separating them were two layers of brick, a few inches of mortar and nine years of silence.

The truth was that once again she had acted in his place, had forced him to come back when he himself had always yearned to do it. She had written him a card and had said come here and he had jumped up like a spring. One letter had brought them together just as another had separated them.

Mattia knew what needed to be done. He had to get out of there and sit back down on that sofa, he had to take one of her hands and tell her I shouldn't have gone. He had to kiss her once more and then again, until they were so used to that gesture that they couldn't do without it. It happened in films and it happened in reality, every day. People took what they wanted, they clutched at coincidences, the few that there were, and from them they drew a life. He had either to tell Alice I'm here, or leave, take the first plane and disappear again, go back to the place where he had been left dangling for all those years.

He had learned his lesson. Choices are made in a few seconds and paid for in the time that remains. It had happened with Michela and then with Alice and again now. This time he recognized them: those seconds were there, and he would never make a mistake again.

He closed his fingers around the jet of water. He caught some of it in his hands and bathed his face. Without looking, still bent over the basin, he stretched out an arm to take a towel. He rubbed it over his face and then pulled away. In the mirror he saw a darker patch on the other side. He turned it around. It was the embroidered initials *FR*, placed a few centimetres away from the corner, in a symmetrical position in respect to the bisecting line.

Mattia turned around and found another, identical, towel. At the same point the letters *ADR* were sewn.

He looked around more carefully. In the limescale-rimmed glass there was a single toothbrush and next to it a basket full of objects assembled higgledy-piggledy: creams, a red rubber band, a hairbrush with hairs attached to it and a pair of nail scissors. On the shelf under the mirror there lay a razor, with tiny fragments of dark hair still trapped beneath the blade.

There had been a time when, sitting on the

319

bed with Alice, he could scan her room with his eyes, identify something on a shelf and say to himself I bought that for her. Those shelves were there to bear witness to a journey, like little flags attached to stages of a voyage. They marked out the rhythm of Christmases and birthdays. Some he could still remember: the first Counting Crows record, a Galilean thermometer, with its different-coloured bulbs floating in a transparent liquid, and a book on the history of mathematics that Alice had received with a snort but had actually read in the end. She kept them carefully, finding an obvious position for them, because it was clear to him that she always kept them in front of her eyes. Mattia knew it. He knew all that, but he couldn't move from where he was. As if, in yielding to Alice's call, he might find himself in a trap, drown in it and be lost for ever. He had stayed impassive and silent, waiting until it was too late.

Around him now there was not a single object that he recognized. He looked at his own reflection in the mirror, his tousled hair, his shirt collar slightly askew, and it was then that he understood. In that bathroom, in that house as in his parents' house, in all those places there was no longer anything of him.

He remained motionless, getting used to the decision he had made, until he felt that the seconds were over. He carefully folded the towel and with the back of his hand he wiped away the little drops that he had left on the ledge of the basin.

He left the bathroom and walked along the

corridor. He stopped in the doorway of the sitting room.

'I have to go now,' he said.

'Yes,' replied Alice, as if she had prepared herself to say it.

The cushions were back in place on the sofa and a big lamp lit everything from the middle of the ceiling. There was no remaining trace of conspiracy. The tea had turned cold on the coffee table and a dark and sugary sediment had settled at the bottom of the cup. Mattia thought that it was only someone else's house.

They walked to the door together. He touched Alice's hand with his as he passed close to her.

'The card that you sent me,' he said. 'There was something you wanted to say to me.'

Alice smiled.

'It was nothing.'

'You said it was important before.'

'No. It wasn't.'

'Was it something to do with me?'

She hesitated for a moment.

'No,' she said. 'Just with me.'

Mattia nodded. He thought of a potential that had been exhausted, the invisible vector lines that had previously united them through the air and had now ceased to exist.

'Bye then,' said Alice.

The light was all inside and the darkness all outside. Mattia replied with a wave of his hand. Before going back in, she saw once again the dark circle drawn on his palm, like a mysterious and indelible symbol, irreparably closed.

46

The plane travelled at dead of night and the few insomniacs who noticed it from the ground saw nothing but a little collection of intermittent lights, like a wandering constellation against the fixed black sky. None of those people lifted a hand to wave to him, because that would have been childish.

Mattia got into the first of the taxis lined up in front of the terminal and told the driver his address. As they passed along the sea shore a faint glow was already rising from the horizon.

'Stop here, please,' he said to the taxi driver.

'Here?'

'Yes.'

He paid the fare and got out of the car, which immediately drove away. He walked across about ten metres of grass and approached a bench, which seemed to have been put there specially to look at the void. He dropped his bag on it but didn't sit down himself.

A strip of sun was already appearing on the horizon. Mattia tried to remember the geometrical name for that plane figure, bounded by an arc and a segment, but it wouldn't come to him. The sun seemed to be moving faster than it did in the daytime; it was possible to perceive its velocity, as if it was in a hurry to get outside. The rays grazing on the surface of the water were red, orange and yellow and Mattia knew why, but knowing it added nothing and didn't distract him.

The curve of the coast was flat and windswept and he was the only one looking at it.

At last the gigantic red orb detached itself from the sea, like an incandescent ball. For a moment Mattia thought of the rotational motion of the stars and the planets, the sun that fell behind him in the evening and rose there in front of him in the morning. Every day, in and out of the water, whether he was there to look at it or not. It was nothing but mechanics, conservation of energy and angular momentum, forces that balanced one another, centripetal and centrifugal thrusts, nothing but a trajectory, which could not be anything other than it was.

Slowly the tonalities faded away and the pale blue of morning began to emerge from the background of the other colours and took over first the sea and then the sky.

Mattia blew on his hands, which the brackish wind had made unusable. Then he drew them back into his jacket. He felt something in his right pocket. He pulled out a note folded in four. It was Nadia's number. He read the sequence of numbers to himself and smiled.

He waited for the last purple flame to go out on the horizon and, amidst the dispersing mist, set off for home on foot.

His parents would have liked the dawn. Perhaps, one day, he would take them to see it and then they would stroll together to the port, to breakfast on smoked-salmon sandwiches. He would explain to them how it happens, how the infinite wave-lengths merge to form white light. He would talk to them about absorption and emission spectra and they would nod without understanding.

Mattia let the cold air of morning slip under his jacket. It smelled clean. Not far away there was a shower waiting for him, and a cup of hot tea and a day like many others and he didn't need anything else.

47

That same morning, a few hours later, Alice wound up the blinds. The dry rattle of the plastic slats rolling around the pulley was comforting. Outside was the sun, already high in the sky.

She chose a CD from one of the ones stacked next to the stereo, without thinking too hard about it. A little sound was all it took to clean the air. She turned the volume knob to the first red notch. Fabio would be furious. She couldn't help smiling as she thought about how he would say her name, shouting to make himself heard over the music and lingering too long over the *i*, jutting his chin.

She pulled away the bed-sheets and piled them in a corner. She took clean ones from the wardrobe. She watched them filling with air and then falling back down, undulating slightly. Damien Rice's voice broke slightly just before he managed to sing *oh coz nothing is lost, it's just frozen in frost.*

Alice washed calmly. She stayed under the shower for a long time, with her face turned towards the jet of water. Then she got dressed and put a little make-up, almost invisible, on her cheeks and her eyelids.

By the time she was ready the CD had been over for some time, but she didn't notice. She left the house and got into the car.

A block from the shop she changed direction.

She would be a bit late, but it didn't matter.

She drove to the park where Mattia had told her everything. She felt as if nothing had changed. She remembered it all, apart from the pale wooden fence that now surrounded the grass.

She got out of the car and walked towards the trees. The grass crunched, still cold from the night, and the branches were heavy with new leaves. Children were sitting on the benches where Michela had sat so long before. In the middle of the table, cans were arranged on top of one another to form a tower. The children were talking loudly and one of them was moving wildly around, imitating someone.

Alice walked over, trying to catch scraps of what they were saying, but before they could notice her she had walked on and headed for the river. Since the council had decided to keep the dam open all year, hardly any water ran at that point. In the rectangular ponds the river looked motionless, as if forgotten, exhausted. On Sundays, when it was hot, people brought their deckchairs from home and came down here to sunbathe. The bottom was made of white stones and a finer, yellowish sand. On the bank the grass was tall; it came up above Alice's knees.

She walked down the slope, checking with each step to make sure that the ground didn't yield. She continued on to the river-bed, to the edge of the water. In front of her was the bridge and further away the Alps, which on clear days like this seemed very close. Only the highest peaks were still covered with snow.

Alice lay down on the dry pebbles. Her bad leg thanked her by relaxing. The larger stones pricked her back, but she didn't move.

She closed her eyes and tried to imagine the water, all around and above her. She thought of Michela leaning over from the shore. Of her round face that she had seen in the papers reflected in the silver water. Of the splash that no one had been there to hear and the wet icy clothes dragging her down. Of her hair floating like dark seaweed. She saw her groping with her arms, waving them awkwardly and swallowing painful mouthfuls of that cold liquid, which dragged her further down until she almost touched the bottom.

Then she imagined her movement becoming more sinuous, her arms finding the right coordination and describing circles that gradually became wider, her feet stretching out like two flippers and moving together, her head turning upwards, where some light still filtered in. She saw Michela coming back up to the surface and breathing, one last time. She followed her, as she swam at water level, in the direction of the current, towards somewhere new. All night, all the way to the sea.

When she opened her eyes the sky was still there, with its monotonous and brilliant blue. Not a cloud passed across it.

Mattia was far away. Fabio was far away. The current of the river made a faint, somnolent swish.

She remembered lying in the crevasse, buried by snow. She thought of that perfect silence. Also

327

now, like then, no one knew where she was. This time too, no one would come. But she no longer expected them to.

She smiled towards the clear sky. With a little effort, she could get up by herself.

Acknowledgements

This book wouldn't have existed without Raffaella Lops.

I would like to thank, in no particular order, Antonio Franchini, Joy Terekiev, Mario Desiati, Giulia Ichino, Laura Cerutti, Cecilia Giordano, my parents, Giorgio Mila, Roberto Castello, Emiliano Amato, Pietro Grossi and Nella Re Rebaudengo. Each of them knows why.

We do hope that you have enjoyed reading
this large print book.

Did you know that all of our titles
are available for purchase?

We publish a wide range of high quality
large print books including:
Romances, Mysteries, Classics
General Fiction
Non Fiction and Westerns

Special interest titles available in
large print are:
The Little Oxford Dictionary
Music Book
Song Book
Hymn Book
Service Book

Also available from us courtesy of
Oxford University Press:
Young Readers' Dictionary
(large print edition)
Young Readers' Thesaurus
(large print edition)

For further information or a free
brochure, please contact us at:
Ulverscroft Large Print Books Ltd.,
The Green, Bradgate Road, Anstey,
Leicester, LE7 7FU, England.
Tel: (00 44) 0116 236 4325
Fax: (00 44) 0116 234 0205

Other titles published by
The House of Ulverscroft:

THE GHOST LOVER

Gillian Greenwood

Josie Price has given up much of her life for the wealthy Haddeley family. Working and living with them, she knows their secrets. So when a young man, Luke, appears and claims, shockingly, to be the son of Kit Haddeley's late wife Alice, Josie helps the family come to terms with ghosts they hoped had been laid to rest. But Luke's arrival casts shadows on both the past and the future, and the ghost of Alice Haddeley hangs heavily over the family. Through Luke, she seems to demand to be both mourned and revenged. It is Josie who holds the key to the mystery of Alice, and it is Josie, beset by guilt, who must resolve the destructive inheritance that Luke brings in his wake.

CARRY ME HOME

Terri Wiltshire

Alabama, 1904. When young Emma Scott claims she's been attacked by a 'black hobo' a chain of events is triggered that will affect future generations . . . In modern-day Alabama, Canaan Phillips has fled an abusive marriage and returned to her childhood home. Canaan's one friend then was her great uncle Luke; now frail and elderly he still lives in a corncrib shack . . . Back in 1905, Emma gives birth to a son, the child she resents, and as he reaches his teens he flees his abusive mother and takes to the railroad. There he finds friendship, love and betrayal — and the true story of his birth . . . In the modern-day, Canaan comes to terms with her past. And, helped by her adored uncle, she learns to love again.